She,
the
Island

ALSO BY IRINA PAPANCHEVA
IN ENGLISH TRANSLATION
PELICAN FEATHER (2016)

SHE, THE ISLAND

First published in Bulgarian language in 2017 by Trud publishing house.
Copyright © Irina Papancheva 2020
      © Edited by Ric Giner and Phil Madden
      © Cover and design by Nevena Angelova
ISBN 9798589570021

Irina Papancheva

She,
the
Island

"She, the island' is a wonderful evocation. Beautifully drawn depictions of real people and events from the history of the Fuerteventura are interwoven with fictional characters who are in love with surfing, writing and love itself. The island is a protagonist, a mysterious siren who captures souls. The book is drenched in enchantment."

Phil Madden, Poet

"I haven't read for a long time such an exquisite, contemplative work, both very human and wise. With an intriguing love plot spread through Fuerteventura's history. Irina Papancheva has described the island so well as a scenery, sensation, magic and mythology that the reader, inevitably, will feel impelled to visit it."

Emil Andreev, Writer

"An intellectual and emotional feast, 'She, the island' could satisfy any taste. It has it all: an engaging plot with many story lines, memorable characters, dramatic turns, and authentic philosophical and psychological interpretations coming from Miguel de Unamuno himself. All of this captured in the mystical landscape of Fuerteventura."

Luis Quimper, Writer

"'She, the island' is a declaration of love to Fuerteventura. It is not just falling in love, but something deeper, coming from understanding and acceptance. Even if one has never been to the island, after reading the book, they would know it. It has a magical softness. Epochs, stories, destinies, realism and mysticism, legends and truths – all are interwoven. The book is not only a homage to Unamuno, a homage which runs through

1

the changing narratives like a red thread, but a statement of respect to a lost past and to the heart of this merciless place."

Radina Ralcheva, Regional Communications Manager, Corning Incorporated

"The book is a unique and valuable addition to the Bulgarian literary tradition. It vaguely reminds me of the research approach of Umberto Eco... All the characters have come to the island with a specific goal – sometimes almost criminal. But they don't find what they are looking for, instead they find... themselves."

Georgi Yanev, Literary critic

"The novel 'She, the island' grips you right from the start. The multilayered dynamics, the contemporary relationships between young people, combined with a reflective, philosophical reference to the past, and storylines which could be made for a film – all of this convinces me that the book will be a success."

Nadejda Deleva, Editor-in-chief, Trud publishing house

"'She, the island' is a multi-layered and polyphonic novel, interesting not only because of the exotic place where the plot unfolds, but also because of the deep revealing of modern relationships in a globalized world, when everyone can meet anyone anywhere. This approach is rare in contemporary Bulgarian literature. As are good titles. "She, the island" is undoubtedly a good title of a good book."

Mitko Novkov, Literary critic

"'She, the island' covers, sometimes allusively, a wide range of topics: personal quests and moral choices; the necessity of perseverance and support, albeit embedded in human nature; the pursuit of spiritual and physical completeness of the experience in its most primitive or rationalised forms; the boundary between the earthly and the sublime; the immense and at the same time fleeting world and diversity of impressions it evokes; and the impossibility of happiness being tamed or grasped. Bulgarian novels, which convey such a colourful palette of questions and interpretations, with their own vision and message, are rare and of real value."

Nikolay Todorov, PhD in Theory of Literature, University of Sofia

"Plato created, I believe, and did not discover Atlantis, and Don Quixote created, I believe, and did not discover, for Sancho, the island Barataria. And I too hope, with the intercession of Plato and Don Quixote or with the help of both, to invent, to create, and not to discover the island of Fuerteventura

(...)

This is my Atlantis. This is my island Barataria!" [1]

Miguel de Unamuno

The same vision came upon Tibiabín. A woman, her daughter's age, wanders around the island, searching for something. She walks among the sands with empty eyes and heart, and searches, searches. All of a sudden the whole island becomes a desert. The woman walks tirelessly, without direction and purpose, walks, walks, walks... She reaches Tibiabín's round stone house. Tibiabín hears a knock on her door. She opens it. The woman is there. Tibiabín takes her face in her hands and looks into her eyes, bleary from staring into nothingness.

"What are you looking for, daughter?"

"The meaning, Great Mother."

"You won't find it in these sands, daughter."

"Then where, Great Mother?"

"Stop seeking. Look the past in the eye, embrace it and let it go where it belongs. In the sands. It's time for you to conceive the present and give life to it."

The woman kneels, weeping, and kisses the back of her hand.

Tibiabín came out of her trance. She shook her hands as if she was rinsing them. She took a bone comb and started brushing her long silver hair. She entered the small room where a young-

---

[1] Unamuno: Articulos y Discursos sobre Canarias, Cabillo Insular de Fuerteventura, Puerto del Rosario, 1980, La Atlantida (p. 66). All the Spanish texts in the book are translated into English by the author.

looking woman was sitting on a hide on the floor, trying to light a fire in a clay pot.

Someone knocked on the door. The younger woman jumped up and opened it. A sinewy man of medium height stood outside. His black eyes stared at her.

"I am looking for Tamonante."

"That's me."

"Ayoce wants to see you."

"When?"

"Immediately."

"Give me a moment."

Tamonante went back inside. The man stayed outside waiting.

"They are calling me, mother."

"Who is it this time?"

"Ayoce."

A shadow crossed Tibiabín's face.

"Take care, daughter."

Tamonante embraced her mother before she left.

"What's the argument about?" she asked.

"Earth."

A year before

They sat on the stone floor in a circle, their eyes full of anticipation, fixed on the dark figure who was rocking gently in the middle. A monotonous, unintelligible sound came from her. It gradually turned into a prayer to the God of the Sun and the God of the Moon. A prayer for a sign, which would prepare them for what was about to come. Her voice soared upward as if it wanted to escape the cave, to reach the heavenly deities and fill the space above the island. Suddenly it lowered, and words rushed in, hushed and secretive. They seemed not to come from the dark figure, but from somewhere in the bowels of the earth.

"Ships are coming. Foreign invaders. Many, many of them. Attacking. The wall does not divide us any more. Shoulder by shoulder, we fight. It's too late. Rout. The foreign invaders rule the island."

The figure became silent and covered her face with her palms.

Silence reigned in the cave.

Tibiabín had foreseen that they would lose their home in the near future. All their efforts were to end buried in the darkness of time. Tomorrow they would not be. There would be no tomorrow.

They slowly got up and left the cave. They did not look at one another nor talk.

A young woman stood to one side and patiently waited for Tibiabín to emerge from her trance. Tibiabín got up, shook herself, saw her and went to her.

"What's the matter, daughter?"

"I want to have a child… Can you help me?"

"Didn't you hear the portent the gods sent us, daughter?"

"I heard it, Mother. What will be will be."

Tibiabín sighed.

"The child comes from the Sun and the Moon and their union, daughter. Pray."

"I've prayed."

"Pray more."

"I have been praying for two years now."

"Is your man aware of your prayers?"

"He is. He sent me to you."

"When was the last time you bled?"

"A week ago."

"Come next Wednesday. After sunset."

"Thank you, Mother."

"Be blessed, daughter."

The sunset bathed the mountain in pink-orange. The clouds glowed, then gradually their colour faded. When the night had swallowed the last glimmer, there was a knocking at Tibiabín's door. The young woman was standing in front of her, looking at her with expectation.

They walked towards the mountain. Tibiabín carried a white bundle.

"This is a secret ritual, daughter. For it to be successful, you mustn't talk to anyone about it, not even your husband."

"Okay, Mother."

"You will wear a blindfold."

"Okay, Mother."

They reached the cave and squeezed inside through a narrow opening. Tibiabín untied the bundle, arranged some stone figurines in a circle, spread a cloth in the middle and sprinkled it with tiny yellow flowers. The woman watched in silence. Was this the Sun? Or the Moon?

"Take your clothes off, daughter."

The woman hesitated a little, then did what was asked.

Tibiabín pulled out a thick cloth and tied it around the woman's eyes. She took her hand and pulled her into the middle of the circle.

"Repeat after me, daughter: I, Sinayadin, call on the forces of the Sun and the forces of the Moon to give me a child. I am giving myself to their fertile energy. I am opening myself to accept it."

Then Tibiabín gestured towards the rocks. A male figure emerged. The man approached them, entered the circle, and embraced the woman. She screamed, frightened, and stepped away.

"Fear not, daughter. The gods are sending you the power of their fertility. Surrender yourself to it."

The woman stopped struggling. The man laid her down on the canvas and took her. Some of the flowers were pressed flat by the weight of their bodies. Those which remained fluttered like yellow butterflies that could fly away at any moment beneath the expressionless gaze of the stone figures.

Thirty-five years earlier

Tibiabín was performing a ritual to summon rain in the same part of the island. The tribe had gathered at the vast, long beach. She dipped her hands in a bowl of water and shook them above the sand while murmuring in an unbroken monotone voice. Her eyes were closed; her face turned skywards, her palms upturned. She was shivering. People sitting on the beach with their eyes closed also had their faces and hands turned to the sky. As they were singing softly, the wind became stronger; the clouds thickened and darkened. The colour of the ocean became ink. Large drops of rain wet their faces, their hair, their hands and the sand, and formed thousands of dancing circles on the water. With their eyes still closed, they opened their mouths and drank the drops with gratitude. Their faces were blissful. Tibiabín's voice faded away, and the people's singing stopped. Eyes opened and bodies moved; the people rose from the sand and withdrew. Tibiabín stood up.

"Tibiabín," a strong, stocky man approached her.

She looked up at him.

"Tonight. In the cave. When the Moon rises."

The man nodded slightly. He glanced at her, turned and walked away.

Another man stood to one side and watched them darkly. Tibiabín went to him.

"What did he want?"

"He thanked me for the ritual."

The man grunted.

"I'll come to you later."

"Tonight the moon is good. I'll perform a ritual. For a child..."

She ran her fingertips through the man's dark hair. He looked away and said nothing.

The moon had risen high. It was huge, full and shining.

Tibiabín combed her hair for a long time. She gathered her stone figures in a cloth bag, put on a white robe and left. She took the path that curved steeply to the top of the mountain, seemingly into the starry sky. Tibiabín walked rhythmically; her white figure with the white bundle in her hands glowed in the night. She climbed without a break until she reached a cave. She squeezed inside. The cave tapered upward to a hole that revealed the fathomless sky over Fuerteventura. A male figure appeared from the shadows inside, approached and pulled her towards him powerfully.

"Wait," whispered Tibiabín.

She put the bundle on the ground, untied it, and took out the stone figures. There were six of them with sculpted faces and distinct sexual organs. She arranged them in a circle facing inward, unfurled the canvas in the middle, and strewed it with small yellow flowers. She stepped over the figures into the circle. The man followed her. He pulled off her robe and took her on the canvas. Moving with his rhythm, she began to moan. Some of the flowers were pressed flat by the weight of their bodies. The others fluttered like yellow butterflies that could fly away at any moment beneath the expressionless gaze of the stone figures. In the volcanic funnel of Malpais de la Arena, the Creation was happening.

An hour later, Tibiabín and the man left the cave and descended the winding slopes. They were walking along the ridge of the mountain when out of its majestic body, a dark shadow emerged. They stopped.

"Are these your rituals for a child? Is this how the gods help you?"

The man's voice was hoarse, low, menacing.

"What are you doing here?"

"Everyone in the tribe will learn about your lies, shameless woman! You'll be tied up and stoned publicly for your sins!"

Tibiabín stepped towards him.

"Please calm down. I am doing this for us. You wanted a child, didn't you?"

The man raised his hand and slapped her. Her head snapped back. Her lover pounced on him with the agility of a wild animal. They exchanged several blows before Tibiabín's husband overpowered the other and gripped his throat. Tibiabín sat sideways, her hands clasped, whispering to herself. At that moment a large dog sprang out of the darkness. It bared its teeth and leapt onto her husband, digging them into his flesh. He rolled away with the dog above him. Her lover stood up, went to her, embraced her, and tried to take her away. She stood frozen, staring terrified at the moving pile from which the moans of her husband came. Her lover, almost against her will, pulled her away towards the village.

The next day, some of the tribesmen brought her the mutilated body of her husband. The dog, which belonged to her lover, was captured, bound, and killed with stones. His dog had been Ayoce's only family.

At that time, two influential men determined the fate of Mahos: Guise and Ayoce. Each had his circle. Tibiabín's husband was a relative of Guise. His death, followed by the murder of Ayoce's dog, made it impossible for the two to share the same territory. Ayoce left, and his people followed him. That year, two kingdoms led by Guise and Ayoce arose on the island. A wall was built between them.

* * *

They had been walking for three hours – silently, self-absorbed. The merciless sun perched high in the sky. Herds of goats grazed the vegetation, and at places, they had stripped the land bare.

Tamonante listened. She made a sign to the man. They turned off the path and reached a place where water gurgled from the earth. She knelt and drank thirstily. The man's eyes ran over her slender figure. Tamonante turned, held his gaze for a moment, and let it go. She stood up and made room for him to pass, her eyelids down. When he slid past her, she felt his breath, more sultry than the sunrays. Small beads of sweat covered her neck.

It was not long before they saw the wall. They walked along it until they reached a gate, guarded by two men. Her companion greeted them and they let them pass through the gate into the territory of Handia.

About fifteen men stood in two groups, speaking softly in the space between the windowless stone round houses.

An elderly man broke off from one of the groups and welcomed them.

"Are you Tamonante, the daughter of Tibiabín?"

"Yes. And you must be Ayoce?"

The man studied her features.

"I called you to help us in resolving a dispute."

"Who are the ones arguing?"

He went to the groups and returned with two men.

Tamonante introduced herself respectfully. The four went to sit in the shade of the nearby palm trees.

"I am listening to you," said Tamonante quietly.

Two hours later, an agreement was reached. The sky was darkening, and a storm was forming in its womb. Tamonante was preparing to leave.

"It will rain. Do you want to spend the night here?" asked Ayoce.

"My mother is waiting for me."

"She knows you're here, right?"

"Yes."

"So she won't be worried. I can't let you go in this weather."

His deep grey eyes looked at her earnestly. Inexplicably, his power did not intimidate her but gave her a sense of calm and security. Tamonante shifted her gaze and met that of her companion, who was staring at her from a distance. A young woman stood to his right and stared at her as well.

Tamonante heard a faint knocking at the door. She got up and opened it slightly. In the moonlight, she recognised her companion. She stepped back inside. He entered, took her in his arms, pulled her white robe down and they collapsed onto the bed.

At dawn, they started on the road back. The same young woman who had stood with him the previous day looked at them from the door of her house with darkened eyes and tight lips.

When they arrived, there was a commotion in the village. Men scurried to and fro with grim faces. They heard a woman crying.

"What has happened?" asked Tamonante.

"This morning, pirates attacked the coast and abducted several women," answered an older man.

"My mother?"

The man looked down in silence.

Tamonante screamed and fell to the ground. Her crying rose to the sky, and neither the embrace of her companion nor the tribe sharing her grief could comfort her.

* * *

Tamonante walked along a cliff overhanging the ocean. Her legs were scratched, her mouth dry, her hair matted, no light in her eyes. In just one day she had changed beyond recognition. Since learning that her mother had been kidnapped, she had not stopped walking, as if exhaustion could lull the pain that gripped her heart. Nothing in this world could soothe that pain. She neared the edge of the cliff. Below, the roiling, angry waves, as if the ocean was also grieving for Tibiabín. Tamonante looked about her, captured her world with one last glance, and then threw herself into the abyss.

THE CALL OF THE OCEAN
OR
THE BEGINNING OF FREEDOM

Marina

She saw him standing a short distance ahead, tall, bright-haired, bright-eyed. He was waiting for someone. For her. She was walking towards him, calm and contained, but also with an inner elan, such as she had not experienced for... an immeasurable time. As she moved closer towards him, the features of his face became clearer: a broad forehead, fine nose, the upper lip slightly thinner with a mole above the left corner. Gripped by sudden tension, she felt the hairs on her skin prickle in the cool breeze of the air conditioner. He was holding a light blue surfboard. He saw her, his eyes laughed, the mole lifted with his smile. Marina felt a throbbing low in her stomach as if the smile had penetrated her womb and shifted something inside. Without taking her gaze off his bright eyes, Marina smiled back, but with slightly more restraint. Only then did she look down. Another step and they were level. One more, and she passed him.

Desert in the middle of the ocean: this was her first thought when they came out. She felt the breath of the sea on her face. Breath, different from the cool breeze of the air conditioners. A disembodied caress in the middle of the rocky desert.

Gerard has encircled her waist with his hand and leads her somewhere. She does not ask where because she knows. She walks with him, surrendering herself to the hand that gently but powerfully pushes her farther and farther away from the airport and from the blue (or maybe green? maybe grey?) eyes of the boy.

Carla

Gerd looked deep in thought. It was as if, in the minutes she had left him to go to the toilet, he had managed to travel far, far away... She followed his gaze. A couple was walking away from them towards the exit of the airport. The woman's dark hair fell in waves on her back, just below her shoulders. She wore a blue linen dress that outlined a slender body and revealed shapely legs. The man's hand rested on her waist. He was taller than her, with silver hair. Nothing to explain the slight wrinkle between Gerd's eyebrows, his motionless expression. What could have attracted his attention?

It sometimes happened that he briefly drifted away. At such moments she had no idea what was going on in his head. Not that she knew much better the rest of the time, but then she did not wonder. In these moments, however, she had the feeling that she did not know him at all, did not know anything about him. She would wake up one morning and see his side of the bed empty without the imprint of his body. And then she would realise that she had made everything up. Everything: their cohabitation, waking up together, early morning lovemaking, the flat, furnished with such enthusiasm (more hers than his), the long walks by the river, the journeys, the surfing, even Fuerteventura... Such crazy thoughts. What would a therapist make of this? Not that she needed one. The analysis she could do herself.

His exquisite profile turned towards her. The fog lifted from his eyes, and his mole twisted into a smile. She felt like covering this mole with kisses. Every time she felt like doing it, but this time more than ever.

She restrained herself. Such public displays were not for her. He grabbed the handle of the suitcase, and the two of them continued to the exit where Enrique was waiting.

He and Gerd embraced joyfully. In his English with its strong Italian accent, Enrique regaled them with tales of waves and surfing, and with plans for the coming days... Gerd and Enrique were like children, excited and eager.

Half an hour later, in the flat. This was their third time on the island, and it felt as if they had never left. Enrique made coffee while they put their luggage in his bedroom. He slept in the small living room-kitchen when they were there.

"How are you, hombre?" Gerd patted him on the shoulder.

"Not too bad. Now I work in a bar. Mostly in the evenings. In the mornings, I sleep late and then – the surf."

"This I call a life!" Gerd laughed.

Did she hear envy in his voice? If he could live such a life, would he prefer it to their orderly existence in Freiburg? She did not want to know. But why these thoughts again? She had probably overstretched herself. The island will bring back her balance, she was sure of that.

The Writer

Salida de emergencia. Emergency exit. The transparent sticker on the window of the minibus made the inscription look like it was carved in the sky, an emergency exit to heaven.

Three days before departing, she had bought a second return ticket with an earlier date. She had become anxious. What if she could not leave the island? If she found herself in a self-inflicted exile? All the photos she had seen of Corralejo showed the ocean, the dunes, surfers, a few commercial hotels and restaurants, and a couple of streets. Except for the ocean, it did not look like a place she would like. Her memories were similar – a promenade, a restaurant where they had had lunch. Nothing else. They got onto the bus and headed for the dunes. A second return ticket. Was this her emergency exit?

"What are you going to do on the island? There is only sand there," a Spanish acquaintance had asked when he heard she was leaving for Fuerteventura.

Unamuno had spent four months here, and his exile, unlike hers, was not imaginary. What did the island do for him? Did it help him face his demons? And how had he mastered those demons, while not knowing the date of his departure?

She did not want to step into this territory. The second ticket was her warranty for peace of mind.

Before she left, she had read most of Unamuno's philosophical books with a pencil in hand. She had underlined some of the sentences and taken notes. During her flight, she started reading 'The Agony of Christianity.' On page 28 she circled the following passage, adding an exclamation mark:

When Lev Shestov, for example, discusses the thoughts of Pascal, it seems he does not want to understand that being a Pascalian does not mean accepting his thoughts, but to be Pascal, to become a Pascal. From my side, again, it has happened many times that, when I've met a person in some writing, not a philosopher nor a wise man but a thinker, when I've met a soul, not a doctrine, I've said, 'But it was me!' And again, I lived with Pascal, with his century and in his ideals, and again, I lived with Kierkegaard in Copenhagen, and in the same way with others. And isn't this the highest proof of the immortality of the soul? Would they not feel in me, as I feel in them? After I die, I'll know if I am to be revived like this in others. Although, even today, don't some of those outside me feel inside me, without me feeling inside them? And what peace there is in all this!

Would she be able to become an Unamuno while on the island? Would Unamuno truly live in her, and her novel? Would they connect in the space, tricking time?

The bus drifted along the road through the dunes. Everything was the same. Everything was different. The volcanic mountains.

The golden sands. The people who climbed the sandhills, strangers in the desert. The vastness of the ocean. A joyful ease filled her. She had returned.

She would find the keys in the Indy café. Her landlord, a young Spaniard, had told her this in a text message. She got out at the stop at the top of the main street and walked down it. It was a long, busy street, with a shopping centre, rock bar, restaurants, shops for different brands... Indy café. The blond woman behind the counter introduced herself as Alma, gave her a set of keys, and told her how to get to the flat. It sounded easy. Down the street. The square on the left.

"Come over for a drink later," she suggested.

"Sure."

The apartment was empty. A kitchen with a bar, high stools and a sea view. Two locked doors in the hallway and one that was open. This must be her room. It was bright, with a king-size bed and a wardrobe. She arranged her clothes, took a shower, and went out.

Miguel

"For the Greeks, exile was heavier than death because those who are far from home cannot be sincere, and those who cannot be sincere in their homeland are not able to be, because they are not really in it." [2]

---

[2] Unamuno: Articulos y discursos sobre Canarias, Francisco Navarro Artiles, 1980, Discurso de los juegos florales

Marina

The beginning of any journey can be so predictable with its excitements and expectations, and its repetitive actions (finding rental cars or taxis; journeys to and searches for the hotel or flat or house; contemplating the landscape and getting to know it, taking it in, attempting to digest it and hold it – if possible, forever – or forget it – if possible, forever; checking in, feeling satisfied – or not; noting the comfort or lack of comfort; looking for a place for breakfast or lunch or dinner; the end of the first day). It has just started, and it is already over. The only space in which it can be kept and experienced again and again is the space of memories. Even the awareness of the current moment cannot keep it from slipping away because the moment we are trying to stop has already passed. But still, every time there is something new, something different that distinguishes it from all the previous beginnings of all the previous trips.

This time it is the feeling, the special feeling that the meeting – no, not a meeting because they have not met yet – that the passing encounter with the boy has brought her. It is difficult to give it another name because it is so sudden and illogical, unreal but alive... the feeling. That is the word she used for it on that Saturday morning in January, shortly after she and Gerard got into the white Audi and took the road to Corralejo.

Gerard tells her something. She is not listening. She only catches occasional words as her eyes, behind sunglasses, scan the rocky landscape. Fuerteventura, Germans, World War II, Franco, Africa, asylum. Suddenly she becomes aware of the silence. Gerard has stopped talking. She takes a look at him; his gaze is fixed on the road. His sunglasses with a fine frame turn towards her and his hand gently caresses her knee.

Palm trees surround the hotel. "White, tidy cottage, two linden trees in front." How ridiculously your memory can surprise you. It strikes suddenly. Before you know it, it has already sucked you in. On the remote island in the ocean, a child's voice has started tinkling in an attempt to recite Ran Bosilek's poem "White, neat hut."

She banishes the memory. It does not belong here. The only similarity lies in the whiteness, nothing else. The hotel has eight storeys, a lush garden, a swimming pool, jacuzzi and dozens of sunbeds. No linden trees at all. The room is spacious, with a view of the ocean, the sands and the mountain ridge behind them.

And the ocean... The ocean has the colour of a postcard: blue-green, azure overflowing into the yellow of the island. Yellow like the dress she bought before they left, which now lies in her suitcase with her other dresses, her underwear, sandals and jerseys, patiently waiting to be worn for the first time. It is as if it had been a presentiment of the island, a hint of what was ahead of them. A sign, but of what? The island, the desert, the straw-coloured hair of the boy? Her eyes take in the ocean and draw her into it. Now they are one. Her lips open slightly, and she gives herself to it.

Carla

There is no time to waste. Time-is-wind-is-wave-is-surfing. Three hours of breaking the waves, the wind, the time, the surf. The moment you are on the board, all doubts, fears and thoughts scatter and disappear like sea foam. Keeping yourself on the board requires your full concentration. It takes *presence*. Here and now. One hundred per cent. An uncoordinated thought and the board slips beneath your feet, the wave knocks you, swallows you and spits you out wherever it decides.

She remembers the beginning, the first lessons. Catch the wave. That is it. But how do you catch a wave? How? You learn. Gradually. It is a feeling. A feeling that you learn to have. To possess this wave, to make it obey you, to make it yours. Like taming a rebellious horse. The horse is a different thing, a being. You make contact. You make it obey. But the wave... How do you conquer an element?

Gerd slides with the coming wave, slightly crouched on the board. He carries himself on it gracefully. The wind stretches his bright hair. Blows in his tanned face. A winner. A master of the waves.

How long ago was that? How had she managed?

She takes the next wave and also stands up. Flying in the spray, the wind, infinity...

The Writer

She had lunch on the square, which was visible from her kitchen window. The restaurants were full. She had imagined a deserted Corralejo in January. Instead, she found herself in a city flooded with sunshine and warmth, vibrant, joyful and hospitable. Quite different from the city in her memory.

The supermarket was around the corner. Everything here is around the corner. Comfortable, easy, calm – and slow. That is how she felt the rhythm of Corralejo in those first hours.

She did the chores for the next few days, then dropped in at the Indy. Alma was not there, but a big man was standing behind the bar: Kumar, the Indian owner. When he discovered she was Bulgarian, he told her of another Bulgarian who cleans his house. That surprised her. She had expected to be the only one on the island, which had more or less turned its back on Europe. She asked him to put them in touch, and he called her. They arranged for the Writer to go and see her the next day at a Sunday market.

"...the chance, which is the beginning of freedom," Unamuno winked at her.

She drank a small beer and met another member of Indy's team. Enrique, an Italian, had moved here because of the surf. His friends, a German surfing couple, had also arrived yesterday from Freiburg.

She spent the afternoon walking on the promenade and lying on one of the wooden platforms there. Not far from her was a statue of a woman with a long dress and an elegant hat. She was staring at the ocean, shading her eyes with her hand. Next to her was another statue of a man, a woman and a child, embracing. This woman's face radiated bliss and gratitude. Next to them, a bucket of dead fish. The statues of the waiting woman and of the woman whose waiting has been fulfilled: that is what she called them on this first day.

A street musician was playing the guitar and singing his arrangements of well-known pop songs. A lyrical and heartfelt performance. She turned her face to the sun and felt the tension that had built up over the past months melting away. The heat, the caress of the breeze, the gentle sound of the ocean... She has arrived in a different place. Different from the confident purposefulness of Brussels, from the crunch of the heavy European machine, the organised gaiety of the after-work parties, the easy communication and the difficult relationships, the shiny sports clubs, the smell of urine on the central streets, the poverty of the homeless sleeping on cardboard, the designer chic of the eurocrats, euro-consultants, euro-lobbyists, euro-successful-people, to whom it seems she now also belonged. It was... different. She wondered what she had wanted the second ticket for. She already knew she would not use it, she would not leave Corralejo in a week, nor two weeks, nor even a month; she knew she might never wish to leave Corralejo... And this knowledge came to her not as a thought but as a feeling. A feeling of peace, freedom and profound harmony that was forming somewhere at the depths of her tired being.

Marina

Pleasure reached every cell of her body. She moaned. Gerard continued moving in her in a rhythmic and controlled way, faster and faster. She opened her hands wide and grabbed the sheet. The pulsing started from her fingertips and, for endless seconds, spread throughout her body together with her scream. She became still, relaxed, and surrendered herself to the crescendo of his thrusting.

Later, as they lay side-by-side, she stared at the picture on the opposite wall. Square and yellow with shades of orange. In the upper left corner was a couple, seen from above, taking a selfie. The boy wore a backpack and embraced the girl. He held the camera with his other hand. Behind them, their shadow resembled an elephant.

Quite a simple composition, but there was something about it that would not let her look away. She gazed at it, mesmerised. Was it because of the predominant yellow colour, which reminded her of the dress she had bought before leaving, or because of the tranquillity and intimacy of the couple? Splashed by sunlight, two young people save a happy moment of their life in a photo. And the moment is saved twice: once in their image and again on the canvas. The sequence does not matter. It was not only that, but the yellow, that yellow like the body of Fuerteventura.

She got up, dressed and followed Gerard onto the balcony. He was resting on a sunbed, smoking a cigarette. He pulled her towards him and kissed her belly through the cotton top. She looked at the ocean, lapping at the shores of the desert. 'The shores of the desert' sounded absurd. But it was true. Her gaze slid down the dunes. They seemed so inviting. Perhaps if she walked out to them she would exit her world, and enter the happy world of the painting.

"I am going for a walk."

"Aren't you tired?"

"No."

The beach was long and wide, with light, fine sand. Half-empty. Abandoned sunbeds, arranged in twos, faced the ocean. Above them were umbrellas, furled and useless. Here and there, a family was sitting on the sand; children buried their hands in it; there were couples of all ages. To the left was a huge hotel, built in three parts. The central section was narrower than the two wings, and it looked like a large chicken with a doomed aspiration to fly. The ocean led to a mountain range whose wavy ridges were its stony continuation. To the right, the desert stretched as far as her gaze could reach. She went in that direction. The wind pulled her hair; she took a band from her little bag and tied it in a ponytail. She saw an empty, wood-built restaurant. The hotels stayed behind her. The dunes stretched before her, pale yellow from the sunlight, rounded and inviting.

The Writer

From the door, a heavy smell of fried mince wafted into her face. The sound of sizzling meat came from the kitchen. A young man was cooking. Average height, with a lean, muscular body, he had his back to her. He wore a vest and shorts.

"Hola."

The man turned. Sharp dark brown hair, grey eyes, straight nose.

He stretched his hand towards her, but his face remained expressionless.

"Fabrizio, nice to meet you."

His voice was flat and uninterested.

"What are you doing here, Fabrizio?"

"Cooking."

"On Fuerteventura?"

"I came for surfing. And I stayed."

"Just like that?"

"Just like that."

"Why?"

"I told you - because of surfing."

"Why here?"

"Because this is the place."

She had no idea yet how often she would hear these answers - paraphrased, but always the same: I came, I liked it, I stayed. She would come to see Fuerteventura as a place that enchants you, dooms you to itself and cannot be completely abandoned. But now, on the first day of her return to the island, this was no more than a vague intuition.

From their brief conversation, she learned that Fabrizio was Italian and worked as a waiter. His flatmate, Juan, was Spanish. He worked erratic shifts at the hospital and travelled a lot; his appearances in the flat were sporadic and unannounced.

The fatigue from the trip and the excitement overwhelmed her, and she went to bed. When she awoke, it was dark outside. Latin music came through the open kitchen window. She looked at the square. A quartet was playing on a small stage. Two couples were dancing salsa. Children were running around them. A little girl in a white dress was spinning in circles, alone. The restaurants were full. She felt like going out and experiencing the Saturday night in this town with a poetic name, to celebrate her newfound freedom... Instead, she went back to bed and fell asleep again.

Gerd

They have been here for less than a day, but it feels as if they had never left. The ocean assimilates you, and it seems like the only reality. The only true reality. Everything else is a dream. Carla had booked tickets for a play some time ago, Life is a Dream. That is the feeling: life is a dream. And surfing is life. The rest is in-between-surfing. In-between-living.

Everything was supposedly the same. But not quite. The feeling after the meeting with the woman at the airport. Her look, her slight smile... He could still see them, hours after they had passed each other. This was something... new. Different. Not that he never looked at beautiful women. Of course, he did. But they just passed by. A fleeting registration of features that pleased the eye. But this one... was still here. She was no magazine model. That was the weird thing. As if the island was playing tricks on him, leaving him dumbfounded.

The ocean swell turns him around, and the strength of his irrational desire to see the woman again gradually fades.

Exhausted, they drink beers at the *Buena Onda*. The sunset softens Carla's features and makes her face shine. Earlier, he watched her lithe body resisting the element of water. He caresses her knee under the table. She throws him *that* look and gently smiles.

Marina

"New dress?" says Gerard, his eyes laughing. "I like it."

She saw it in the window of a small boutique in the Marolles, in a sunny moment on an overcast Sunday when Gerard was playing golf. She had not planned to go shopping, only to walk, listen to street musicians and wander around the flea market on Place de Jeu de Balle, containing pieces of a myriad of worlds; sink into the Sunday oblivion of the artistic heart of Brussels. She strolled down Rue Haute glancing carelessly in the shop windows and at the people passing by, her eyes dwelling long enough to catch one detail or another: the colour of a person's eyes, a smile, a restless lock of hair, the cut of someone's clothing, hands holding hands, some antique furniture, groceries, a dog, a yellow dress... a yellow dress. She stopped in front of the window and stared at it with slightly narrowed eyes, as if to see the future, to see herself in this dress and everything she would go through while wearing it; to judge what she would feel like as *the woman in the yellow dress* and what that woman might be capable of. She entered the shop. The saleswoman took the dress off its mannequin and handed it to her. She liked its touch on her body. One hundred per cent silk, the label said. The silk stroked her skin with all of its hundred per cent. She looked at herself wearing the dress, in a large antique mirror with a frame and wheels. The saleswoman was also looking at her.

"Yellow is the colour of happiness. It suits you."

There was no need to convince her. Marina took out her credit card and paid.

Marina and Gerard drove across the desert to Corralejo. They passed down the main street and parked in one of the side streets, then walked back to it. Shops, bars, restaurants. Sales signs everywhere. They reached the pedestrian area of the city and continued down to the pier. A statue of a woman in a long dress, with her hand to her forehead staring at the ocean. She radiated hope and expectation. Beside her, another composition showed a woman hugging her returning sailor and their daughter. She looked at them. The woman who had welcomed her beloved represented her past. The eternally waiting woman, her present. She wanted it to be the other way around. But it was not. She was the woman, staring at the horizon of the past and hoping for... what... a miracle?

They sit in one of the waterside restaurants. In front, a man is playing his own arrangements of popular songs on a guitar. "Rooooxaane..."

"I like Corralejo," says Marina. "It has... atmosphere."

Gerard smiles and presses her hand.

The sun sets, colouring the horizon in pink-orange: the orange light that makes so many tourists ask Emiliyan if he has used photoshop on his photos to only get a curt: "No." He is tired of explaining. How can he ever convince them that everything in his photos is as it is, a saved moment of the reality of Fuerteventura, as God created it, and as he has learned to capture it with his camera, gradually, consistently and flawlessly?

Marina sips the white wine that Gerard has chosen, and takes in the pinkish-orange sky with her eyes, while he tries to draw her into making plans for the coming days.

Gerard

Her tranquillity, the brightness of her eyes, her light smile: these were enough to make him feel happy. Happy and grateful, not for the cruel chance that brought them together, but to the providence which linked their fates. She was his beginning and end. Was such an experience of love only possible in maturity? He did not know. It happened like that. He had been in love with Viviane. He loved her, and, with love and tenderness, they had made two children. But obligations, fatigue, habit, demands, and her eternal dissatisfaction burned up the love. Their marriage resembled a field after a summer fire: the fire is gone, only embers and smoke are left.

With Marina, it was different from the beginning. Not as elemental and sweeping, but deep. Conscious. Evoked not so much by her delicate beauty as by her air of gentle mystery; her dreaminess and sadness. It derived from her femininity, which manifested itself in everything, from her clothing to the way she spoke and behaved. She was reserved, exquisite and friendly in an unobtrusive way. He felt good with her. He felt himself.

That had not changed. Three years later, she still lived encapsulated, following the same trajectories that maintained her apparent balance. At Christmas, he thought that perhaps the time had come for a transition, for her gradual return to life and, who knows, maybe to joy. A colleague of his had spent his holiday on Fuerteventura and recommended the island as a great place – still not too touristy, with large beaches... Once he had been to Tenerife with Viviane and the children, but that had been too commercial for them. It quelled any desire to try the other Canary Islands. Besides, Viviane developed a taste for the sort of islands and destinations that needed a ten or fifteen-hour flight to reach. With two children, the holiday began in such a stressful way that by the time they finally managed to relax, it was time to go back.

He saw pictures of Fuerteventura online. The yellow of the island reminded him of the wheat fields of his childhood. The desert landscape exuded serenity and timelessness, different from the typical European scenery. Without leaving the continent geographically or exhausting themselves with endless flights and airport stop-overs, they would find themselves in *a different* place. A suitable place for the start of the transition he was hoping to inspire in Marina. So he proposed that this year, they should spend their winter holiday on Fuerteventura. Now, as he sees the island's beneficial effect on her already on this first day, he feels his decision was the right one.

The Writer

In the morning, rested and refreshed, she returned to the promenade. The previous night's liveliness had given way to the kind of Sunday calm you can experience in any city, but especially in cities that suffer from mass insomnia on Saturdays – an insomnia which she had slept through. *There will be other Saturday nights*, she told herself. The streets were half empty. Early-rising tourists were running along the promenade. The staff of the restaurants were preparing for another long day. Here and there someone was drinking coffee. On the upper end of the beach, not far away from the platforms where she had lain yesterday, a man in a bathing costume and a peaked cap was sculpting a sandcastle. She stopped and stared. The man was shaping the castle down to the smallest detail, fabulously authentic. She saw herself building a sand tower on another beach. Hers would be far more abstract, purity of line completely absent, but compensated for by curling intricacy. Small roses like those that her mother piped onto the cakes of her childhood. Now the tower is erected, fragile and delicate. Along comes a wave and sweeps it away. Where did she go wrong? Perhaps the site was not the best, or the density of its structure.

There was a box with some coins next to the man. After the usual long rummaging in her bag, she took out a euro. The man thanked her, reached into the jar beside him, and handed her a small glass ball in iridescent yellow and blue. She held it up to the sun, and its colours shone. She turned it in her fingers, and they moved animatedly, showing the birth of the cosmos out of primordial chaos. She dropped the germ of the cosmos into the chaos of her purse and went along the street. The tide had moved out, and wet rocks glistened in the sun, uncovered and accessible. She reached the beach, where young people in surfing suits sat in a circle, looking at the teacher who was explaining the rules of windsurfing. After a while, they all stood up and started exercising. She turned and found herself in front of the Indy.

She drank a tea, talking with Alma and Kumar, then walked lazily up the main street in the direction she had come from yesterday and took the road to El Campanario.

Carla

Carla brushed her teeth thoroughly, in front of the mirror in her blue cotton nightgown. Yesterday's anxiety had dissipated and now it seemed laughable. Just one day, but what a change. What an effect this island had had on Gerd. Last night they had made love like at the beginning of their relationship: spontaneously, joyfully and breathlessly. Like being hungry. The sea, the sun, the waves: in a single day they had given Gerd the stimulus he had been missing in recent months. Fuerteventura was an inexhaustible reservoir of life-giving energy.

Their home city was also a special place. The Black Forest is said to be an energy centre. It is not surprising that spiritual practices are so popular in the area. But on Fuerteventura the energy moved differently for them. Whereas in Freiburg its direction was closure, encirclement and centring in the home, on the island what was happening was expansion, dilution and connection to the natural elements, turning nature into a home. Carla needed both.

Marina

They heard about the Sunday market in El Campanario from the receptionist. The many stalls in the narrow streets sell jewellery, souvenirs, photographs, paintings and such like. Alongside the stalls, there are cafes as well as shops, attempting to attract customers with their seasonal discounts.

The plethora of objects in different sizes and colours both disturb and hypnotise her. She passes from booth to booth, holding one item after another in her hand as if to feel its energy but, unable to decide, returns it. She spends longer with the glass angels hanging on their transparent cords. Pale purple, pale pink, white angels, with elongated bodies and rounded wings. Angels of modernity. "Do you want to buy one?" Gerard asks. She is silent. Hesitant. "Which one do you like?" She takes a pale purple one. The woman wraps it and gives it to her with a smile. "We all need an angel. Perhaps this is yours." *Mine flew away long ago...*, she thinks. Gerard pays and they continue their way.

Around the corner, photographs of Fuerteventura attract her attention. In particular a triptych of flying birds. Such energy in their movement! Such coiled dynamic life.

"Do you like it?" asks her the man behind the stall, in Spanish.

"Are they yours?"

"Yes."

"They have... presence. Spirit..."

"Thank you very much," he says in a very expressive voice, emphasising each syllable.

He is attractive. Charismatic. Younger.

Behind him stands an older woman with blond hair, tied in a ponytail.

"This is only part of my work," the man says. "I can show you more if you are interested."

Yes, she is interested. He turns to the woman and tells her in Bulgarian:

"Dari, could you give me the folder."

Marina is not expecting to meet any compatriots! It catches her off her guard.

"You are Bulgarians," is the only thing she is able to say as if it is not obvious.

"Obviously, you too! And we might not have found out until the end," the man smiles calmly.

"I didn't know there were Bulgarians here."

"Oh, there are at least twenty of us."

"Today we're even expecting a writer," the woman joins in.

Marina looks inside the folder. She likes his other work, but the triptych with the birds remains her favourite. He offers her a deck of photos and invites her to pick one. She takes one out carefully and turns it over. A vast deserted beach, surrounded by cliffs under a dramatic sky with dark clouds, merging with the boiling ocean. And, in the midst of the abyss, a lonely white wave.

The photographer raises his eyebrows.

"Cofete. A special place."

The Writer

In El Campanario there are streets, a circular space with a stage surrounded by restaurants, and many stalls offering paintings, jewellery, photographs and any number of products created by human hands and imagination.

She follows a street along a line of restaurants and cafes. In one corner stands a blond woman of around fifty. This must be

Darina. Having seen the Writer's quizzical look, she smiles and extends her hand. The Writer follows her to the stand with photographs, behind which a tall, dark-haired man stands speaking to a woman in Spanish. When their conversation is over, he approaches them.

"How happy you look! I rarely meet such Bulgarians - so smiling and radiant," he turns to the Writer

"Really?"

"This is Emiliyan," Darina introduces him.

"Are the photographs yours?"

"All of them."

She looks at them attentively. They have captured all the different conditions of the island: sunsets, rocks, waves, a triptych with flying birds... Magical and authentic, the soul of Fuerteventura stares at her. She wants to have them all.

Emiliyan tells her he has lived here for eight years but does not fully know the island yet. And she? What can she hope for in the short time that she has allowed herself? They agree to meet later in a restaurant on the promenade and she goes to take the bus to the dunes.

Marina

She walks on the beach. The fine cool sand caresses her feet. The clouds, which covered the sky in the morning, have scattered and the sun is now shining with its maximum force for January. There are people in swimsuits or shorts, walking and lying here and there. Among them a woman, wearing jeans and a pink cardigan, is exposing only her face and bare feet to the sun. She has a small laptop on her knees, her fingers rattle rhythmically on its keyboard. She looks up, directing her dark sunglasses to her and smiles slightly. Marina also nods.

A blond girl in an orange swimsuit runs along the beach. The upper part of her suit has ridden up her neck like a bow tie. Her hair is scattered over her shoulders and back. Marina shifts her gaze from her to the dunes. This model of a desert gives her a sense of timelessness.

Nothing
      has ever
           been
               nor
           will be
       anything
    else but
sand.

Where did this thought come from? From the sand? From the nothingness? She repeats it like a mantra. There is a rhythm to it as from a pounding drum. Noth-ing has ev-er be-en nor will be any-thing el-se but sand. Ta-Ta-tar-ta-ra. A child's drum. Sandy hair and a high little voice, which rhythmically recites: "I am mama's sun…" She shakes her head to banish the memory of it.

Nothing
      has ever
           been
               nor
           will be
       anything
    else but
sand.

She likes the dunes more than Corralejo, Brussels or Sofia. Especially more than Sofia. She walks and walks, and she feels like staying here forever, on this island, combining the timelessness of the desert and the vastness of the ocean; the whisper of the waves and the silence of the sand. In this bareness, one hears and sees oneself better.

The sudden noise of an engine. Two small beach-buggies go past, two men driving but she cannot see their features from this distance. *The island is a mini-world, a playground, in the mini-desert grown-up children drive buggies.* What nonsense goes through her mind, but how good it makes her feel. Easiness. Easiness. The buggies have disappeared behind the dunes and the sound of their engines gradually fades.

Gerd

A day without wind. A true rarity on Fuerteventura. You can count the days like this on the fingers of one hand. Well, perhaps both hands. What are we going to do? It is no good for surfing. The ocean has turned into a lake. No, no good at all... What to do... I have an idea. A funny one. Well, not as much fun as surfing, but cool. What? You will see. Jump in the car. We will go to the dunes.

They park near the one big hotel and walk towards the other one. The one that looks like a wardrobe in three sections. A wardrobe containing the luxurious lives of all its inhabitants, in rooms like drawers. Hop, one life here. Hey, another life there. And several lives together, as couples and families do not count as one life anyway... everyone has their own cloak of thoughts, emotions, feelings, secrets... For a couple of days, he has become quite a philosopher. Carla looks at him. He reads a question in her eyes. But he is tired of responding to her need for security and love. It seems to him that he is party to an unspoken agreement obliging him never to leave her, and her never to show a lack of understanding, tolerance or patience. Perfection, however, is more tiring than any flaw.

"We have arrived," Enrique says, pointing at some buggies.

Gerd looks at him with bewilderment.

"Are you serious?"

"Of course!"

Five minutes later, they are speeding away in two of them. Carla sits behind Gerd. When they reach the sunbeds, she steps out. She strips to her swimsuit and relaxes on a sunbed. She takes out her suncream and meticulously applies it, first on her face, then to her body.

"Well?" Enrique raises his eyebrows.

"Awesome!" exclaims Gerd.

"Vamos?"

"Vamos! Hasta pronto, meine liebe," shouts Gerd towards Carla and sends her a kiss. She giggles and watches them until they drive out of sight. Then she rests her head and closes her eyes under the gentle caress of the sun.

As the speed increases, Gerd's scepticism disappears completely. This really is fun! Suddenly he is five again, riding the bumper cars in Freiburg. He drives around a square; the fifteen square metres become a whole world where he passes mountains, villages, cities, borders, seas and oceans. He turns in a circle, but in fact, this is a spiral, and at every turn a new territory awaits him, a new country, a new continent, until he passes into this exact circle where he is driving through the desert of Fuerteventura with his fearless companion, both uncatchable and unbeatable. Yuhuuu! Yuhuuu, Enrique yells back and they spin along to the next dune-mountain-conquest-over-the-nine-mountains-and-across-the-eight-oceans. And so they continue to the end of the desert. They make a turn and drive back. At the foot of the highest dune, he looks up and sees her. A thoughtful princess, sitting in the tower, where she waits to be rescued. Her face is directed towards the sky. This lasts only a moment. Disturbed by the noise of the engines, she bows her head. He sees her dark wavy hair and the blue of the sky above them. Like an angel leaning over him. His eyes slide over the blue linen dress. And he remembers. The airport.

Carla

She did not know how much time had passed until she heard the growl of the engines again. The sun had been shining intensely and she could not move from such bliss. She only opened her eyes when the noise stopped. Then she turned and froze. A woman was sitting behind Gerd! Carla noticed she was pretty, older than them, perhaps, wearing a blue dress.

Her gaze shifted from Gerd's companion to him – examining, questioning.

"Hola, mi querida. Your sweetheart has just saved a princess. Let me introduce you, princess..."

"Marina."

"Marina, this is Carla. This Italian gigolo is Enrique. And the humble persona of your saviour – Gerd the German."

Marina curved the edges of her lips in an embarrassed half-smile.

"In fairytales, after rescuing the princess the hero marries her... right?" asked Carla, supposedly joking, though her voice did not sound like it.

"In our story, they all go together to drink a beer," Enrique said, pointing at the wooden restaurant among the dunes.

Marina looked in the direction of the hotel.

"Nooo, don't even think about leaving," Enrique insisted, "you are obliged to have at least one beer with your saviours."

Marina hesitated, then walked with him. Carla and Gerd followed them.

Gerd

Enrique was lagging behind. Gerd boosted the motor to gain ground and reach her first.

"Buongiorno, Princhipesa!"

"Buongiorno...," she smiled, a little uncertain.

But her eyes! Her eyes looked at him without embarrassment. There was no uncertainty there, just deep tenderness.

"Apologies for being so late," Gerd switched to English.

"It's OK. I was waiting for you."

"Well, jump on the horse then," he showed her the empty seat behind him.

Enrique arrived and also stopped. A half-astonished half-asking smile that comes with the understanding that you have missed something appeared on his face.

Marina hesitated, got up slowly and sat behind Gerd. Her hands embraced his waist.

"Off we goooo!"

He pressed the accelerator and the buggy shot down the dune as fast as it would go.

Normally, it would never have crossed his mind to invite a stranger into his car, even if that car was just a buggy. For one thing, he had a girlfriend, and for another, that girlfriend was waiting for him even now. But at that moment everything stopped. His whole rational, social and emotional experience disappeared, and his learned reactions to the familiar situations of life flew away with it. It was as if it was not him. Someone else spoke to the Bulgarian and invited her into his buggy, someone who had borrowed his body and his spirit. Yet at the same time, it seemed to him that, in doing so, he was being his real self, more than he had ever been before.

Carla

Only one table was occupied. There was an older man with thinning hair sitting at it together with a younger woman. Enrique greeted them both and their group joined them. Introductions, beers, toasts... Both women were Bulgarians who lived in Brussels. It sounded like a joke. But it was true, and Carla did not find it funny at all.

It turned out that Gerd's Princess, Marina, was married to a Frenchman who was waiting for her in their hotel. He held a senior post in the European institutions. She also worked for the EU, but as a freelance translator. The other woman, whose name she missed, was a writer working on a book about a Spanish philosopher who stayed on the island. The Writer was calm and sociable. She asked them questions, listened and showed interest. Carla found her quite pleasant. But Marina bothered her. There was something vague and appealing about her locked-in, silent presence, which made Carla instinctively distrust her.

It seemed to her she was taking part in a show without being aware of her role in it; that everything she was saying were lines memorised from another play; that, in the space of just a few minutes, the decor, the characters and their positions had changed so radically that she was not sure she would ever see the world again as she used to know it. Their world. Hers and Gerd's.

Gerard

His first impression was confirmed in the following days. The decision to come here had been a very good one indeed. The island was having a beneficial effect on Marina. She would come back from her walks in the dunes with a peaceful expression, exuding serenity rather than her usual sadness.

While she was out, Gerard lay by the pool with a book. In recent months his work had been very intense with the new project and he needed this rest.

That day, however, Marina was taking more time than usual. He got worried and phoned her. She did not reply immediately, and when she did, he could hear voices around her. She said she had met some people, but she would not be late. Spontaneous encounters were not typical of her these days. She had locked herself in and avoided close contact, especially with strangers.

When she returned a little later, he saw no change in her behaviour. But her eyes and face: something had lit her up inside, or so it seemed to him.

She told him about the German couple, their Italian friend and the Bulgarian writer. It was not really clear how they had met, but that was not so important. More important was that the present reality had taken precedence over the past... at least for now. He suggested she invite them for dinner. She replied vaguely but did not refuse. She went to bed and stared for a long time at the yellow painting on the opposite wall.

Marina

She had not tried to make new contacts for years. Moreover, she had purposely avoided them. She felt better inside her secluded space. Only there could she experience the past. Only there, remembering for the thousandth time every little memory, every insignificant incident, could she recreate the reality as it was *before*, as if it had never changed. In that reality she lived in a small flat in one of the best districts of Sofia; she had a husband, whom she loved, as well as an astonishing, beautiful daughter:

blonde and smiling. 'White, tidy cottage...' Day after day she was perfecting the impossible skill of arresting time. That other life became increasingly real, as though she was living it and dreaming her current life.

Meeting Gerd had upset the balance between the two realities. With this new emotion, the reality of her being weighed heavier and became alarmingly present. A desire grew in her: the strong and overbearing desire to see him again. And when fate, providence and the island met them at the dunes, and he invited her into his buggy, she lost her ability to think. All she could do was obey – take his hand, get into the buggy and enter the momentary, sweet illusion that yes, she is this princess locked in the tower, and he was the prince who came to rescue her on a white horse. In this case, a dark green buggy. In the short minutes of driving down to the beach, with her arms wrapped around him and with the wind in her hair, she felt happiness. It shifted any thought and emotion, and turned her into a beating heart. When in the next moment they stopped by the sunbeds and he presented the nice-looking young woman to her as his girlfriend, this heart briefly stopped in clinical death. Then it came back to life with a slower rhythm. As if it was not normal for him to have a girlfriend, like she had a man. What would have changed if he did not have one? She felt uncomfortable. Part of her wanted to leave. The day's events were more than she could take: the unexpected meeting with the boy from the airport, the discovery that he had a girlfriend, and then this woman, whom she had earlier greeted, and who turned out to be Bulgarian... Apparently, it was impossible to avoid the Bulgarians on this island, which otherwise blurred the feeling of being in Europe, and created a sense of some place exotic and remote. It was far easier for her in Brussels, where there were many more Bulgarians – but also more opportunities to control the circumstances and avoid them. On Fuerteventura, however, the chance was waiting behind every dune and engaged with her whether she wanted it or not. The only thing that kept her there were Gerd's blue-grey eyes, which watched her with keen interest. The presence of his girlfriend did not diminish in any way her attraction to him. In the ensuing self-analysis, she attributed this to the *feeling* that the first meeting with him had brought. A feeling which, until two days ago, she thought she would never experience again. That invigorating, joyful, painful force, a mix of longing, tenderness and ecstasy.

The desire to look into his eyes again. To hear his voice. Only that. No more. Is it a crime? Is it wrong? When a desire appears after years of absence, it cannot be ignored and smothered as it germinates. That is, it could... but it should not.

And as this "cannot" crystallised within her, she agreed to Gerard's proposal to invite her new acquaintances to dinner.

Carla

She had not seen Gerd like this for the seven years of their relationship. Being so familiar with another woman. Taking her into his buggy... That was not typical of him. Not at all.

Carla noticed the way she looked at him. Married or not, she definitely liked him. That is normal. Human. Gerd is an attractive man. She is not the first nor will she be the last. Let her like him as much as she wants. But he... why had he allowed her into their day? Into their life, albeit briefly? It was natural for him to like other women, no matter how unpleasant the thought was... However, it is one thing for a woman to make an impression on you, but another to meet her, and it is an altogether different thing again to take her to your girlfriend. Probably the last one should be reassuring. Why did it not reassure her then? Where did this anxiety come from? Was it intuition or paranoia? She decided not to poison herself any more. She told herself that these thoughts came from her, not from reality. The reality was that Gerd was hers and she was his. They belonged to each other. There was no power to change that. She shook her head to get rid of the thoughts. She inhaled. Exhaled. Visualised light splashing through her body. Her face relaxed. She opened a beer and went out onto the balcony, where Gerd and Enrique were continuing their surfless day.

The Writer

The sharp tone of the phone shook her out of her nap. She had fallen asleep in her clothes as she was reading. A message from Enrique. "Hey, Writer, where are you?". "Am tired, won't make it tonight ..." "Will pick you up in 15 min." She started answering him not to bother, but stopped, got up and began to prepare for going out.

An hour later, she was sipping a mojito and watching a surfer skillfully descending in the tube of the wave. Like a skater on a ramp. Only this ramp was mobile, alive and dangerous like an open maw. One wrong move and you can sink into it and never come out. In the stories of those who have experienced clinical death, there is often a tunnel with light at its end. What do you see at the end of the wave-tube-tunnel? To what sort of a realm does it lead? Is it the same or another underwater world? Do the souls of those who drown go to another beyond? Do the souls of the surfers, swallowed by the ocean, continue their surfing in infinity? Is this their paradise – unmolested, carrying on the waves of eternity?

"What are you thinking about? Has the surf inspired you?" asked Enrique.

"Have you ever been in the tube?"

"No. It takes a lot of experience to enter the tube. They say, however, that the feeling is indescribable."

"And the fear?"

"When there is trust, there is no fear. And in surfing, you must trust."

"Whom?"

"Yourself. The board. The wave."

"And those who died? Didn't they trust?"

"Maybe not enough. Trust starts with knowing. If you don't know yourself and the ocean enough, you shouldn't go into the tube. Also in life, trust is not always justified. Does this, however, mean we should not believe?"

"You know, I dance tango. And it doesn't work without trust either. No trust, no tango."

"Let's see if it applies to salsa!"

Enrique took her hand and she followed him to the dance floor. They carried themselves in a series of slips, spins, playful glances. Alma and Kumar, Gerd and Carla danced next to them. It was their third bar tonight. In the previous two, Kumar had warmly greeted the barmen and then joyfully shouted: "Chupito, chupito!". They had drunk one or two chupitos at each place. There were flat screens almost everywhere, which showed shots depicting surfing giant waves. A continual inspiration and incentive for the insiders. Later Carla told her how Gerd met Enrique at an Erasmus in Spain. Then Enrique came to Fuerte, got obsessed with surfing, and moved here. Three years ago they visited him and also got hooked.

Wave, board, tunnel... The words shook off the dust of the familiar and shone with newly acquired sense. She had come to write a book about Unamuno and the island. Instead, she had not stopped listening about surfing. And had not written a single line of the novel.

Carla

The call came on Monday, while they were relaxing on the sand and had the sandwiches Carla had made. She saw a foreign prefix, but never thought it could be her. She had not expected her to be so bold. To call her?!... Marina invited them to dinner with Enrique and the Writer. She could have pretended that she never received this call. Something was whispering in her ears that this lie, and more precisely this hiding, would have been noble. Rescuing. Good not only for her. But also for Gerd, and the Bulgarian, and her husband. Although none of them knew it yet. Gerd had pricked up his ears as she spoke and looked at her inquisitively. There was no way to hide it. He pretended he did not remember who she talked about - there were two Bulgarian women there. But had he driven both in his buggy... Both Enrique and Gerd responded positively - why not see how eurocrats live? As if it was not clear. As if it was so interesting or exciting. But she did not want to start pointless arguments. The forbidding makes the desire stronger, she knew it well. She returned Marina's call and –with well-disguised reluctance – confirmed the dinner.

The Writer

She stood by the railing on the roof of the building and contemplated the horizon. Rocky hills enclosed the city outline behind the last buildings. The sun was just where the mountain and the rooftops met. She looked down. There were people walking in the street. A skater passed, made an ollie and turned around the corner, the sound of sliding wheels reaching her for a while. Thin white cobwebby clouds hung over the ocean, where the blue was turning pink. A long grey cloud slowly moved left behind the buildings to the point where the sun had set. She already knew that this was not the end of the sunset, but only its beginning. Sunsets over Corralejo, when the weather was clear, were like a spectacular light show. Bright and stunning. Just for a moment the solar radiance became intensely pink-orange and lit up the whole sky, colouring the white of the clouds. The light sprung from behind the buildings and spilt out to the horizontal and vertical of the sky. She had seen similar light in some biblical paintings, in which the artist had managed to depict the dissolution of the heavens, the multiple layers and the shine from the Lord's halo. But even these paintings waned before the sunset of Corralejo. Breathless, she felt at one with the Creation. Another skater passed and the sound of the wheels again echoed behind him. On the roof of the neighbouring building, two large dogs ran, on the building behind it pigeons hovered around their hut. The colour of the sky changed every second. The pink hue melted into orange, gradually becoming grey in the clouds. The violet colour of the sea dissipated, replaced by the lead of the darkness. The last sunbeams slowly died to give way to the night. The moon grew brighter and brighter in the gathering darkness. The show was over. She sighed, shivered from the breeze, which had become more tangible after the sunset, picked up her laptop from the towel next to the chimney, took the towel as well and went down to the flat. The bathroom door was open. A shirtless young man was vigorously brushing his teeth. He turned his head towards her, fixed her with his green stare and gave her a foamy smile. Juan. Something between her womb and heart fluttered like a bird in a cage.

"Hola!" she greeted him.

He nodded, still smiling, and continued brushing.

Carla

A wave chased Gerd with its jagged maw, reached him, struck him and swallowed him with the board. His head appeared on the surface after a moment and he began to row back inside, waiting for the next wave. He descended it lying on the board, got up and reached the shallow waters.

They had been surfing for two hours along one of the small northern beaches. She was tired. The previous night they had again passed by Buena Onda and Banana Bar, had drunk beers and talked with other surfers, then had made love half-asleep. Days became nights became days in its repetition of surfing, surfers' bars, conversations about surfing, living for surfing - which never bored them... Nothing else existed. Nothing else was as real as this life - short, saturated, packed into their limited time, but continuing in them after their departure in the interval to their next arrival. Back in the orbit of Freiburg, they looked at their photos from Fuerte, watched movies and videos, on YouTube, with surfers mastering giant waves, spoke with Enrique via Skype and planned their holiday. Their life had changed. And they had changed with it or vice versa, but - regardless of the sequence and the dynamic - nothing was the same. The surfing and the time spent on the island were a new bond for their relationship, another place, beyond the physical space, in which they met in a different way and which was just for them, only them, because no one else had experienced it as they had in their togetherness. This sharing ensured its privacy from others. All the others. For the first time, Carla felt that synchronicity and ease between them, when Fuerte and the surf entered their life. Previously they had lived in a banal plot, in which an ordinary, not particularly beautiful nor talented but stubborn and purposeful girl dreamed of meeting the prince. The girl turned into an ordinary, not particularly beautiful, actually rather plain young woman, who however, still steadfastly sought the prince and prepared for meeting him. One day she really met him and no force could stop her from being with him, to love him and to devote herself to him. Even the absence of a special interest in him was not an obstacle and the determination of her striving overcame his lack of interest. Their relationship, which began as a slight deviation from the prince's carefully grown preferences - because it is clear to everyone that princes look for princesses, or at least exceptional women - grew into a partnership with an increasingly dominating flavour of the fateful "until death do us part."

Gerd's parents (hers had died long ago), relatives and friends cemented the impression that they were made for each other - such harmony and understanding do not happen often, and when they happen, they should not be wasted, because this would mean losing 'the Chance' that is given once in a lifetime. And should you miss it, you are doomed to lifelong self-pity and bitterness.

Fuerteventura has become the promised land of their relationship and surf provided an additional passion between them. Common passion means shared. The passion for surfing, transformed into a passion for one another. Together they were swept away by the fury of the ocean and together they took their first wave. "We love something together" might lead to "we love one another". For many couples, this is a child. For them, it was surfing.

But now this bond is not strong enough. Everything seems the same on the surface. But it is not. Gerd is not fully with her, she senses it. Since he met Marina she feels that he has only mimicked normality. His thoughts and emotions are elsewhere. But she does not want to talk about it. It's like Pandora's box, this conversation... So she also continues to mimic the normality of their Fuerteventuran existence. And anxiously awaits the dinner with the Bulgarian–French couple.

Miguel

"A truth is indeed at work in us only if, after we have forgotten it, we've turned it into our natural quality – then we really possess it."[3]

Marina

Gerard and she were sitting in the restaurant garden when Gerd, Carla and Enrique arrived. While they exchanged the customary kisses, she breathed him in. A scent of sun and ocean. She had sensed it that day, on the buggy, clinging to his back. She woke up at night and tried to recall it, to find it in the memory of her sense of smell, preserve it like something innocently taken away from him. A small theft, in which there was nothing criminal, nothing stolen...

Gerard, as usual, gave an initial push to the conversation - from Freiburg and Germany through Brussels, Fuerteventura and surf, to their acquaintance. She left him the initiative with relief. It was one of the first things that attracted her to him in the early days of their relationship - his ability to master the situation in a calm non-imposing way, but setting the direction. Later, when they began to live together, this allowed her to inhabit that world, located in the time-space of the past, but experienced by her as present in an intensive and focused way. Gerard, being the

---

[3] Miguel de Unamuno, The childhood of Don Quixote, Publishing house "Zahari Stoianov"

present, without realising this, had become the best guardian of her past. With his natural sociability, he guaranteed the unobtrusiveness of her silence and the inviolability of the world hidden behind it.

Tonight she followed the conversation. Not so much the words as the facial expressions and the eyes, the reactions, the movements of hands. Meanwhile, the Writer had arrived with a half-hour delay. She apologised, saying she had to finish writing something. She sat next to her at the place where previously Enrique sat, but who had gallantly given it up for her. She ordered a glass of white wine and a salad and joined the conversation with ease. They were sitting in the following order: at one end - Gerard, on his left - Marina, on his right – Gerd, next to Marina – the Writer, next to Gerd and opposite the Writer - Carla, at the other end of the table, between Carla and the Writer - Enrique. The conversation moved like a ball that the three men and Carla skillfully threw among themselves. The Writer also managed to catch the ball, rotate it thoughtfully in her hands and toss it suddenly in an unexpected direction. Marina felt like a silent referee in this game. A referee who only observes and registers but does not interfere. Gerard was in his element - the young company definitely pleased him, and the idea of being accepted by them and of making them feel good, obviously stimulated him. Gerd seemed confident, his voice was vibrant, he was smiling. Every time their eyes met, it surged heat in Marina, and she wondered if the sweetness she saw in his eyes was only for her or was inherent. Carla participated convincingly, shared viewpoints, but looked thoughtful even when smiling. Her eyes sought an answer to unspoken questions. At times Marina felt them on her face like caterpillars - crawling, probing, studying. She met them briefly or ignored them. Enrique was relaxed, smiling, jocular. His tone became noticeably more alive with the arrival of the Writer. His dark eyes darted to her and stayed a little longer than normal. She showed interest in everyone, listening and responding with a friendly restraint.

Gradually, the group split into two. Gerard, the Writer and Carla on one side and Enrique and Gerd on the other. Marina remained in the middle and could hear phrases of both, depending on the direction of her attention. On the left, Gerard's voice dominated, on the right – Enrique's. She noted that if she repetitively shifted her attention from one group to the other, a new conversation was constructed, accessible only to her.

... German submariners went to Handia to relax... We can go to this beach tomorrow ... Gustav Winter, haven't you heard?.. Should I buy this board, what do you say?... Dubious history and unclear ... Even so, I think it's worth it... But still it isn't coincidental that the old capital is called Betancouria... Endless summer, I loved it, imagine one day we do this, chasing the summer on our boards, how does that sound?... He met his second wife here, much younger than him and built the castle in Handia... Do we need to go so far, when here we have everything we need, an endless surf season...

She apologised, got up and walked to the hotel. On the way out of the toilet, she looked at herself in the mirror. She wore the yellow dress, which accentuated her complexion. Gerard said that her skin had a honey colour. She stared at her face, not at its features but at its expression. She found something new. Or maybe old but long forgotten? A shadow of dreaminess. A shadow of hope. For three years she had inhabited only the space of the past, while the space of dreams is always the future. Looking forward had become unusual for her and therefore exciting and a little scary. She felt pregnant again - in her womb, like a child, the *feeling* associated with the boy had taken hold. Gerd. She sighed, came out of the toilet and faced him. He stood in the hallway and looked at her. She walked straight to him - silently, innocently, and when she almost reached him, ready to say something polite and insignificant, he raised his hand and stroked her. She looked at him, frozen. Everything stopped. There was only this moment when his hand slid down her neck, shoulders, chest, gently and tenderly followed her contours, wrapped her waist and pulled her close. Her body flared under the movement of his hand. She felt his lips, their butterfly touch. They stood motionless, with rapid breathing, a small eternity. Suddenly they heard footsteps, he stepped back and ducked into the men's toilet. She leaned against the wall to overcome the excitement, to assemble herself, to return. The Writer appeared.

"Are you okay?" she asked.

"Yes, yes, I'm fine... I'm just a little bit dizzy... from the wine."

The Writer looked her in the eyes.

"A very good wine, indeed," she said after a pause. Back at the table, she tried to look natural, that is serious, self-absorbed, neutral. She made an effort to hide the happiness overflowing in her, brazenly, boldly, sinfully. Gerard reached out, grabbed her hand and squeezed it. She caught Carla's eyes - tense and still questioning. Marina asked her something about her centre for spiritual practices in Freiburg, in order to contain this wave, to direct her attention elsewhere, to put it in a rational framework. Carla started explaining, but she did not hear much. She nodded, imitating interest and trying to guess the right questions.

Gerd also returned. He sat next to Carla and wrapped her waist with his hand, examining Marina. She avoided his gaze as best as she could. But the effort was too great. She felt naked and was waiting with dread the moment when someone will notice it and scream it out. She apologised for her fatigue, said goodbye and walked to the hotel. Someone behind her called her name. The Writer. She reached her.

"On Sunday morning I will be with Emiliyan in El Campanario. Come. I would be delighted," she said.

"Ok... we'll speak. I apologise for tonight. I don't feel well."

She was not asleep when Gerard returned. She kept her eyes closed in the dark and listened to him undressing. After a while, he tucked himself into the warmed bed. He shaped his body to hers and took her in his arms. She felt his wine breath on her face. He began to kiss her - insistently, passionately...

The Writer

In the morning after the dinner with her new acquaintances, she left for Puerto del Rosario.

The first days on the island had involved her in double dynamics – slowness, in which time runs not noticed. She had come with a purpose, but the island laughed in her face: *my plans for you are different*. She liked it. She very much liked to leave herself to it, and to what it had to offer. It was different from the full calendar in her smartphone. The books she had brought also reminded her of Unamuno. Whenever her gaze fell upon them, she felt guilt and embarrassment, as if she was betraying him.

Now, she finally went back to the root cause of her trip. The book. Unamuno.

Two statues, one at the beginning of the street and one in front of the house museum, etched him not only in the spiritual but also in the physical realities of the island.

The woman in the museum greeted her politely. They walked around the rooms. The gaze of the Writer fell on the antique wooden furniture, elongated framed mirror, single bed with a white cover of knitted lace, rocking chair, and rested on the desk with a small table lamp, two ink pots and quill stand, a picture of Unamuno with another man and two children, sheets, written in his handwriting... The museum administrator pointed out two birds made from newspaper, perched among the objects on his desk: "He constantly made paper birds," she said. And discreetly walked away.

As she was leaving, she bought "From Fuerteventura to Paris", written by Unamuno during his stay in Paris, and his "Letters from Exile". When the woman heard that she was writing a novel about him, she pulled out another book and handed it to her with a smile: "A gift." Its title was "Unamuno: articles and discourses about the Canaries."

"You know, they say...," her voice lowered and became conspiratorial, as if she was sharing a carefully guarded secret, "They say that a young woman, a writer like you, followed him here... She came to the hotel, but he sent her away. He asked the receptionist to give her shelter until the next ship arrived."

Marina

She walked again through the dunes. This time she went further. She turned to go back and saw the birds. They flew low, in ever-changing directions while staying in the flock. They made circles, crossed each other, grouped together. She went closer. Hundreds of birds perched in the hollow. They rose a few metres and landed again. She recalled the photo of the Bulgarian. And the Writer.

It was Saturday evening. Sunday, the Writer had said. She did not want to meet people, to talk, to peer into their lives, to let them into hers... Yet, unlike past years, an impulse rekindled in her. A hope. Vague, unnamed, gradually delineating its borders. There was something in the Writer, in the insisting and caring way in which she had said: "Call me", awakening this impulse. Something stronger than her resistance to communicate with Bulgarians and to remember Bulgaria. The Writer did not live in

Bulgaria but in Brussels, like her. However, many Bulgarians lived in Brussels and she did not interact with them.

She took out her mobile, found her name, stood still for a minute or two and put it away again. There was no need to call. She said she would be in El Campanario. If she felt like going, she could do it spontaneously

As she was hesitating, her phone bpiped. A message from the Writer: "I am with the Germans and Enrique at Buena Onda. Come. "

Enrique

Buena Onda was, as always, busy. Gerd, Carla and Enrique were drinking beer and discussing their surfing day. The Writer appeared in a short red dress, flat shoes and a beige raincoat. She gave them kisses and sat next to Enrique.

"How is the surfing going?"

"Life is not only surfing" he said indignantly.

"It isn't?"

The three of them looked at each other and burst out laughing. The Writer ordered sangria.

"Where are you with your writing?" asked Carla.

"Nowhere."

"How come?"

"Just like that."

"Writer, get rid of this writing!" joined in Enrique "You'll write, when you're back in Brussels. Now you're here, on the island, don't write, but experience it."

The Writer smiled and was about to say something, but Gerd stepped in.

"Enrique, when have you become such a philosopher?"

"I've always been one. Well, maybe not quite like... what was the name of the philosopher in your book, Writer?"

"Unamuno."

"Not like Unamuno, but... when will you try surfing?"

"I didn't come for that."

"Hmmm, I've heard this before. Now, these people are among the greatest addicts."

"I keep a distance from any addictions."

"Ai-ai-ai, Writeeer, think twice about what you gain from this distance, and do you gain anything at all."

"Pardon?" - her smile disappeared and she looked at him with interest.

"Addiction often starts with passion. And what is life without passion?"

"An ocean of possibilities that passion eliminates. Because such focus abandons the rest of the world. The rest of life. This is limiting."

"I would say it is expanding."

"Really?"

"Yes. Because the deeper you get and give yourself to this passion, the more you see and understand its object. This knowledge gives width. And when unfocused, you remain on the surface of life. Without depth. In a passion you can experience the whole of life. But in a life without passion, you don't experience any-th-ing."

Before the Writer was able to answer, Carla intervened:

"There is truth in his words. Surfing changes you. It's with you everywhere."

"Aren't you getting tired of it? The repetition of the same action?"

"That's the thing – it's not the same. Each wave is different. And the approach to it is different. Surfing means to be in rhythm with the ocean. It's like a dance. Like falling in love."

Carla looked at her as if she was challenging her.

"This should interest you, Writer! Surfing like falling in love. That feeling down in your belly, remember?" Enrique leaned slightly towards her and stared at her.

The Writer swallowed dryly and looked away.

"Sort of."

"Well, in surfing it's not sort of, it's a full and constant experience. Non-stop infatuation with each wave, with 'the Wave'."

The Writer listened thoughtfully.

"Turn your back to this philosopher whom you came to write about, and let yourself go with the wave of real life, the one that is here and now. It carries risks, true, but what's life without risk?"

A little later Enrique suggested they call Marina and Gerard. Carla tried to talk him out of it, but Enrique was determined to win her over. Gerd was staring intensely at the screen on which surfers drifted on huge waves with such ease, as if they were born on the board, and stayed silent. The Writer took out her mobile and sent a message to Marina.

Miguel

"There are indeed people who appear to think only with their brain, or with any other organ of theirs, adapted specifically to thinking; while others think with their whole body and with their whole soul, with their blood, with their bone marrow, with their heart, lungs, belly, life."[4]

---

[4] Miguel de Unamuno, Essays, Publishing house 'Science and Art', 1983, „The man from flesh and blood'

Marina

Marina finished her sangria and ordered another. It seemed to her that this woman, his woman, the German, was examining her with her cold blue eyes, trying to see the core of her soul to a depth which even she does not dare to reach. But the drink gave her a burst of calm and courage and she met her eyes. This time Carla shifted hers. Marina felt good. As if she had achieved a small victory over the blunt frankness of her eyes.

"What exactly is your book about?" she turned to the Writer in Bulgarian.

"About Unamuno, the Spanish philosopher and ..."

"I've read Unamuno."

"Really? Finally, someone not looking at me blankly when I say his name."

"I graduated in Spanish philology. How did you decide to write about him?"

"I was on the island years ago. The landscape stunned me. Someone told me that Unamuno had been exiled here. I was working on another novel then. Last year I came back to this idea. But I didn't find much information about his time here. So I decided to come back. Do you like him? Unamuno?"

Marina looked pensively in front of her.

"It was thanks to him that I met my ex-husband... I knew he had been exiled to the Canaries, but I had forgotten that this was the place."

"Won't you tell me?"

A shadow crossed Marina's face.

"It's a long story."

"I love stories. Especially long ones."

Marina sipped her sangria.

"This one... I'm not sure you'll like it," she said in a while.

Gerd no longer watched the surfers. He joined the conversation of Gerard, Carla and Enrique, but was mostly silent. Occasionally, he shot Marina an oblique look. She felt droplets of sweat breaking out under her white dress. She took out a fan and opened it with a brusque gesture.

The Writer

Fabrizio scurried between the kitchen and his room.

"I am moving," he announced.

"Where?"

"To another flat."

"Alone?"

"No, but I'll have a bigger room. More comfort. I have plans..."

"What plans?"

"I don't want to be a waiter forever! I'll start my own business. I'll organise holidays for surfers."

"Aren't there many people doing that?"

"Not enough. And the number of those coming for surfing is going up. I'll do a nice website..."

They heard a door opening. Juan appeared.

"Hi," he said, looking playfully at the Writer. He opened the refrigerator, took out bread, butter, ham and cheese and began to make a sandwich.

"Are you here for the surf as well?" She tried to sound natural and to look at him with neutral eyes.

"No, I am doing a specialisation at the hospital in Puerto."

"What are you specialising in?"

"Paediatrics."

"Finally someone who is not here for surfing… You don't surf?"

"I've tried. But I've no time. I wish I could... And you? Have you signed up for a course already?"

"No. And I'm not planning to..."

"You came to Fuerte and won't try surfing? Isn't your book about surfers?"

"No... It's about Unamuno."

"Unamuno?"

"Yes, the Spanish..."

"Ai-ai-ai, Writer, I know who Unamuno is. He was exiled here like me, only for him it was four months, and for me four years."

Juan swallowed the last bite of his sandwich, jumped up, grabbed his rucksack and left.

Marina

She woke up with the idea of the triptych with the birds. The sight of a flock in sudden ascent held her spellbound. The synchronous movement of their wings, the splicing, the throaty sound that they produced, the harmony in their forming and reforming. The triptych had succeeded in capturing it all. Almost. The sounds were left to the imagination. Or to the memory.

It was Sunday, the day of the market in El Campanario. The Writer had renewed her invitation the night before. She had promised nothing, but now she felt a desire to go. To buy the triptych. To possess something of the birds, of their flight and freedom.

A little later in El Campanario they found the Writer speaking with Emiliyan. The Writer hugged her warmly. Gerard was examining the photographs and discussing something with Emiliyan. Then he paid, waited for him to pack the triptych and handed it to Marina solemnly.

"It's yours, my love!"

She smiled faintly and thanked him. They left the Writer and Emiliyan and walked down the alley.

"Strange birds," said Emiliyan.

Gerard

They arrived in La Oliva fifteen minutes later. A small town of a few streets. Gerard had checked the sights and had made a plan. Marina, as usual, did not mind following him.

He parked in front of a building and they walked towards it. The Museum of Grain. A young woman greeted them, gave them a leaflet and left them to it.

The past of Fuerteventura stared back from the photos. Veiled women and men with straw hats and bright clothes. Haystacks amid the rocky landscape. Camels. Donkeys. The agricultural livelihood of the island. It would not have occurred to anyone that such a deserted rocky land could be so fertile, give birth and feed its people. As they walked through the museum, Gerard commented on the various tools and Marina listened to him absent-mindedly.

He was raised in the wheat fields of the South of France. Wheat had been present in his life, had been more than wheat, had been the landscape of his first years. Wheat and vineyards. Bread and wine. During grape picking, he had kissed his first girl. Among the wheat, he had lost his virginity. His relationship with the land was primordial. He took the South with him to Paris and then Brussels. Sometimes he would see the wheat in his dreams and when that longing turned into a calling he headed to Montpellier. Especially while his mother was alive. But also after her death. He visited her grave and it gave him a sense of that protected space, which she had always been able to secure for him. Thanks to the care of the housekeeper Michelle, the house still looked like his mother had just gone to the garden and would soon return. Since he started living with Marina, they spent most of their holidays there - she did not wish to go sightseeing or visit places with many people. Their days passed by the swimming pool and walking in the countryside. Sometimes they dined out. But more often he prepared the meals and selected the wine they had in the garden. Once in a while, his grown-up children visited them for a day or two. Gerard saw how Marina calmed down during these holidays and how the shadow of sadness on her face brightened. This pleased him - his birthplace gave power not only to him but also to the woman he loved.

Gerd

Gerd felt more secure in the ocean. The waves were his strong female partners and whilst he was flying among their white curls he felt the freedom which he had always sought. Freedom, which recently he had been increasingly thinking, he had failed to achieve. Enrique was free. He had left everything in Italy and had moved to the island for surfing. But he, could he not do the same? To draw the line, to pack up and stay here forever? As an IT developer, he could, theoretically, work from anywhere. Nothing to keep him. Nothing but the orderliness of his life and Carla. Perhaps she would be able to move her practice here. To offer yoga and massage to the tourists. Surely they would manage. They would earn less, but would be free. Would they be free? He – would he be free if he brought the invisible web of her love with him?

He asked himself these questions, lying exhausted on the sand. It seemed to him that his feelings were awakening after a long sleep. And the first thing they saw were the dark eyes of the Bulgarian. This silent woman was an enigma and awakened a desire to penetrate her sadness and shake her from within. Her husband seemed a good sort, harmless and a bit of boring.

Apparently, he had not been able to achieve what Gerd believed he could do. Marina had not pushed him away then, at the hotel. On the contrary. Her eyes were calling, inviting him.

Carla was still in the water. He took her mobile from her bag, found the number of the Bulgarian and wrote it down.

The Writer

Voices and laughter drifted from the kitchen. Juan had his back to the door. A young woman sat opposite him. The Writer's gaze quickly swept over her long bright hair, grey eyes, golden skin, straight nose and raspberry lips stretched into a dazzling smile... something tightened in her throat.

"Meet our new flatmate," Juan turned to her.

"Lola," the woman stretched out her hand.

Lola worked in one of the many perfume shops in Corralejo. Her glittering eyes darted at Juan, whilst his danced between Lola and the Writer, flirtatious, laughing. After a short while, the Writer retired to her room, took one of Unamuno's books and started to read.

Miguel

"It's interesting what happens with the thoughts of man. Often in our minds many thoughts are swarming, vegetating in the darkness, plain, incomplete, without knowing each other, mutually avoiding each other, because in the darkness, thoughts, as well as people, fear each other, torn and divided, they sleep each in its own corner, avoiding any encounter. But then suddenly a new thought, spraying light, penetrates and brightens every corner. It sees the other ones and they see each other, recognise each other, rise, get together, unite around the newcomer, hug, make a brothership and start living a full life."[5]

The Writer

In the evening Enrique was waiting for her at the pier, next to the statue of the waiting woman. They went to Mojito and – ignoring the tautology - ordered mojito. Having exchanged their usual talk about their day, surfing, writing, Enrique said:

"Writer, I'm sure you will be delighted to hear that our meeting tonight has a mission."

"Has it?"

"Oh yeah. You are involved in a love conspiracy."

"Love conspiracy?"

"Exactly."

"Who else is involved in this conspiracy?"

"Me... Gerd and your Bulgarian friend Marina."

"She is not exactly my friend."

"From tonight she is. Because you are spending the evening together. You have had dinner in a small, Italian, of course, restaurant, you have walked the streets of Corralejo, then you have had cocktails at a seaside bar and you have not noticed how suddenly it was after midnight ..."

"Interesting. And if I decide to go long before midnight?"

"You will not do that to your new friend, dooming him to a solitary drunkenness."

"What if I decide to go long after midnight?"

"Then Gerd and I would have met you in our guys-only night out, exactly when Marina is leaving and Gerd, being a good friend, would have left us alone."

The Writer looked at the dark ocean.

---

[5] Miguel de Unamuno, Essays, Publishing house 'Science and Art', 1983

"What has silenced you now?"

"Interesting, now I found myself in someone else's plot ..."

"Well, you can't always orchestrate things. Life would be to boring this way, don't you think? But enough about this. Let's talk about something more interesting. For example, why is a beautiful and intriguing woman like you alone on this island?"

"Writing is not a group experience."

"How many pages have you written since you have been here?"

"Writing does not happen only when you write."

"Look, you do not have to justify yourself. Besides, I am pleased that you are alone here..., as long as someone is not waiting for you in Brussels."

"What does that have to do with you?"

"Don't pretend you don't understand."

Enrique stretched his hand across the table and touched her fingers. She withdrew her hand.

"You know I like you. One doesn't often meet women like you on this island... not alone."

The Writer said nothing. She stared at the ink coloured ocean sway, where the waves died, white.

"Won't you say something?"

"Enrique, I like you, but... I'm not looking for an island affair."

"What are you looking for then?"

"Nothing. I look for nothing."

"Why did you go out with me?"

"Because you invited me. But now I feel tired and I am afraid I won't be able to share the rest of your guys-only evening."

She took out five euros, left them on the table and briskly walked away. Enrique followed her with his eyes until she turned the corner, finished his mojito and went off in the direction of Kiwi.

The flat was dark. The Writer entered the kitchen and, without lighting the lamp, looked out of the window at the lights outside, at the couples who dined on the square, at the running children, at the group who played another number, at the ocean which approached the shore in relentless control, at the distant, shining stars, at the ripening moon.

To how many had adultery become the island scene? How many confused people were sheltered, encouraged and concealed? How many meetings, how many separations? It seemed to her that the air of Fuerteventura vibrated with feelings, desires, passions, hopes - realised or not - which filled the space and drove her crazy. She looked again at the sky and noticed a shadow, light like a disembodied cloud. A shadow in the shape of a woman with a bulging belly, as if she was pregnant.

Miguel

You are born and you grow, mysterious moon,
dwindling and dying, your avaricious light,
pale mirror of mortal fortune;
always, sad, you give us the same face
your cradle swing in the corner,
a wave that Sahara will return.[6]

"It's an image of the Moon, which floated on a lake of clouds like a boat, above the sea, a night when we went to wait for the rescue ship. On Fuerteventura the Moon is born on the horizon where the sea meets the beaches of the Sahara."[7]

---

[6] Miguel de Unamuno, "De Fuerteventura a París", Editorial Excelsor, 1925
[7] Miguel de Unamuno, "De Fuerteventura a París", Editorial Excelsor, 1925

Marina

The feeling of impossibility. And a condensed desire that pulsates within her - from the loins to the womb. The boy has a girl. And she has a man. This road passes through two broken couples and four broken hearts. They watch each other silently. She turns her eyes away. He raises his hand and caresses her neck. His fingers slip into her hair. She closes her eyes. He takes her in his arms and then presses her against him. She feels his breath near her temple. His hands glide over her body. She lets herself to him. Then suddenly pulls away. She fixes her dress. She leans on the rock and stares into the ocean. Her breathing gradually calms down. He looks at her.

"Don't you want me?"

"I want you."

"Then?"

"It's pointless."

On the way from La Oliva she had received a message from him. He would wait for her tonight at the bus stop near the main street. She should say that she will be going out with the Writer. She swallowed, looked in front of her and said to Gerard:

"The Writer suggests that we meet tonight."

"Wonderful, she seems nice."

"Yes... she seems."

She messages him back: "OK."

Gerard had told her she was very beautiful. He had embraced and kissed her. He had wished her a nice evening and had gone to bed with a book. She had jumped into the car and sped through the darkened sands, glowing gently under the moonlight. Moving like the birds. Like the winds of Fuerteventura.

She sees him at the bus stop. He is wearing jeans and a white sweater. He kisses her lightly on the lips. She presses the accelerator and the white car takes them in no particular direction.

They travel in silence. She stares at the road ahead, lit only by the heavy stars and the round moon. He looks at her profile. He reaches out and caresses her neck. Electricity flows through her body. It seems to her that she would shine in the dark. His hand covers hers. Her hand feels at home. A feeling that she disappears and only that hand remains, gripping the gear, but actually, helplessly nestled in his, in a wild, shameless, painful happiness.

Ahead into the moonscape of Fuerteventura, framed by the mountain ridges, ahead towards the infinity of nothingness.

The road narrows and the ocean opens in front of them - silver and inviting. Marina stops and gets out of the car. Gerd grabs her hand and they descend the steep trail down to one of the many beaches on the island, that will remain forever unrecognised and unnamed, an anonymous accomplice. The beach is small and surrounded by cliffs, not yet covered completely by the rising ocean. The waves bite the shore and slowly withdraw only to return with renewed force, ever more predatory.

He sighs and sits on a rock. After a while, he gets up, comes closer to her and pulls her into his arms. She embraces him in return. They stay like this, pressed against each other, as the wind scours them.

He kisses her hair and temples. She does not dare move, clinging to him.

And then... Then everything is becoming searching lips, hungry hands, one single body, one single moan.

Carla

They walked across the island. The sun was strong, their lips were dry from thirst, but there was nowhere to take water from, there was no one around, they were all by themselves on this rocky piece of land, thrown in the middle of the ocean. They walked and walked. She did not know where they were going, she only understood that they should not stop. Suddenly, a woman emerged from behind a rock, like a mirage. She had long dark hair, dark eyes, and a chiselled face. She was wearing a yellow dress similar to the one Marina wore. She was holding a glass container, filled with water. She lifted it and drank. Drops of water dribbled from the edges of her mouth down her neck. They got close to her. Gerd stopped, Carla caught up with him. The woman smiled. She handed the vessel to Carla and she began to drink thirstily. She choked on the water. She opened her eyes and saw Gerd holding the woman in his arms and kissing her passionately. She tried to stop drinking, but she could not. She was coughing, but they paid no attention to her. She grew faint. Everything was blurred before her eyes. The earth opened like soft lava and she fell into it.

She woke up at Gerd's touch. Her whole body was dripping in sweat. "It must be very late," was the only thought that went through her mind, she grabbed his hand and went back to sleep.

The Writer

She was still in bed when the phone rang. Marina.

"I'd like to see you. Is tomorrow convenient?"

For a moment, she felt tempted to ask: "Really or like last night?", but she stopped herself.

"Early evening in Corralejo?"

"Great."

She heard movement in the flat. She got up, took a shower, put on jeans and a shirt and went to the kitchen. Lola had lifted her long legs onto the couch and was drinking coffee. The Writer prepared tea.

"How are you, guapa?"

"Good, and you?"

"Very good. I have a day off."

"Why are you on Fuerte?"

"I came, liked it, went home to Zaragoza, packed my stuff and returned."

"Was it that simple?"

"Yes. Should it be complicated?"

"You're certainly not here for the surfing..."

Lola smiled.

"No. Because of the colours. The ocean. The sunsets. And the time, which has stopped."

"You lived somewhere else till now?"

"With my boyfriend. But we broke up."

"Are you sad?"

"A little. But it'll pass. Tomorrow I will get my cat."

"The flat will become full of cats ..."

"Let Juan deal with it. But he's crazy enough to handle it."

The Writer again felt a contraction in her throat. When did Lola get to know him so well? Probably, while she was out, meeting all the people and doing all the things that had suddenly filled her island life.

"And you? Are you alone?" Lola looked at her with curiosity.

"We could put it that way..."

"A pretty woman like you would hardly stay alone for long."

The Writer said nothing. She washed her cup, wished her a good day, took the laptop and book and left.

Carla and Gerd sat in front of Indy.

76

"Ah, there you are! I was already beginning to miss you." Carla said "Last night I almost called you, but I got lazy. Gerd and Enrique abandoned me. Won't you take a seat?"

The Writer looked at Gerd. His face did not flinch.

"I was on my way to the dunes ..."

"It'll be a quick coffee. Gerd is going to the supermarket, you'll keep me company."

Gerd left them and took the direction of HiperDino.

"What is happening with you, Writer?"

Carla's bright eyes examined her.

"Not much. I have a new flatmate. A woman."

"Ah, right? Is she nice?" her voice became lively.

"I would say stunning."

"Is it only the two of you?"

"No. We have another flatmate. A guy. Stunning as well ..."

Carla smiled knowingly.

"I see. The appearance of a stunning female flatmate is probably the least desired circumstance when you already have a stunning male flatmate."

"Probably."

They looked at each other and laughed.

"Look, Writer, the circumstances should not be an obstacle when the intention is strong."

"Shouldn't the intention still be shared?"

"It's desirable, but not mandatory. Don't get distracted with unnecessarily staring at reality. This usually leads to problems. Focus on your desire. If you want this man, take him."

"The man is not an amoeba."

"The man is a confused little animal that can be tamed with the right approach."

"Any man?"

"Anyone. Do you think that Gerd ever ran after me? If I relied on him, we would never have been together."

"And don't you think that this carries the risk that some day his nature will wake up and he will run off to chase another?"

"Some day, some day... Some day the cord will be so tight around his neck, that he wouldn't be willing nor able to escape anymore. The intention is important. It gives direction and makes things happen."

"And how will my intention see to it that the stunning male flatmate would not fall for the stunning female flatmate?"

"Stop thinking that way! Forget the other flatmate! Act as if it's just you and him. You and him. No one else."

She gazed at the blue of Carla's eyes, was just about to say something, but stopped herself.

From that evening on, she joined Lola and Juan in the kitchen and got engaged in their conversations with more and more genuine naturalness.

Miguel

"The truth, the truth! Like a crown and the crowning of everything, the truth! The earth of this ascetic island does not lie; Fuerteventura tells the truth to people, tells its people, its children, the truth, barren and devoid of flesh, the skeleton of the truth. The one who lies here is the sky, that gets covered with clouds, without raining. But the earth, the bones of the earth, the skeleton of the earth? The truth, crown and crowning of all human life; nothing but the truth. Which happened to be the greatest illusion.

(...)

This land, this noble land, devoid of flesh, tells the truth to its children; it does not deceive them. That's why they love it."[8]

---

[8] Unamuno: Articulos y Discursos sobre Canarias, Cabillo Insular de Fuerteventura, Puerto del Rosario, 1980, Palabra de verdad

"And what greatest illusion is the truth! The truth is the greatest deception. Because the truth makes us believe that there is something more after it, something far beyond it.

(...)

Yes. Life might not deceive us; but the truth, the naked truth, the truth of those whom fools call pessimists, it does not deceive us. And this powerful truth, this truth of the strong wind is the greatest comfort and the greatest joy. There is no other smile like that of the skull. And that smile says that behind the truth is the after-truth.

Fuerteventura has no word for honour, it only has a word for truth."[9]

Gerard

He carefully spread butter on the baguette, cut in two, put a piece of smoked salmon in the middle, pressed together the two halves and took a bite. He drank champagne and looked at Marina.

"You didn't tell me anything about the evening with the Writer."

Marina sipped her coffee, stared into the azure stretch of the ocean and said calmly:

"I was not with the Writer."

"No? So who were you with?"

"With Gerd."

"Gerd? The German? And his girlfriend?"

He stopped chewing, coughed, sipped champagne and swallowed the bite.

"A stupid question. Of course, his girlfriend wasn't there... Carla was her name, right?"

---

[9] Unamuno: Articulos y Discursos sobre Canarias, Cabillo Insular de Fuerteventura, Puerto del Rosario, 1980, Palabra de verdad

"Does her name matter?" a slight irritation appeared in Marina's voice.

"Of course, it matters. As it matters that I'm Gerard, your husband... anything matters at this moment. The moment where happy ignorance leaves to never return."

"Is it necessary to dramatise?" she looked him in the eyes.

"I don't dramatise, not at all," he was trying to sound under control, but the slight trembling of his voice betrayed him. "Just thinking aloud."

"Nothing has happened. The moment has passed. The words have faded away. Let us continue the day like all the other days."

"Why are you telling me?" He was no longer trying to hide his pain.

Marina thought before answering.

"Because the lie would kill us. You are my best friend."

"But yesterday you lied to me."

"Yes. I had to."

"And what about him? The young German? What is he to you?"

She took a breath, held it for a moment and let it out.

"I don't know yet."

She got up, put her chair back and walked to the dunes.

The Writer

The Writer and Lola sat on the couch. Juan was standing while eating and watched them playfully.

"I don't know what's going on with me, but I constantly need sex," he said.

"Very interesting," noted the Writer.

Lola was smiling faintly and glancing at him.

"Interesting? Painful. Today I saw a chick in the hospital. She was a killer. I immediately checked her name in the file and found her on Facebook. But she was married, pfuuu!"

"Does that bother you?"

"I don't play around with married women."

"Oh, you've got principles," joined Lola.

"Of course. And I've never cheated."

"Well done. Nor have I."

"And you, Writer? Won't you tell us?" That was Juan again.

"I have nothing to tell."

"You're very secretive. Is there someone waiting for you in Brussels?"

"As if this would matter..."

"What do you mean – as if it would matter?"

"Well… it doesn't matter."

"Hmm, you're very mysterious."

She went to the window and looked out.

Juan approached her:

"Look at this" he handed her his mobile.

The Writer watched a short video of a surfer passing through the tube.

"Cool."

"Isn't it?"

She handed him the mobile and touched his fingers.

Lola observed them from the couch, chuckling.

The Writer returned to her. Juan took his laptop and plopped down between them. The Writer felt his thigh next to hers. He entered his Facebook profile and started showing them his photo session, posing in underwear. The two women joked and teased him. Their hands touched briefly and quickly pulled away, their eyes were sparkling - Juan and Lola, Juan and the Writer, Lola and the Writer - semi-conspiratorial, semi-competitive.

Someone got up first, it was late, they said "good night" and went to their rooms.

Carla

Gerd appeared to her more distracted than usual. In his vague words, in his look and touch, there was no presence. As if he did everything mechanically, unconciously, without participating. She knew him well, so well that she read any change in his expression, every nuance of his voice, the unsaid in what was said.

Even in the surfing, he was different. He often lost his balance, swept by another wave. Then lay on the sand long and silently. He said nothing

He had had such moments of switching off before. But now, especially after his outing with Enrique the other night, they had become more frequent. It seemed to her that this had something to do with that Bulgarian. She told herself that it was insane to think so, that Marina was here with her husband, nothing could happen... But the thought kept eating her from within, relentlessly and methodically.

Then she did something that she had never done before. She went out of the water before him and, while he was spinning in the centrifuge of the ocean and trying to gain control over the board, checked his mobile phone. She found nothing. Nothing at all. "Sick fantasies," she tried to reassure herself.

Gerd would go out with Enrique again tonight. Guys-only, again. He did not tell her directly but hinted it. If you are tired, you could stay and rest. Of course... She looked searchingly into his eyes, but he held her gaze, pulled her towards him and gently kissed her hair.

They would go around the bars and chitchat, they so rarely saw each other, had a lot to catch up on.

Carla and Gerd dined early in the flat. Gerd was going to fetch Enrique from work. She lay and watched him getting ready.

How he dried his hair, put on cologne, combined jeans with t-shirt. There was something so thorough in this routine preparation, which she had witnessed hundreds of times over the years, that made her stomach shrink. Seemingly it was the same, but why did it appear to her that it was not. That nothing was and would not be the same anymore. She wanted to tell him: "Don't go, stay with me. Enrique will understand. I need you. To be with me, to love me...", but she stayed silent and stared at her book. Gerd kissed her and left. The door slammed, her lips trembled and tears tricked down her face. The tip of her tongue licked them mechanically. Their taste was like the taste of all tears – bitter, salty.

The Writer

She came home in the afternoon and lay down. A door slammed. Feeling restless, she wrapped herself in a shawl and went to the kitchen in her silk nightgown. It was quiet. She stood by the window. The door opened. Juan. He greeted her and began to prepare a late lunch. The Writer sat on the couch, silently watching him. She wanted to go to him and stroke his strong arms, but could not move from her seat.

"So what, Writer? How do you say in Bulgarian: 'Do you want to ...'" - and he made an unequivocal gesture, pointing at himself and then at her.

The Writer said it, he repeated the words and gestures.

The Writer laughed, but felt stiff. It was impossible for her to say "Yes, I want it!", to take three steps towards him, to touch him, to take him, to give herself to him... instead she got up and walked to her room, leaving its door ajar. After a while Juan appeared:

"You want to...?"

"Come here, I'll give you a spanking."

"Nooo," he ran back to the kitchen.

The Writer stood in the frame of her door and they yelled from both sides of the corridor. Lola's door opened and her tousled head appeared. She looked sleepy.

"Oh, sorry, I didn't know you were here!" said the Writer embarrassed and returned to her room.

After a while, Lola joined Juan in the kitchen. The Writer could hear their voices: hers - gentle and endearing, his - slightly husky, strong.

Marina

They met at sunset next to the waiting woman and walked towards the harbour. After the usual questions, they fell silent. They reached the retaining wall behind which the ocean opened. They walked up the path along the wall and rested their bodies against it. It was still warm from the sun. The warmth penetrated their bodies, while the wind whipped at them. Waves crashed violently, turning into a sparkling white foam.

Marina closed her eyes and surrendered herself to the feeling of the wind that went through her raincoat, her thin dress, her lace underwear. The wind which could blow everything and leave her emptied, rekindled, cleansed. The strong wind of Fuerteventura. Tautology, she thought. Like saying the strong wind of the strong wind. What nonsense. Nobody should talk about strong wind on Fuerteventura. Or the wind at all. Because the wind is understood, it is the first condition, the unconditional pre-requisite. It is enough to say Fuerteventura. This exhausts everything. And all conversations about winds become meaningless and redundant.

"It's meaningless and redundant...," muttered Marina, her eyes closed.

"What?"

"To pretend that nothing has happened."

"And has it happened?"

"Yes, it has... I'm sorry I did not call to tell you... to ask. It must have been... uncomfortable to find yourself in this situation... without your consent."

"It was... surprising but not shocking."

Marina opened her eyes and looked at her.

"Why?"

"Because I saw your eyes. And your look in front of the toilet."

"What was it?"

The Writer thought.

"Excited, embarrassed, happy..."

"I might have recalled something..."

"Yeah, quite, in the toilet... You don't look like a woman with happy memories."

"You know nothing about me."

She said it quietly, staring at the horizon.

"No. Just my fantasy of you."

"And what is this fantasy?"

"About a sad woman who walks among the sands and looks for something that cannot be found."

"Cannot be found... What else?"

"It doesn't matter. We don't have to do that. Only you know."

"What?"

"Who you are. Where you are. Why you are doing what you're doing. Others can only fantasise."

"I'm not sure. Sometimes I think that others know and I fantasise. Gerard knows much better than me the answers to my questions. So I told him."

"You told him?"

"Yes."

"Was it necessary?"

"It was inevitable. Lying to him is like lying to myself while looking in the mirror."

"But him? Are you thinking about him?"

"Of course. That's why I don't lie to him. He's leaving on Sunday. I'll stay another week. I'll rent a flat in Corralejo. You know, I haven't been alone for years... the thought of it terrified me. And now... I long for it."

"What will happen to your marriage?"

The sky had coloured pink, which gradually permeated the white clouds. They walked towards the benches along the ocean and sat. The sunset was preparing for yet another performance, its twenty minutes of fame that would illuminate the evening and the lives of all those whose senses were open to it. The rest did not interest it at all.

"I don't know. We'll see. You know, I was married before Gerard... I told you that. Everything seemed constructed in a way that it would never crack. With the necessary doses of love, sex, affection, care. With all the ingredients required for a memorable story."

Marina's dark eyes looked thoughtfully at the Writer.

"Didn't you mention Unamuno?"

"Yes, Unamuno...," Marina smiled more to herself than to the Writer. "I was at a discussion about forgiveness. Pompous words about the ability to forgive, to understand that we are all one and should there not be condemnation, there wouldn't be offence, hence no need for forgiveness. And the Bible says: 'Do not judge, or you too will be judged.' The act of forgiveness becomes redundant because nothings leads to it and... etc. new wave bollocks. I listened, listened and couldn't keep myself from reacting. I got up and said that according to Unamuno punishment is necessary, and only after that comes forgiveness, because only then it will have a moral effect on the forgiven."

"I remember this...," muttered the Writer and put a strand of hair, which the wind was tugging insistently, behind her ear.

"Yes... There was such a strong reaction. Some had not even heard of Unamuno. I listened to them a little and quietly left. Outside, a man caught up with me, 'You impressed me,' he said. 'I much appreciate Unamuno. I didn't interfere as it was pointless... These people would not have understood. But I would like to talk with you. May I invite you for a coffee?' And we had a coffee then, immediately. And on another day we got married."

"And on another day you divorced?"

"That's right, that's what happened. That's the whole story."

"Why do I think that between these three days so much more had happened..."

They stared at the ocean, at the running waves - busy women, whose lives passed in seconds, from birth to white hair. All that remained of them before being swept away by their impatient sisters: "Why are you rushing to your death?" thought the Writer. "At least your death is white. Frothy like champagne."

"The life of the waves is so short. But filled with passion," she said.

"Indeed... Now I have to go. It's nice being with you, Writer."

They rose from the bench, hugged and Marina ducked through the streets towards her parked car.

Gerard

Gerard came out of the garden of the hotel and walked to the dunes. The sand sparkled from the pink glow, which spilled over the ocean as far as the mountain range. He walked and wondered what had been happening in his wife's head during all those days in which she had taken her solitary strolls in the sands. His wife, who was now in the arms of the young German... What has he been for her? A bridge, leading her from a tragedy to a love? Has this been his role in her life? His mission? Is this why he met her ten years ago in Avignon? Is this why he had to bring her to this island?

Pink-orange-yellow, the sunset generously gave itself once again for a short moment, a moment comprising an eternity. Is it possible to grieve in the face of this primaeval beauty for lost or unrealised loves? The sunset brought a wordless promise: "Everything has been and will be again. How much have I taken in on this island, how many stories, how many sighs, how many tears and groans .. Everything passes, only I stay."

Gerard rambled, and with each step calm set inside him. The pain slumped somewhere deep inside him only to be replaced by humility. Humility before the spiritualised beauty of the sunset, before the wisdom of the island, before the permanence of the ocean. The wind whipped his face and this sobered him: Marina was right, nothing significant had happened. Life goes on.

The island was a woman. A woman who gave him solace, advice and embrace. And this woman would not leave him. He sat at the foot of a dune and watched the ocean, which changed its colour from pink to pewter.

He had met Marina at the festival in Avignon, where he used to go for a day or two to see a play and be immersed in the joyful artistic atmosphere. After the performance of the Bulgarian troupe, he saw the actors in a restaurant in which he was having dinner and went to congratulate them. Marina was their interpreter. Having expressed his compliments, he started talking to her and she invited him to join them. Dinner was over and they continued in a bar. The conversation drifted light as a feather, stopping here and there. When they fell silent, it was late, part of the troupe had gone home and the bar was half-empty. The next day, they saw each other again. On the third day, he took her to his favourite restaurant and told her he really liked her. She lowered her eyes for a moment, then looked him squarely in the face and said that in two months time she was getting married.

"Where is your engagement ring?"

"I am having it adjusted, it was too big."

"Isn't this a bad omen?" he raised his eyebrow ironically.

"I prefer to think it was poor judgment on the part of my future husband." Her voice contained hardness he had not heard before.

"Of course, I'm sorry for the inappropriate joke. Your future husband is a lucky guy. To your union!"

The crystal glasses chinked and they drank.

In the morning he left. She was also leaving in a few days. They sent emails, first more frequently, then once every few months. The next summer, she came back with the troupe and they saw each other again. A gold ring glinted on her left hand, her belly was slightly swollen. His gaze rested on it a little bit longer, she looked down as well, stroked it with her hand with the ring and smiled. She sent him a photo of the baby who grew up to become a charming girl, Neda. Meanwhile, he moved to Brussels. She was successful in the competition for freelance interpreters at the European institutions and periodically flew to Brussels for two-three days. They went out for dinner and concerts, she talked about her family life, he - about his latest girlfriend, whom he never introduced to her.

On a sunny afternoon, his phone rang and he was surprised to see her name. She had never called him. Her voice sounded as if it was not of this world.

"Something... terrible... happened. Can you... come?"

That evening he landed for the first time at Sofia airport.

The sunset ended its performance. It became suddenly cool. The wind threw sand in his face and laughed at him. He looked at the sky studded with stars, shuddered, stood up and walked to the hotel, just as Emiliyan cast his first hook for the night, on the rocks slightly further down, the cigarette of Darina gleaming behind him like a firefly.

Miguel

The sea projects the night in its depth
and the night the sea; the moon, absent;
they kiss their eyes and foreheads;
the kisses leave a mysterious trace.[10]

Gerd

He was waiting for her at the same place. He jumped in the car and kissed her breathlessly. She returned his kiss, hit the gas and drove toward El Cotillo, following the GPS. His hand gently massaged her neck. She watched the road ahead and drove in silence. They passed a big white mill, which seemed abandoned amidst the wilderness.

They sat in a restaurant in the centre of town overlooking the raging ocean. Two-metre waves were running towards them and spilt over the little square and yet another statue of a woman staring out to the sea. Marina shuddered. "Don't be afraid, they can't reach us," Gerd squeezed her hand. They ate slowly, sipping white wine, holding hands and jumbled a mixture of memories and plans as naturally as if they had known each other for years.

As they walked from the restaurant to the hotel where Marina had reserved a room, Gerd pulled her into the shadow of a house and sought her lips. They kissed, clinging to each other as if, should they stop, the world would fall apart and they would never be able to find each other among its remains. When they parted to walk the last few metres to the hotel, Marina had the feeling she saw a shadow. It was so quick that it was not possible

---

[10] Miguel de Unamuno, De Fuerteventura a Paris, Editorial Excelsor, 1925

for her to judge whether it was real, but she was left with the memory of a shadow of a woman furtively watching them. She felt the cool fingers of fear up her spine and pressed her body against Gerd's.

In the room, the self-forgetfulness of the moment replaced any fear. In the moonlight streaming through the window, Gerd took her in his strong embrace, framed her face with his hand and kissed her. Their lips, mad butterflies. Gerd slipped down the long zip of her dress with eager fingers. Her hands took up his T-shirt and unbuckled his belt. Gerd impatiently unhooked her champagne coloured bra and her breasts rose like a couple of moons. He pulled off his trousers hastily, pushed her to the bed and penetrated her without taking off her lace panties. They took each other with frenzied tenderness, in which teeth and claws slipped on the flesh of the other but stopped their cruel onrush just before crossing the fine line between pleasure and pain. They bit each other's lips and bodies, froze breathlessly, joined to the limit, to continue again their mutual search, discovery and penetration.

When later, exhausted, they lay in each other's arms, Gerd spoke:

"Can you imagine? Staying on this island, you and me, to experience this daily."

Marina was stroking the back of his hand, curled into his heated body.

"Do we need to hurt each other with fantasies?"

"Why fantasies?"

He lowered his head to her face and stared into her eyes, glittering in the darkness.

"It seems to me, that I have known you and that you now know me like no other, beyond all the facts of our lives, beyond any rational reasoning."

"Yes..."

"Would you? Would you be with me?"

A sigh escaped her lips.

"Gerd... and what, when... this element passes? Two, maybe three broken couples, four broken hearts."

"Does it have to pass? I'm not sure. With you, I breathe like never before. It's irrational but real."

His voice echoed with boyish enthusiasm, full of excitement and conviction.

Marina was silent. It was enough to listen to him.

"Would you?"

"'I would' is my spontaneous answer. But the rational answer would probably be different. And not just for me, but for you as well, when you see the tearful eyes of Carla and hear her sobs."

"But is it better to stay when your heart wants something else. Is it fair - to you, and to the other?"

Marina drew spirals on his chest.

"I don't know... I only know that we are at the gateway of pain... and there is no other way than to pass through it. The question is whether we will go through it alone, or whether we'll drag with us the people who loved and supported us for years."

Gerd ran his fingers through her hair.

"You wouldn't tell Gerard?"

"I've already told him."

"You've told him? Then what involvement are you talking about? He is already involved!"

"Lying hurts more than the truth. He has a right to know and decide... But it's one thing to say, and completely different - to leave."

"But what would it be like not to see you again? That's what I don't want to find out."

He squeezed her in his arms.

"Freiburg is not far from Brussels."

"No... But I prefer to stay with this image - you and I on the island, together."

The Writer

The conversation with Marina settled in her thoughts, wrapped in the sadness of that woman, opaque and tangible like fog. Love, even impossible love, in the beginning at least floats on a cloud of intoxication. But she could not escape the feeling that this cloud would carry hail.

In the evening she went out with Lola and three female friends of hers. They also lived on the island and like her worked in bars and shops. Attractive women of different ages with well maintained bodies, provocative clothes and heavily made-up faces. They ordered cocktails and indulged in the festive rhythm of the night. It was difficult for the Writer to share their gaiety. She was friendly, but she was still possessed by the idea of a man and a woman merged in a newborn love only to return to a world swept by an apocalypse.

Lola and her friends, whose names she did not remember, were dancing, talking animatedly and laughing. Two young men approached them. Not long after, they moved to Kiwi, where they met Juan with a friend and two girls. He was delighted to see Lola and the Writer and introduced them, while stressing mischievously: "My flatmates". The girl next to him looked at him with disbelief. A salsa started and the Writer took his hands. He danced well and she let herself be led, suddenly oblivious to all the sinful loves and broken hearts. Their faces touched for a moment, their hands slipped around each other and connected again after another spin, their eyes met, followed by playful smiles in the language of dance, joyful and wordless. The song ended and they parted as quickly as they had come together. The Writer looked around, but Lola and her friends were gone. She went out and searched for them in the crowd. She returned to the first bar, they were not there either. She walked back to Kiwi.

Someone grabbed her by the waist, she spun around and found herself face to face with Enrique.

"Heeey, Writer, what are you up to alone at this hour?"

"I had company, but I lost them."

"So now you're with me."

"It didn't occur to me that it may be so straightforward."

"Writer, you will become ugly from so much thinking. What will you have?"

"Whisky without ice."

Enrique went to the bar and returned with two glasses. Juan was still there with his company and occasionally their eyes clashed, only to withdraw startled. Enrique and she were sipping their drinks, looking around and slightly swaying. Juan and his folks were leaving. He threw her a last look and waved, she nodded back. She escorted him with her eyes. Another island night was entering its maturity and it seemed that it would not be any different from those before or those after. The Writer was finishing her whisky and thought of leaving, when someone pulled Enrique. He turned and saw Carla.

Carla

Carla watched TV, read, tried to sleep. No joy. She got up and looked out of the window at the star-studded sky, to the bustling streets, to the ocean's lazy swell. She felt like a princess, forcefully separated from the world in her tower. It occurred to her that unlike the princess, there was nothing to keep her in that room, that the night of Fuerteventura was just as much hers as Gerd's, and that instead of lying and suffering, she could go out and enjoy it, because she was writing this tale and only she could release the princess from the darkness of her thoughts and fears. A walk, a drink, a short timelessness would be enough. Was that not healthier than the sleepless expectation of Gerd's return? Of course, it was.

The night smiled at her like an accomplice, and with a subtle gesture took away all her previous suffering. Carla felt joyful excitement, looked around and took the promenade by the ocean. The wind immediately pounced on her, as if it had prowled for her around the corner. It pinched her cheeks and ruffled her hair. Her eyes filled with tears, different from those which had wet her face just an hour ago. She wiped them and continued. She walked past the row of bars and restaurants, turned and went to the two-story building which attracted the nightlife lovers with a few trendy bars. There was a risk of meeting Gerd and Enrique, but so what? Gerd had not told her where they were heading for her to be considerate in choosing her route. As always, there were many people in front of Kiwi. She squeezed among them and entered. She headed in the direction of the bar, bought a beer and stood away from the dancing people. She had not been out alone at night for years, since... before Gerd. The last time was probably that night when things between them finally happened. It was so long ago... She remembered her determination, born from her fruitless attempts to have him, from the months of courtship, phone calls, hopes and non-realisation. It was a Saturday night, she had no plans, had spent the day thinking hard of how to break this circle and release her desire. She had talked to him the day before, she knew he would go out with friends in the evening. There was nothing to lose, everything to gain – him or merciless clarity. She wore a dress, put on some makeup, which was not usual for her, and walked to the busiest bar in Freiburg. She hastily finished one drink and ordered a second, and with that in hand made her way through the crowd. Familiar faces here and there. He was with friends, standing and looking around. He did not seem excited at seeing her. She lied to him that she was supposed to meet a friend but could not find her, and asked if she could stay for a while with them. He introduced her to his companions, one of them even showed more than polite interest. Once the drinks were over, someone immediately bought more. She stopped checking her watch and looking around for her "unreliable" friend. The night progressed, they lost count of the drinks, their mood grew more and more exuberant. She danced, laughed, felt attractive and free. Gerd also seemed to enjoy himself.

"I want to dance with you," she said and hung around his neck.

She let go of him only in the morning when he was leaving her home. That evening they went out on their first date.

And now, seven years later, she was alone in another bar on this unreal island with a European nationality and African soul, searching again... For what? Him or merciless clarity?

Her gaze drifted between dancers and onlookers. Why did she have the feeling that she had returned to the starting point, when everything was vague and imminent? But now? Has everything already been experienced? She tried to chase away the shadows of those memories and to reconnect to that other sensation – the one of a night filled with unspoken promises... Was that the Writer she saw in the crowd? She was not alone. There was a man next to her. As she made her way towards them, she recognised Enrique. All her fears had been on vain, all her concerns - meaningless. She did not see Gerd, but he had to be around. She reached Enrique and took him by the elbow. He turned and his face took on a guilty expression.

"Where is he?" Carla almost screamed.

Enrique did not know what to say. How to lie to her? Alcohol does not help with such improvisations.

"Where?"

She turned and walked out with the beer in hand. The Writer followed her.

Miguel

"Love, my readers and brothers, is the most tragic thing that exists in this world and in life; love is a child of deception and gives birth to disappointment; love is consolation in desolation, the only remedy against death, because it is, was, its sister."[11]

The Writer

She lay with her eyes closed on a recliner at the beach in front of the dunes with her back to the ocean. The experiences of the previous day lined up in her mind, bright and intense like flaming torches. It seemed to her that her body would glow from the tension built up over the last twenty-four hours. An inferno of others' and her own desires, longings, anguish. Several years ago in these same dunes, a young woman had told an older man: "Every night I dream about my husband." "At this point in the films she catches the next flight," he had replied in a choking voice. The Writer could still see them now, lying on the beach and leading this conversation, while the strong wind of Fuerteventura was trying to bury them alive in the sand. She crushed the memory into an invisible ball and let today's wind carry it away. She imagined how a huge wave comes and sweeps her away together with the flames, whose tongues penetrated the most remote corners of her soul. And how only smoke and tears remain of her, which the ocean, benevolently, gathers. The sun barely caressed her face with its anaemic rays. She snuggled into their begrudging warmth and tried to shift her focus from the

---

[11] Miguel de Unamuno, Essays, Publishing house 'Science and Art', 1983, „Love, compassion and person"

emotional to the sensory experiences. The wind, which pressed against her back with unskilled tenderness, the dappled sun touching her lips and eyes, the endless whisper of the ocean, the perfect crest of the dunes... Fuerteventura was a mother, whose embrace calms. Any suffering was like affectation before the antiquity of this wise woman. A feeling of being at home replaced all that had overwhelmed her just a moment ago. She dozed off. When she opened her eyes, she saw four camels, tied to one another, passing a few metres from her like a mirage. A boy with a straw hat, colourful shirt and medium length khaki trousers led them. The camels moved smoothly, shaking their long necks. One of them turned and looked at her with its wide-set, almond eyes, its large nostrils twitched and it occurred to the Writer that it smiled. As if it was laughing over the insignificance of her torment. "What for?" asked the eyes of the camel with mocking tenderness, "For a vain man who doesn't know what he wants? Remember how he showed you his photos! For him? Really?!" The camel turned its head and continued.

She followed the camel caravan with her eyes as it hid behind the dunes, took out her laptop and began to type. Her days on the island tumbled into words, sentences, paragraphs.

The previous night she had reached Carla outside the bar. Carla had lost her senses. She threw the bottle on the ground, it shattered into pieces and the beer flowed like transparent blood. She was sobbing, shaking. The Writer tried to hug her, but she pushed her away, hid her face in hands and slid down next to a column. The Writer knelt beside her and stroked her blonde hair.

"Why? Why?" was all she could hear "I can not ..."

She pulled her into her arms and Carla finally let herself be embraced. She continued to cry like a child, but then gradually quietened down. She pulled away and wiped her reddened eyes. She started breathing deeper.

"I need a drink," she said.

They got up and went to the Buena Onda. They ordered whisky.

"He's with her, right?"

"I don't know. I was with some friends, I lost them, I met Enrique, then you came..."

"There is no one else for him to be with... It's not like he has a dozen friends on this island. He told me... lied to me, that he would be with Enrique."

"Only he can answer you... It's pointless to torture yourself now."

"And what? What if I find out that he has been with her? I already know it. But what would this mean for us? I can not imagine life without him. I do not want to imagine it."

Her lips trembled and her eyes welled with tears again. She sipped the whisky.

"The thought that now he is with her ..."

"The fantasy."

"I gave this man all my affection, I gave him everything, I hoped, I believed, that he had grown to love me, that he can love me, that he at least will stay in my life... I lost my parents when I was six. Grandparents and aunts raised me. Rigour and discipline instead of caress. I thought I'd created this protected place with him. And that Fuerteventura was our paradise found... Why is love so complicated and unfair?"

"Dear Carla, I am the last person to give you the answer."

"You writers create people, relationships and denouements... You *have to* have an answer," her voice rose.

"The answers of literature and the answers of life do not always coincide, even more often they disagree...," the Writer spoke in a flat voice. "I sound rehearsed," she thought.

"Why do you write then? Isn't this hypocrisy? If you don't have answers, what are you wasting your time for?"

"Writing is an intuitive process, Carla. It is a necessity. And love... is illogical and inconsistent."

"Why am I continuing to talk in cliches?" she thought.

"Nonsense, Writer! Love is an intention, decision, dedication. Everything else is like the wind. Food for the narcissistic souls of selfish people, incapable of love. The eternal pursuit of the thrill, the obsession with falling in love is the opposite to love. Why do men... Why doesn't Gerd understand that?!"

"Maybe because of the nostalgia for childhood. Falling in love is the childhood of love."

"Damn childhood! A source of traumas and neuroses! I believed we had achieved maturity in our relationship. Robust self-sufficient maturity. I was hoping..."

Carla hid her face in her hands and began to sob again.

"Carla," the Writer stretched her hand across the table and touched the back of her hand "if he is your man, he will remain yours. If not, there is nothing you can do."

Carla stopped crying, took her hands off her face and looked at the Writer intently with narrowed eyes.

"He IS my man. I have no hesitations."

She wiped her eyes and drank the rest of the whisky.

"I'm sorry... Thank you."

She waved over the waiter, paid, she and the Writer embraced and went their separate ways.

The Writer crashed in her bed and immediately fell asleep, exhausted. Four hours later she woke up to giggling in the hallway. Two voices intertwined. "Come onnnnn, come onnn...", the male one insisted, drunkenly. "Ha-ha-ha, nooo ..." the female one curled thinly. "Come onnnn please ..." Smack-smack-smack. A knock as if from bumping into a wall.

She looked at her mobile. It was 6 am. She climbed out of bed and opened the door. Lola and Juan were in the hallway. Her hand was over his shoulder, but both were barely able to keep straight.

"Hello."

"Hello ...," they were startled.

"How was the party?"

"Veeery nice."

"She can't dance, ayayayay," laughed Juan.

"Bullshiiiit, what do you know," Lola grinned.

"Come on, show me," said the Writer.

They took their hands and Juan began to turn her. It was difficult for them to keep their balance and they could not stop laughing.

"She's doing pretty well," concluded the Writer.

She went back to bed and closed her eyes.

The exchange of words continued for a while. Then two doors slammed.

The Writer clutched her eyes. She was breathing fitfully, as if a hand had grabbed her throat. Tears slid beneath her clenched eyelids and wet her pillow. Her breathing gradually calmed down and she sank into a soothing sleep. She woke up a couple of hours later. The flat was quiet. She took a shower, had breakfast and left.

When she stopped writing, the sun had passed its zenith. The wind became cool. She shuddered. She went back to Corralejo, entered the first surf club she saw and signed up for a lesson the next day.

Later Juan found her on the roof where she had come to watch the sunset. She replied coyly to his greeting.

"Sorry about this morning. We were drunk... and did not know you were there."

"Where should I have been?"

"I thought you had sex with the man I saw you with."

"An interesting suggestion..."

"Why not?"

"Yes, why not..."

"I didn't get any ..," he sighed sadly.

"This means only one thing."

"And it is?"

"You have not played your cards right."

While she uttered this, she stared into his green eyes.

The sunset burst and lit up the sky in all the shades of yellow-pink-orange.

"What do you mean?"

The Writer did not answer. She stood, staring at the horizon, as if she had not heard his question. He mumbled something and walked into the building. When the last glow faded, the Writer followed him. In the kitchen she found Lola, who also watched her anxiously:

"Sorry about this morning. We were drunk."

"No problem."

"I hope you're not angry..."

"I'm not angry."

She went to her room and closed the door behind her.

Marina

Marina was restless. The phone call that Gerd received at the end of the evening was like lightning cutting through an impenetrable night. She noticed how his face tightened while he was talking with Enrique, and how hastily he began to dress. She thought she would not see him again and her throat went dry. Even his farewell kiss was nervous, hurried, as if stolen. She waited until he disappeared in the darkness and started the car. Gerard was reading, when she came home.

"Why aren't you sleeping?"

"I'm not sleepy."

She undressed, lay down in her half of the bed with her back to him and closed her eyes. At dawn, he took her in his arms and made love to her with persistent tenderness. As the day broke her hopes began. She expected some news from Gerd - if not a phone call, at least a message so that she knew what had happened. But the mobile remained indifferently silent. She was wondering whether or not to go to Corralejo to see the Writer or Enrique. The Writer did not pick up her mobile and she did not have Enrique's number. In the afternoon, she went for a walk. She sat on top of the dune where Gerd had invited her into his buggy just two weeks ago, which now seemed to her like years, and stared at the ocean. The wind had calmed and there were small waves. She realised that in the recent days she had hardly thought about her. It happened for the first time and she felt like she had betrayed her. She covered her face with hands and tears ran between her fingers. Her shoulders were shaking. She slid down the dune on her back, the sand squeezed through her hair, under her clothes, in her shoes. She didn't have the strength to get up and return to the hotel, to look at Gerard, to pretend that she had not forgotten her, that she had not allowed the feeling to replace the memory... She had told him that nothing had happened. But as she lay buried in the sand, she realised: everything had happened. The habitual shelter of the monotonous grief was replaced by the uncomfortable nakedness of the expectation. She wiped her tears and stared at the ocean again.

The Writer

The jeep drifted across the rocky landscape of Fuerteventura. A space framed by a chain of mountains, impassive, almost unreal. Loud music - alternative, intense, rhythmic – filled the jeep. Combined with the landscape, it created a film-like sensation. They were five with the teacher – the Writer, yet another Italian and a couple of Belgians.

The car stopped on the edge of the hill that sloped to the beach. The ocean spread out before them. Huge. Immense. Intractable.

"What's the first thing you look for when you go to the beach?" the teacher asked and made a sweeping gesture towards the ocean.

"The waves?" someone said.

"The flag?"

"Exactly. The flag. When the weather is safe, there is no flag. The yellow flag like today shows not only the waves but also the currents. See the rocks there" – he pointed – "you see how water moves in two directions - in and out? This is the current. It's very dangerous and you should keep away from it. It could suck you in and then you will have to be saved. Be careful and avoid it."

They took the boards under their arms and walked down to the beach. It was long and wide, from it the ocean opened to an infinite horizon. The shallows were filled with small Lego-like figures, beginner surfers, who tried to stay on the boards. They managed for a moment, then they fell and disappeared beneath the waves to re-appear after an instant, and to continue their efforts to synchronise the board with the power of the wave.

"There are different types of wave. The green wave is strong and dangerous, it will take you and swirl you inside itself. The white wave becomes foam. It takes you out. Keep the board always by your body, parallel to it. If it is in front of you, it's dangerous. The wave can hit it so hard towards you, that it could injure your ribs and then you won't be able to surf for days."

"As if on the scale of human misery not surfing for days ranks highest," thought the Writer.

"Always protect your head with both hands. These are training boards and are soft, but those you will surf on later, are wooden and can injure you. There are three steps in surfing. Once you decide which wave to take, the first is to lie down on the board. Your toes must reach the sharp end of the board, your chest is curved upward. You paddle with your hands. Turn your head back to see where the wave is. When you lift the end of the surf, you do two more strokes with your hands and stand. To stand up and keep the balance however, don't look at the board or your feet. First, put the tied foot forward, then the other. Your hands should be just below your ribs. Look ahead. The body follows the eyes. You shouldn't think of the board. You and the board are one. It shouldn't be the ocean who decides but you. You need to know at all times what you want and not leave yourself to its whims. The control must be yours."

"How easy it is to say that. You need to know at any time what you want and not leave yourself to its whims. But moving from knowing, to being capable of, and to doing?... How could you take control from the ocean? How?"

Balance was the key to happy surfing. Just like in life, but literally.

They ran on the beach. They jumped on the spot. They trained on the sand getting up on the board.

"We will go without boards so that you first feel the ocean."

The water was cool. But the surfing suit decreased the feeling of wetness and chill.

"Ride along the waves," ordered the teacher.

She turned her face to the beach. The other beginners continued their training. She faced the ocean. The wave was gaining speed. She waited for it and went with it. Next thing she was underwater. No control whatsoever. She felt like a plaything in the powerful grip of the ocean. She came to the surface and struggled to her feet. The next wave was already coming. She went with it again.

"Try to keep your head above the surface," advised the teacher.

She tried and almost succeeded.

"We will go for the boards."

They walked to the shore.

She fixed the cord to her leg and fastened it, as instructed.

"Take the boards. Enter."

She took the board by her side and carried it to the ocean. Inside, she tried to stay stable. But even before she went with the board, she knew that everything was beyond her control - the board, the wave, even her own body. What control in front of this open maw dashing towards her? She stood facing the shore, glancing backwards to select a wave. Here it is. She turned and tried to lie down on the board. It did not work out. The wave devoured her. A terrifying feeling. She spun like in a centrifuge. The board had gone in another direction. She thought she would die. Now the board will return and hit her. She covered her head with hands as the teacher had shown them. She managed to come up the surface. The salty water was in her eyes, nose, mouth. She coughed. The board returned to her. She grabbed it and tried to put it back to its side position. It was not easy, but she succeeded. Then the next wave knocked her down again. She lost her hold on the board, but she got it back quickly. She lay for a moment on it, but before she started to row with her hands, the wave reached her. After a few centrifuges, she dragged herself ashore, threw the board on the sand and relaxed on it. The sun came out from behind the grey clouds and shone on her face. She took it with gratitude. She was breathing heavily. She lay for a while, ate two bananas, drank water and walked back to the ocean. This time she managed to stay on the board a couple of times and to paddle to the shore, carried by the wave. She felt the lightness of being at its crest. It was a partnership, flight, union. And the wave was no longer an open maw, instead, it gave her wings. That's it. Suddenly, she knew why those infected by the virus of surfing travel to faraway destinations.

Because of the *feeling*. Finding the wave with which to fly.

And she had only lain on the board. What would it be like to be standing?

While she was resting, she observed how high the tide had become, each wave closer to her.

The teacher waved to her. She got up, took the board and walked towards him.

"The tide is with us. Don't try anymore where the waves are so strong. Go from here," he pointed a strip of sand that just a while ago was the boundary between the ocean and the coast, and now had turned into a mini-island.

He held the board so that she could lie on it.

"This one isn't good... nor this one... and this one lacks power. But this one is good. Go! Start paddling! Go! Paddle!"

She rowed while striving to maintain the proper position of her body – like the asana "cobra" in yoga. The wave carried her.

"Come on, stand up!"

She could not. She remained motionless on the board. Only her hands were still mechanically rowing. She was already on shore. She got up, took the board and went back to the teacher.

"Okay. Now try to get up."

She laid on the board again, waiting for a good wave.

"Go ahead. Come on, go ahead. Stand up."

She stretched her tied left leg forward. She took a breath and without stopping to look in front of herself, stood up. In the short instant of her flight on the crest of the wave, any thoughts had left her. Her senses were possessed only by the feeling. The feeling of lightness and absolute freedom.

Carla

She pretended to be asleep when Gerd returned. She lay with her back to the door. He slipped in next to her and hugged her. Again she wept soundlessly. Tears slid into her parched mouth. She swallowed them as if they were a life-giving liquid. She tried to calm her breathing, to soothe the pain, to fall asleep. Gerd's breathing quickly became rhythmic. Hers followed.

She woke up around nine. He was still asleep. She dressed and went jogging. Sport always helped. It mobilised her. It gave her strength.

She reached the dam, climbed the steps, pressed her body against it and stared at the ocean. Huge, powerful, containing the waves which rolled in different directions. She wanted to get strength from it. Likewise, to be able to take a grip on the feelings flooding her soul. Sun rays filtered through the dramatic clouds and bathed Lobos in their light.

She continued along the alley towards the wind generators. Their blades were spinning furiously. She reached the round garden, passed it, and went down to the small beach. Pushups, yoga, meditation. She was already more relaxed, able to face Gerd. She ran back. The wind scattered the clouds and the sun warmed Lobos. Without thinking, she took the quay of the harbour. She reached the tourist office and asked how much the return ticket to Lobos was. Fifteen euros. A boat was leaving in five minutes. Mechanically, as if it was not her, she bought the ticket and jumped into the boat. It glided away from the dock and headed for the island. She did not think. Her body had decided for her, she had only followed. After twenty minutes they arrived. She took the path circling the island. She was all alone, the only inhabitant. She felt both adrenaline and a growing sense of peace. The environment of Lobos was as varied and surprising as life. Volcanic rocks, low shrubs, even trees. The landscape was changing and her feelings were changing with it. There could be anything on an island - beaches, vegetation, outcrop, rocks, residents, newcomers, visible and invisible world, but none of these co-habitants affected its integrity. And so it was with relationships. Each one was a separate island. Like hers with Gerd. What happened was part of the diversity. It would pass, but the island, their relationship, would remain. The pain faded. Her anger dissolved with it to give way to the love, to the endless ocean of her love for him. She reached the lighthouse building, climbed to its terrace and the ocean spread in front of her with its infinity. She sat down and stared long at its moving waters.

She was walking through a rocky area when she noticed the stone composition over a hill. It looked like a headless female torso. She got closer. She saw two distinct profiles at the level of the woman's armpits, male and female, looking in opposite directions. As if the headless woman was hugging them. She shivered. She remembered that dream in which she was wandering alone in the desert. Wasn't it a prediction? The soul always knows. She took out her mobile to take a photo of the composition and noticed that there was no coverage. Gerd must have been worried.

On her way back she stopped at the museum. Seals once lived on the island. Hence the name, Lobos, water wolves. But people had exterminated them. Yes, this also could happen on an island. Invasion of aggressive aliens. She went down the pier, reached its edge and looked out. Across the water, the hotel where that woman, the alien to their island, was staying, rose like an ugly pyramid. She imagined her, calm and happy with her conquest. Like a powerful wave, her anger rose again. She knew what she had to do.

In Corralejo she caught the bus to Puerto del Rosario and got out at the stop by the hotels.

Marina

She did not know how much time had passed while she was lying at the foot of the dune, covered in sand and with wet eyes. She heard steps, raised and turned around.

"Carla? What ..."

"Why Gerd?"

"I don't know. These things..."

"Gerd is the only thing I have in this world. The only one. We are destined for each other. He'll never leave me."

"I don't want him to leave you."

"What do you want then?"

"I don't know. Look, Carla, something terrible happened to me. I had not felt joy for ages... I had lost the connection with life. Gerd woke me up from this... lethargy."

"I don't want to know! I don't care! To me, you're the one who broke into our relationship."

"But I didn't break in. Gerd invited me. You should be having this conversation with him, Carla, not with me."

"Don't tell me what to do! If I wanted to talk to him, I would not have been here."

"What do you want from me?"

"To leave him alone."

"And if he contacts me?"

"Don't answer."

"Why?"

"Because of me."

"Carla..."

"Imagine that your daughter was going through this. Would you have inflicted it on her?"

Marina tried to calm her breathing.

"Would you?"

Carla's light blue eyes stared at her accusingly.

"Go to hell, Marina!"

Carla turned and rushed across the sands. Marina shivered from the cold touch of the wind, which had returned bold and reckless. She got up and walked to the hotel, dragging her feet as if they were sandbags – heavy and unwieldy.

THE SILENCE OF THE ISLAND
OR
OUR ATLANTIS

Miguel

The feeling that has not left me ever since the servants of this cretin who runs our country took me away. What is happening in my wretched country would have been grotesquely funny had it not been so tragic: that you can be taken from your home in front of your entire household because you have dared to tell the truth. The feeling that corrodes me all the way from my house in Salamanca to the station, on the train to Madrid, in the hotel, from which they don't let me go out, on the way to Cadiz, in the next hotel, on the deck of Atlante... A feeling of disgrace, which gets partly dissolved by the sight of the sea.

Later I write to Concha:

"The trip was delicious. The sea like a sleeping lake. The captain was the Catalane D. Jamie Gelpie Verdager, a very clever man, cultivated, with a generous and free spirit. A lieutenant, a commander and three captains came on board and kept us good company. All understood the new absurdity – it is nothing but this - in which we were thrown by this cretin of Ganzo Real. One of the captains was going to Fuerteventura, where his wife is. He was very supportive and told us many interesting things about the internal state of the army. He was from Africa. I joked with Soriano that we would organise an independent federal republic of Fuerteventura."[12]

After five days on Las Palmas, they board us on the ship and we set off to Fuerteventura.

---

[12] Cartas del destierro, Entre el odio y el amor (1924-1930), Collete y Jean-Claudde Rabate, Ediciones Universidad de Salamanca, 2012

The Writer

I arrived in Fuerteventura on a Saturday in January with a small case, containing my laptop, a few clothes, a crumpled map of the island, a couple of books by Unamuno and an old notebook.

I came with two return tickets. Why two? At the last moment, I got scared by the idea of being all alone on the remote island, of finding myself in exile on the island of a foreign loneliness, different from the familiar, domesticated and integrated one. The foreign loneliness is a dangerous territory. I didn't know what to expect from it. What would be its face, its habits? Whether it would smile spitefully or would snarl menacingly. Whether it would hit me during the day in the middle of a beach, whether it would sneak through the sounds of an old melody or would wake me up during the night and grip my throat with sweaty fingers... I could only guess. I didn't know what to expect from myself either, when I see its unknown face. Would I feel fear or a desire to woo it, to be drawn into a glass (or more) of mojito, sangria, whatever, or into that insistent and strong sadness which makes you enter the ocean and swim towards the horizon without turning back? I didn't know and I didn't want to find out. The second ticket was my emergency exit. A promise to myself that I won't have to enter the ocean.

Unamuno had not chosen to come here. Nor did he know when he would leave. What had he got out of his stay? Or of himself? That is what I was hoping to find out. Unamuno is a titan of the spirit, a thinker, a philosopher, a colossus of talent and emotion. I am an ordinary coward.

But an ambitious coward. I would not dare to face the ghost of the unknown solitude but I have loaded myself with the challenging intention of writing a novel about the colossus on the island. An intention which appeared to me more and more impossible to execute. Particularly among the sophisticated dissipation of Brussels, particularly after the hours of reading Unamuno and staring at the blank page. Hence, after a hectic and successful year of being a consultant, I booked two flights to Fuerteventura, and two days before I left I added a third one, and allowed myself a creative break.

I arrived at the island exhausted, hopeful, fearful and empty. Empty like a white sheet.

Miguel

"I received the order of deportation on 21 February, exactly 50 years after I heard one of the first bombs falling next to our house in Bilbao. Maria should remember; we were together on the porch – this ridiculous bombing started by our bureaucrats, amid lies and nonsense and concerns; who knows whether on 21 May the civil liberation of Spain and its civilisation will be celebrated in our Bilbao, so that I can celebrate the civil liberation of Spain and its civilisation."[13]

The Writer

From the moment I set foot on the island, I came out of my organised life and found myself in the space of Chance. If Unamuno is right and Chance is the beginning of freedom, on Fuerteventura I was unusually and unexpectedly free. Naturally, I did not realise this immediately. In the first minutes after my arrival, while looking for the van which was supposed to take me to Corralejo, and later, while I was travelling, I was focused on the

---

[13] Cartas del destierro, Entre el odio y el amor (1924-1930), Collete y Jean-Claudde Rabate, Ediciones Universidad de Salamanca, 2012

feeling. The feeling of being back here. Comparing it with that earlier feeling of being here for the first time. The feeling of having returned. What was it? Ease. Freedom. The sun, caressing my face. The wind in my hair. The waves crashing over the shores of the desert.

My first moment on Fuerteventura was the last one of my relative independence. Of objective observation, of almost impartial knowledge-recollection. Next I was in the bar to take the keys to the flat where I rented a room. Then, I did not yet realise that I had taken off my will and intention like some unnecessary clothes and had entered into the magical world of the island completely naked. Like the nudists who lounged and swarmed around its endless beaches. Indeed, I was not alone. On the bare island, we were all naked. And each next step of ours or an apparent volition would lead to the inevitable denouement. I had come to write a novel. In fact, I was the heroine in a novel. The novel being written by the island.

Miguel

"Puerto Cabras, Fuerteventura, March 11, 1924

Dear Concha,

It's seven in the morning. From my bed, I saw the sun rising over the sea and then the outlines of three camels against the backdrop of the sea. We enjoy absolute tranquillity.

Yesterday they brought us from Las Palmas. They expected that we would ask for something, but we are determined not to ask for anything that we are not entitled to by law. Here again, we raised the issue that the state should cover our costs. We did not pay the hotel in Las Palmas, neither the journey to here. They may imprison us, but not oblige us to pay for jail, and in the circumstances, this is jail.

(...)

The island is sunk in sad poverty; something like desolation. Almost no trees and the water is not enough. It looks like La Mancha. But it's not as bad as I describe it. The landscape is sad and empty, still, there is some beauty in it. But I have never seen an ugly landscape. These empty hills remind me of the back of a camel. Yesterday we made our first trip by car to Antigua. We will also make some trips on camels. We should visit Chamotistafe, Loscilihate, Liskamanita, Leguate, Lekspirague, Ampuyenta and some more. (...) The names of the villages here are similar to those of humans in Palencia. And we will study the habits of the camels. I will see if I can get them to pass through the eye of a needle.

The people are wonderful and welcoming. And all are aware of the nonsense of Primo. And more precisely Anido, who is the real author of this."[14]

The Writer

I took the keys from Alma, entered the flat, left my luggage in my room and was already living in Corralejo. That's right, that's how it was. I immediately started living there, in the way in which some friendships, some loves and some feuds start - with sudden, unconditional reciprocity. I was not a tourist. I was not a visitor. I was not an outsider. I was a woman who lives in Corralejo. I entered this role with unexpected ease. I settled myself comfortably into it. I went to the supermarket, cooked and immersed myself in the simple rhythm of my Fuerteventurian being.

From that first day, each person I met took me to the next, each story was a part of the plot, fully linked to the previous one. I lived Fuerteventura. We all lived it. Or maybe she lived us?

---

[14] Cartas del destierro, Entre el odio y el amor (1924-1930), Collete y Jean-Claudde Rabate, Ediciones Universidad de Salamanca, 2012

Brussels ceased to exist. With a precise gesture, an invisible hand wiped it off the map of my emotional memory along with all the people who inhabited my life there.

Two days later that same life of mine was full of new people and of the feeling that I have known them for years.

Miguel

"Puerto Cabras, Fuerteventura, March 13, 1924,

I am writing this from one of the islands called the Fortunate ones - and this one, Fuerteventura, really is, because there is neither cinema, nor football teams, nor boy scouts. Instead, camels prevail - it is a piece, torn from West Africa. Here, together with the east wind, comes the sand of the wind samum from the Sahara."[15]

The Writer

Alice entered the Mirror world. Lucy entered the wardrobe. I entered the island.

What was magical about it? Everything in its habitualness. The landscape, combining the desert, the bare cliffs and the ocean. The whiteness of Corralejo. The slow time. The light. The climate. The sunsets. The people I met. Everything.

It all started with that, the Corralejo as I discovered it and the Corralejo from my memory were two different cities. Five years ago, it appeared to me to be a small, uncomely and uninteresting place. We had lunch in a restaurant with a view of the harbour and left immediately. Nothing but the name matched my memories. Now Corralejo fascinated me immediately. A city of

---

[15] Cartas del destierro, Entre el odio y el amor (1924-1930), Collete y Jean-Claudde Rabate, Ediciones Universidad de Salamanca, 2012

surfers, skaters, street musicians and cats. The surfers were everywhere - in the ocean, in the bars, in the huge screens, from which the moving eye of the wave-tunnel looked at me. The skaters flew in the streets and the rattling of their boards on the asphalt reached me anywhere in the city. The musicians had distributed themselves among the streets and the bars and restaurants in front of which they performed their repertoire. I was passing from melody to melody, from song to song. Cats lounged under the sun in quiet enjoyment of life. They preferred the rocks over the dam that separates the city and the ocean. They curled up on the hot surface and ended up looking like big breathing buns. But you could also see them on the tables of restaurants early in the morning, and elsewhere. The other day one was seated next to a puddle among the stones by the sea. The puddle looked like a miniature lake which has captured the reflections of the cat and the clouds. The haiku of life.

Corralejo is a town created for joy. The numerous restaurants and bars along the seaside promenade and through the inner streets, the port, the dam, the playgrounds, the ocean made it a place glorifying life in a quiet, charming and self-sufficient way. A city with a magical name. Coral-echo. If only corals could produce echoes... The echo of the name. Corralejo. I checked on the Internet its etymology. There was no information, but I found the following text in a numerological website: "The number of life's path of the name Corralejo is 7. The significance of this number is: highly intelligent, sometimes philosophical and imaginative. You have psychic talent and you can enjoy your loneliness. This is a quality of the lonely. Since you don't accept things easily, without checking them, your path leads to learning, tests and analysis. Sometimes it will be better for you to have more faith. Without faith you become cynical. You were born to seek the truth. All spiritual and mystical things attract you. You like natural beauty - the ocean, the grass, the plants, the flowers. You always leave a sense of mystery in others. And it is hard for you to reveal yourself in front of them. With your perfectionism, you are devoted to mastering the unknown and the accumulation of knowledge." This is the city with which, slowly and irrevocably, I began to fall in love. It seemed to me that we matched.

What had happened to the plain town from my memory? Had it changed beyond recognition, or had I?

The answer did not matter. I was there, I lived it and without realising, without thinking and rationalising, I had voluntarily entered into the role, predetermined for me in the novel of Fuerteventura. The one of the Writer.

Miguel

"Puerto Cabras Fuerteventura, March 11, 1924

My dearest Concha,

Our life here passes in a profound peace. Yesterday we strolled along the sea and we went to eat seafood. What distracts us is the expectation of letters and the walks along the pier where we observe the steamships arrive. People are very kind. The notary, the judge, the priest keep us company. We walk with them - all of them valuable people, including the military." [16]

The Writer

I came alone to write a novel. During the first week, however, I almost didn't get anywhere near writing. In the novel, in which I lived, Corralejo was a city where people meet, communicate and experience their strongest, most profound and long suppressed nature. And as I had left my will overseas, I was not left with

---

[16] Cartas del destierro, Entre el odio y el amor (1924-1930), Collete y Jean-Claudde Rabate, Ediciones Universidad de Salamanca, 2012

anything but to obey. Obedience was exciting, engaging and tasty. It tasted like freedom and had a breath of enigma.

Chance offered me the opportunity to share a flat with two young men - an Italian and a Spaniard. "Good fellows," the owner assured me before booking online. I met Fabrizio as soon as I arrived. Good looking, swarthy, friendly-distant. His life revolved around surfing, but he wanted more. He had plans. Following them, he moved out of the flat a few days later. The Chance winked to me behind his back.

The meeting with Juan could have been the inciting incident in an exciting island romance. The Chance, however, had decided something else. And Fabrizio's place was taken by the attractive Lola.

I had to take my keys from the Indy bar where I met Alma, Enrique and Kumar, the owner. Alma was a beaming Argentine, around forty, who loved her job, nightlife and dry martini. Enrique was an Italian surfer who had dumped his well-paid job in Turin and had come to Fuerte to live his passion, making a living as a waiter. His friends, a German couple, had arrived on the same day as me. His brown eyes immediately looked at me friskily. And Kumar, the good-hearted Indian, hence the name of his bar, knew another Bulgarian woman Darina, who cleaned his apartment.

The Chance again had sent me to Julio's restaurant shortly before Enrique appeared with Gerd, Carla and Marina, and involved me in the labyrinth of relationships, which had begun to build between them.

I was fully in possession of Chance. And I felt free.

Miguel

"Puerto Cabras Fuerteventura, March 26, 1924

On Sunday we went to Tujneje, then to Tiscamanita and Gran (!!!) Tahaal. We saw a very beautiful property among the alfalfa - for when we bring here Ganso - maintained with salty water. Now wells shine with this water.

The sea is something which those who know Kantabriko do not expect. A calm lake. In the last few days, the full moon was very beautiful. The earth is deserted beauty. Goats and sheep lick stones and pull dry blades of grass. Mountains without a single tree. And at every step a stately camel. Children of camels are called guelfo (or guelfa) and later, after four years, mahalulo. We will take pictures of ourselves on camels. And we will make a trip to Betancouria on camels."[17]

The Writer

I slept through my first night on Fuerteventura. But I woke up rested, blessed and grateful. From the kitchen window, I could see the square, the pier and the back of the waiting woman. Pleasantly deserted, the city was luring me. I got dressed and went out. The air radiated with a soft golden light. The ocean was withdrawing with mighty splendour. Across the sea, Lobos and Lanzarote, shrouded in the haze, looked like ghosts. I felt elation and peace. A crystallised, alive, vibrant feeling. I walked slowly, my senses taking in every detail. I dropped one euro in the small bucket of a man who had built a solid sandcastle, and he gave me

[17] Cartas del destierro, Entre el odio y el amor (1924-1930), Collete y Jean-Claudde Rabate, Ediciones Universidad de Salamanca, 2012

in return a glass ball in iridescent blue and yellow. I turned it against the sun and I told myself: this is my world now, this joyful, shining mix of colours, that's how I feel.

Darina's thoughtful eyes, her shy smile and the restrained heartiness with which she invited me to accompany her to the stand in El Campanario. I did not ask her what she was doing at that market. It was enough to know that I am not the only Bulgarian on the island, and that this other Bulgarian is inclined to see me and even reveal to me some of its secrets. But before she said anything I figured the most important thing from the photos at the stand. Here, that's how Fuerteventura can be loved, because only the deep and complete loving gives the patience, the attention and the eyes for catching its conditions, its regal moments. I looked at the photographs with bated breath, when the tall, dark-haired man behind the counter came over and told me in perfect Bulgarian: "How joyful you look! I rarely meet such Bulgarians."

Darina was smiling beside him and her eyes subtly examined me.

"I have been here for eight years and I still can not say that I know the island," said Emiliyan slowly and distinctly, staring into my eyes. But I had not come to write about the island. I had come to write about Unamuno and hoped that he would give me the cards to unravel his relationship with the island. For me, Fuerteventura was only environment, landscape, location. Emiliyan, however, shook his head and kept looking at me. It seemed to me that he wanted to tell me something but could not find the words, or was not sure that I would understand him.

We agreed to meet later in the "office", as they called café Latino, because of Emiliyan's refusal to go anywhere else. I left the colourful world of El Campanario without realising that something crucial for me and my novel had just happened. But it was not me who was writing this novel, right...

The desert tempted me with its whiteness and tranquillity. I remembered the dunes. On that same wide beach, I had told a man years ago, that every night I dreamt about my husband. But that was in another life. In this life, I slipped off my shoes and walked barefoot on the mildly warmed sand. I walked and walked and walked...

Nothing
      has ever
           been
                nor
        will be
      anything
    else but
sand.

Indeed. Simple and profound as any insight. This one was very valid, especially in the desert.

I sat on the highest dune and slid down. The grains of sand penetrated under my clothes, stuck to my skin, remained in my hair. I walked back to the beach all sandy and shining. I sat on a sunbed and began to write on my small laptop. A dark-haired woman with a pleasant face passed and our eyes met. I greeted her, she nodded faintly and continued to the dunes. My battery was running low. I closed my laptop and went to the restaurant. Julio, the owner, an elderly man with a weathered face and smiling eyes, brought me a goat cheese salad and bread. I was the only customer, we started talking and he sat with me. He was born in Corralejo and had spent his entire life here. I praised his bread. This made him feel good. The bread was made with gofio, flour from milled corn. "In the difficult years... thanks to this flour... we survived." He spoke slowly, heavily, with pleasure. Fuerteventura had been the granary of the Canarias. Hence the many windmills.

I was to discover later that Unamuno wrote a whole essay about the gofio and called it a prehistoric meal, "from before bread." Skeleton of bread. So he called it. At the end of this essay, he asked: *"Has gofio created the Mahos or the Mahos created gofio?"* And replied: *"Both. And they both were created by Fuerteventura of the strong wind."*[18]

"Unamuno was a very natural, earthy man, they say. He made friends with the locals. He went fishing with them. He passed by here on the back of a camel... These giant hotels and umbrellas were not here then. Only sand, ocean and Unamuno on his camel," said Julio. He paused and then added "Corralejo has changed a lot over the years. All the hotels, shops, tourists, surfers... I am one of the very few remaining local people."

A pair of pigeons were courting around the nearby table. One landed on the back of the bench, the other was making fine steps on the ground, puffed up and lovingly cooed.

Two couples walked into the restaurant. Of the first, I recognised Enrique from Indy. Beside him was the woman who had passed me earlier on the beach. The other two had to be his friends, the Germans that he had mentioned. Enrique greeted Julio warmly, kissed me and all of them sat at our table.

The Germans, Gerd and Carla, were in their early thirties. Gerd was a handsome guy with his blue-grey eyes, a mole above his upper lip, chiselled features, short light hair and an elongated, muscular body. In recent years I had developed a special affinity for German men, and despite the noisy glory of the French and Italians as lovers, I had a theory that the Germans were the uncredited Don Juans of Europe. Carla radiated openness and had a confident demeanour that made her attractive and interesting. Sporty, with short hair, light blue eyes, a slightly snub nose and determined chin. The other woman, Marina, looked older than

---

[18] Unamuno: Articulos y Discursos sobre Canarias, Cabillo Insular de Fuerteventura, Puerto del Rosario, 1980, El Gofio (p. 70)

them, about forty, with enigmatic, ethereal beauty. Dark wavy hair, tied in a ponytail, expressive brown eyes, olive skin, full lips and a classical feminine curvy figure. She seemed concealed and reserved. She didn't say immediately that she was Bulgarian, did not express any joy in the fact that we were not only compatriots but both lived in Brussels, nor responded to my invitation to see each other. She often looked at her mobile, sipped her beer and was silent. After a while, having spoken by phone in French, she walked away with the excuse that her husband was waiting for her at the hotel. It didn't become clear to me what the relationship was between her and Enrique and the Germans. They didn't seem to come from the same world nor to be close to each other. Enrique told me about their acquaintance while we were travelling by car to Corralejo among the white sands in the glow of the sunset. He suggested that I go out with them in the evening. I answered evasively. I did not want to promise, to engage myself, to leave my new-found freedom. But again, as if it was not me who was making decisions, a few hours later I was immersed in the nightlife of Corralejo. It was a crazy night. Hopping from one bar to another, emptying successive chupitos, the festive mood of Kumar, the warmth of Alma, the flirting of Enrique, the increasing closeness with Carla, the blue-grey eyes of Gerd... And surfing accompanying us everywhere - visually from the large screens and contextually in our conversations. Enrique walked me home at dawn. I slipped into the flat, closed the door behind me and rested in my bed, exhausted and happy.

Miguel

"Puerto Cabras on Fuerteventura, April 3, 1924
        Dearest Concha,
        Our detached and peaceful life continues in the company of these good friends, mostly the wonderful family Kastaneyra - a

family of men, say it to Piero Bances - and of the priest Victor San Martin. The last few days the director of Le Cotidien, his wife and an editor from Paris visited us and spent six days here.

(...)

We walked a lot by the sea, which is great. (...) I will become a sailor. My companions hunted kabriyas and I fished metaphors. This is a true sanatorium. The weather is perfect, an eternal spring; food is very healthy and good. I am sending you some pictures.

(...)

I wanted to send you another very nice picture of Betancouria, where a camel drinks water from a rubber tyre next to a palm tree, but the French took my only copy to publish it in Paris together with the other ones taken by them. The best of them contain a camel, the most decorative element here, much more decorative than Primo de Rivera, and certainly a lot smarter."[19]

The Writer

Anyone I met took me to the next person, each story was a piece of a novel, integrally connected to the previous one... Exactly.

I arrived without knowing anyone. Three days later I participated in at least three storylines.

First storyline: two couples, surfing, Indy, sands

Marina and Gerard. Carla and Gerd. So different that one would hardly imagine them together. They don't have anything in common. The former – even-tempered, mature, upper class. The latter - young, eager, riding the waves with their boards. The captivation of the former by the desert and the playing with the ocean of the latter suggests that they

---

[19] Cartas del destierro, Entre el odio y el amor (1924-1930), Collete y Jean-Claudde Rabate, Ediciones Universidad de Salamanca, 2012)

would never meet. But they have met. An Italian friend-surfer and a mysterious writer complement the diverse group. What can be the bond between these characters, not belonging together, but love... or passion... or something that can not be called anything but... a feeling... The feeling.

Second storyline: two women, Don Juan, cat, flat

At the beginning, the Writer lives with two men - Italian surfer and a stunningly attractive Spanish doctor. Just like in a woman's wet dream. But reality intervenes. The surfer moves out and the irresistible señora and the elusive cat enter the frame. The doctor flirts with both women. Both like him. The three of them lurk, approach each other, gain distance, purr, meow... like cats in heat. The real cat, Lola's cat, stares at them with her green eyes. The three of them toss and tumble in their beds with longing bodies. Only the cat passes from room to room, stands unseen in a corner, then reappears. The longing bodies continue to toss and turn...

Third storyline: Bulgarians, a camera, an island, books

A Bulgarian woman, who used to be a librarian in her homeland, cleans homes in Corralejo. And passionately reads for the rest of the time. A Bulgarian man, who could be her son, lives with her and spends his days shooting and sharing the island, his great love. Someone's quick thought would immediately see intrigue in this partnership. But quick thoughts often stumble over the truth. And the truth is that the relationship between the two is that of a Don Quixote, taking photos, and his, in this case, tripod-bearer. The beloved of the photographer lives thousands of miles away and visits him twice a year. During the rest of the time, she shares his life via Skype. An instant friendship arises between the librarian, the photographer and the Writer...

Three storylines. Have you noticed anything? Exactly. The one for which I had come was missing.

Miguel

"Puerto Cabras, Fuerteventura, April 14, 1924

(...) So far, thirty-three years of teaching day after day - and at that time I am less missed by my class - and more than thirty years writing, my pen combining the two Spains that the waters of the sea divide - and how I smile here, on Fuerteventura, to our tragic weaknesses – and putting together the blood of the spirit, the language.

My life here, on this island of Fuerteventura, is a life full of dreams and expectations. On this bare, dry, skeletal island the climate is a treasure trove of health, and the people - a treasure trove of nobility. The island is really happy because it has no cinema, nor football teams, nor boy scouts."[20]

The Writer

The truth is that in our short encounter I did not notice anything. Only some nervousness in Marina, boyish excitement in Gerd, confident restraint in Carla. Enrique was too busy flirting with me. When they entered the restaurant and Enrique walked towards Julio and me, I felt irritation. I had just got closer to the island, I had peered into its past through the crystal eyes of Julio, and these intruders would separate me from it. I did not want to know them. I wanted to get to know her, the island. Unamuno called the ocean the sea. And not just a sea but she, the sea. And for me, Fuerteventura was *she, the island*. Since the very first time. Well, not in those words. But with that feeling. As a white witch, she had healed my soul. Its essence interested me. Theirs not.

---

[20] Cartas del destierro, Entre el odio y el amor (1924-1930), Collete y Jean-Claudde Rabate, Ediciones Universidad de Salamanca, 2012)

But they came and sat at the table and locked me in the invisible circle of their relationship. And I had to stand between them and reflect them.

Only at that dinner, I caught the shadow of their prohibited reciprocity. In the shy eyes of Marina and her silence, enfolding her like a protective cloak. In the absence of any contact between her and Gerd. In the cautious gliding of his gaze over her face and chest. In the way Carla looked at him, then her, while talking about surfing, thoughtfully stroking her hands. When at the end of the evening I found Marina in front of the toilet with a flushed face, frenzied eyes and heavy breathing, I already knew. Not with my mind. But with the jealousy that has invaded me like a sudden wind - inexplicable, non-directional and mixing everything. It was only a moment. I chased it away as fast as closing windows banishes the wind. But the memory remained.

I was not surprised when two or three days later, Enrique informed me of the real purpose of our date. He invited me to go out and this was the first thing he said. I left, not because of irritation, but because of this jealousy. Not of Marina and not of Gerd. I was jealous of the generosity of Fuerteventura to two sinners.

In this context, my crush on Juan was inevitable. Pre-destined. Not only by his foamy smile over the sink, his slanted green eyes on the face of a Hollywood actor and his body of a model, nor because of his intimidating, provoking behaviour, but rather by the setup of the island and the atmosphere of impossible loves, intimacy, longing, passion, created by Fuerteventura. She was laughing at us. She has cloaked us in her cliché without us realising, and was gently pulling our strings.

Juan, Lola and me. We gathered in the kitchen in the evening and got tipsy from the attraction between us. A sweet and mind-blurring drink it was. Our laughter and teasing were flowing from one to the other, touching each other like we did not dare, penetrating each other. The tacit agreement that nothing will happen, that we will maintain this perfect triangle unbroken, excited us like a drug. Until that morning in which their drunken kissing in the hallway woke me up and the triangle collapsed.

Miguel

"Puerto Cabras, Fuerteventura, May 26, 1924
   My dearest Concha,
   Nothing new, the expectation continues. My health is perfect. My life is very simple: sunbathing in the morning, lunch, siesta, chess with Mr. Flitch, reading, socialising, dinner, night walk and sometimes a trip.
   (...)
   I'm too lazy and do not write much."[21]

The Writer

Everything in Corralejo changed after my meeting with Marina, the surfers and Emiliyan and Darina. Everything. Corralejo ceased to be just a beautiful town in the middle of the ocean and has become a structure of parallel universes that overlapped without disturbing one another. Every place brought its emblematic or hidden meanings, suspected or not.

   Buena Onda and Banana Bar were meeting points of the surf culture. And the places where Enrique, Carla and Gerd spent their evenings. Once we were all in Buena Onda, including Marina and Gerard. It was after the dinner at their hotel in the dunes. I decided to be an observer. I spoke with Marina about Unamuno, but secretly, like a thief, was looking for a hint of intimacy between her and Gerd. The way in which they did not look at

---

[21] Cartas del destierro, Entre el odio y el amor (1924-1930), Collete y Jean-Claudde Rabate, Ediciones Universidad de Salamanca, 2012)

each other, nor did they talk, and the rapid shift of Marina's eyes when they met his, told me more than any intentional flirting. Gerard was a nice man. Relaxed, steady, sociable... and he loved her. But this did not seem to be enough. Why is something not enough when we already have it? Marina with her calm hands, veiled with sadness, being absent in her presence, soft, unobtrusive but also impossible not to be noticed... I can still see her now. I can see her walking next to me towards the marina, the wind messing her hair, she tries to control it, to stop its flight, to make it obey... I see her staring at the ocean with a body pressed against the warm dam with the unfocused gaze of a person who has nothing to lose. She turns to me, strands of her hair touch me, playful creatures, she hides them away again. I hear her voice, thick and low, trying to pass through the wind and bring the words. I remember the feeling of doom that struck me after our parting. How come, when I started talking about the surfing sites, I ended up talking about Marina? I do not know... Enrique teased me, seducing me to try surfing, dressing the experience in all sorts of metaphors and analogies. Carla sang along with backing vocals. Only Gerd showed no interest in my potential conversion, but his silent awe with which he stared at the screen, as if trying to become one with yet another surfer dancing on the board in the tube of a giant wave, was more convincing than the most sophisticated metaphor.

We continued in Tequila, Kiwi and Waikiki where the nightlife lovers gathered. We drank chupitos, danced and exchanged a few words. I was amazingly... free.

Talking about surfing, watching surfing, including two or three documentaries that Enrique gave me, the drinks with my new friends and the invariably negative answer to the question of whether I would not give it a try foretold my little surfing adventure.

Instead of a novel about Unamuno I wrote the following:

"The green wave is the wave that the surfer must catch. This is the only wave for surfing. The wave of white water is already a broken wave, it has lost its power and has no face. The beginners should catch the waves with white water because they are easy to capture, they are not as powerful, threatening and steep. In the reefs, the steep waves can be very dangerous if the water is shallow. The good surfers choose these waves because of the tube that forms there. The shallow bottom helps its formation. But only the really good ones can surf in the tube. Because if you fall in the water, the wave can crush you to the bottom.

Before the lesson, Enrique sent me links to films about surfing. In 'The Endless Summer' they said that the perfect place for surfing in the wave is through the white water - where the wave breaks. This place is called a curl. The main objective of surfing was to always stay in the curl - as close to the white water as possible, but without being caught by it. The ultimate goal of all manoeuvers in surfing is to stay in the curl. In 'Step into Liquid' the surf masters literally dance on the board in an effort to keep their balance on it, in the foot of the wave-monsters. Their feet frantically move back and forth across the board. If those dancing on live coals are called fire-dancers, the ones dancing on water are exactly these surfers. It turns out that the wave is a curly-haired woman, in front of whose face, in her curls, move those who have dared to flirt with her. Isn't this a different image of death? In which all of us, tiny figurines, brave or not, surf in front of its huge face, in the curves of her curls, trying to keep balance, to survive, to be as free as we manage in the tunnel (which has been) assigned to us. And only the most skilled (reckless? adrenaline junky? crazy?) ones manage

not only to stay but also to dance on their boards in the
moving body of the ocean-life with breathtaking grace."

Mostly the locals, the people who lived in Corralejo, dropped by Indy cafe. They exchanged a few words with Kumar, Alma and Enrique, as they ate freshly prepared food or had a drink. Tourists came as well, attracted by the promotional offer - free tapas with each drink in the evening. For me Indy was the stop on my way to or from the dunes or some other island place. I stayed for a quick drink and went on.

In the minimalist Mojito with its four or five tables, relaxing music and a view of the ocean and the boats, I loved to write in the evening over a glass of wine.

All these places had another presence or completely stopped existing in that Corralejo which I experienced with Emiliyan and Darina. I met them in the "office", we ate something sweet in the "German snacks", a bakery whose owners were Germans, we grabbed the "best pizzas in town", from a central Italian restaurant and we ate under the stars. In this Corralejo the main events were not the waves caught but the sunsets, the ocean with all its colours, the wind direction and whether it favours fishing, the low and high tides, the pebbles found on our walks...

Miguel

"The foamed waves at high tide are called sheep, and rabbits; in English sea horses; in French moutons."[22]

Sheep of the sea, generations
of men or sonnets appear;
the creations pass, the nations pass,
the sea remains, keeping its secrets;

---

[22] Miguel de Unamuno, De Fuerteventura a Paris, Editorial Excelsor, 1925

calming her foam in our hearts
they might be tired, but never still.[23]

The Writer

The dynamic consumption was Emiliyan's concept. When he and Darina invited me to join this very personal ritual of theirs, I wasn't exactly clear what to expect. Emiliyan, however, didn't care to explain.

"The dynamic consumption cannot be told. It must be experienced," he said brusquely.

An hour before the sunset they waited for me in front of HiperDino in the main street. Emiliyan bought a bottle of vodka, another one with ice tea, and sliced ham and cheese. Me – cola, in which I poured part of the vodka, and raw almonds.

"Now, Writer, I can tell you what the plan is."

"I am burning with curiosity."

"Hide your sarcasm please, we need to be serious. Because the dynamic consumption is a serious thing. This is what we do: we walk, stop at certain places to have a sip and a bite, then we continue walking."

"Isn't it possible to just sit on the pier or on the beach and have a modest picnic?"

"No, Writer, because then the consumption won't be dy-na-mic."

"And why does it have to be dy-na-mic?"

"Because it's more enjoyable. And it's harder for the alcohol to get you. The result is a cultural way of getting drunk."

"A cultural way of getting drunk... Ok... So be it. Are we going?"

"Not yet. Drinking starts here."

---

[23] Miguel de Unamuno, De Fuerteventura a Paris, Editorial Excelsor, 1925

Emiliyan took a sip from the vodka and passed the bottle to Darina. He repeated this with the bottle of ice tea. I took a sip from the bottle with coke. And on we went.

We walked along the entire seaside alley with a few more stops for consumption, always guided by Emiliyan.

"Consumption," he said with a theatrical intonation.

We stopped, took out our small bottles, drank, ate from the snacks and continued.

The fire of the sunset illuminated the sky in pink-orange. We stood with our backs to the ocean and watched it speechlessly, until it died, leaving behind only the live coals of the stars. Emiliyan made a gesture and we were off.

"The Germans are a great nation," he started talking in his calm and convincing way. "There are no others like them. Such strength of spirit, discipline and love of working. To rise from the ashes of their demolished country and to become again one of the greatest economic powers... I bow to them. They do have dignity, these people. They have spirit and creativity. So many great discoveries have been made by them."

He stopped at a restaurant to leave a photo for a Dutch couple. Darina and I were waiting in front.

"I am back to work tomorrow," sighed Darina. "In Bulgaria I worked in a library, I was among the books. I so love reading... While here I clean. What to do? Life."

"Why don't you go back?"

"I cannot. What am I going to do there? We won't manage... I hope to be able to go back at least for Christmas, as I have not seen my people for a couple of years."

"Her people" were a husband, two married daughters, two grand-daughters and a grandson. She saw them on skype every other day. Face-to-face once every two or three years.

Emiliyan came back and we continued. We turned towards the centre and took the main street. We had made a circle. While drawing it we had said so many insignificant and meaningful things. And we talked again lively, laughed out loud. The tourists threw short half-curious, half-reproachful glances at us.

Emiliyan was right. The dynamic consumption cannot be told. His eloquent leadership, the heartfelt and patient presence of Darina, the walking around the town with innocent plastic bottles in hand, the conversation meandering from one topic to another, the laughter, the stops for consumption here and there… This was a practical philosophy and art in action. A Fuerteventuran version with a Bulgarian heart of the Chautauqua in "Zen and the Art of Motorcycle Maintenance". But a lot more unsystematic and chaotic in its content. Like an artwork which is being spontaneously born in a shared authorship.

"Now we're going to the best pizzas in town!" Emiliyan announced.

We stopped at an Italian restaurant and took three Margaritas.

"We're going to the port. A nice view and a shelter from the wind," directed Emiliyan.

We sat on a bench. The wind had calmed down. In front of us was the ocean with the boats tied in straight lines. I remember how I was chewing the pizza, grilled on live coals, and felt that my life was being filled with perfect calm and simplicity.

Miguel

Like a wife, I finally embrace you,
oh naked sea, heart of the world,
and in your eternal look I sink completely.
In it I will wait my last term![24]

"Fuerteventura is where I got to know the sea and where I achieved my mystical first communion with her, where I

---

[24] Miguel de Unamuno, De Fuerteventura a Paris, Editorial Excelsor, 1925

absorbed her soul and doctrine. And I call it 'her, the sea' rather than 'him, the sea', because the male seas are the Mediterranean, the Adriatic, the Indian, the Baltic, etc.

But - and this counts   for the future- the sign or the configuration of the planets and the stars, under which a person is born and their self is created, sets their entire fortune."[25]

The Writer

On another day Emiliyan and I passed the port where our dynamic consumption had ended. He made a sign for me to follow him. We descended to the first quay where the boats were arranged. He opened the latticed door.

"Now speed up. Don't stop. So they think that we are the spoiled children of rich people who come here with the intention of buying. Fast pace shows determination. Let's see what awaits us here. Elvira – it does not attract me especially, it seems too narrow, I think not, Ocean Dream - yes, I suppose it suggests a certain reverie with these little windows, I agree, I agree, oh, here it is, here it is, Donnata, plenty of space, comfort, and large windows that won me over immediately, but here, again, immediately after that comes Rosalia, a beauty, a real beauty you are, Rosalia, yes, yes, yes, Rosalia, I would not reject you with that clean design. Let's go back. Now we go to the real thing."

I couldn't stop laughing. We descended to the next berth.

"Let's see now. Aneta - no, you don't win me over with these tiny windows, Anastasia - yes, you have everything, small benches to sit in front, a terrace up there, fine, but Margarita whipped me up - what a stance, everything has been thought of, these French windows are perfect, bringing a lot of light, and a sofa, yes, Margarita, you have me! Yes, true, Rihanna is also a

---

[25] Miguel de Unamuno, De Fuerteventura a Paris, Editorial Excelsor, 1925

good option with this table and chairs, it is definitely welcoming."

"What would happen if I stepped on it, jumped over and stretched out? How easy!"

"Oh, be sure that even though you can see no one, wherever they are the owners have secured a perfect view to their yacht, and at the moment you put your foot on it, they will take action. A few years ago that would not have stopped me, but now I would not advise you to dare. Hey, what's so funny now? Come on, we are finished with the inspection."

We stopped at the "German snacks" and bought a piece of cake. We headed to a bench overlooking the pier, on which a man sat, but, according to Emiliyan "he was going to leave soon." Only two women happened to be faster and took the bench. Our nice wooden bench with a backrest.

"We are left with those," I pointed to the stone ones without backs.

"No, no. I see another one like the one that we missed, empty. Over there, a hundred metres further."

"You cannot make me walk that far!"

"Come on, come on, get mobilised! I think about having maximum comfort in the shade, so that the sun doesn't aggressively burn my profile and prevent us from enjoying the beautiful view. The only danger is that the couple in front of us could be faster, but judging by their pace, I think we will be safe. If they had such an intention, they would have speeded up and would have had a more purposeful appearance. The bench is ours."

Already on the bench, he pointed at the ocean.

"When they start talking to me about the colour of the ocean, I get sick. Do you see that on the left it is blue, because of the sky, then there is an abrupt boundary and it becomes lead-grey. But the grey is also nuanced… There is no single ocean's colour. The ocean is constantly changing."

emembered his words a few days later on the beach with
.unes. The ocean was azure in places, greenish in others, dark
.e under the clouds on the right, silvery blue, where the sun's
.ays caressed its surface, pale chartreuse to white where the
waves were crashing. Erratic, vain and irresistible like a woman,
like "her, the sea."

On another evening, we bought a small bottle of whisky,
mixed it with coke and had a "mini-consumption", as Emiliyan
put it. On a bench next to Buena Onda, he told me his story.

He had arrived in Fuerte to visit an acquaintance after five
long years on mainland Spain. His attempt to start a small
business in Bulgaria had ended in failure, but also with an
important meeting. Eva was ten years younger than him and for
the last six years had been sharing his life from a distance, while
being a student. Her graduation was imminent and both of them
were expecting the moment when they would share the same
space. The bitter question was which space. Eva was to seek a job
somewhere in Europe, prioritising her career. The assumption
was that Emiliyan would follow. In saying this, his voice lowered
until it faded away completely, and his gaze fell upon
Fuerteventura's land.

The first thing which attracted him in the island was the
climate. The lack of winter was a sufficient condition for him to
stay. Through that same acquaintance, he had met Darina who
had become his flatmate and closest friend here as well as his
faithful tripod-bearer.

Gradually he had discovered Fuerteventura and had become
a prisoner of the desire never to leave her. On a bench, he had
found a forgotten camera. And he began to photograph her, to
study the craft in detail until he had developed expertise and
sensitivity, making it possible for him to preserve her conditions
and to offer pieces of her soul to the world – the way he had got
to know her. He had not walked the cities of the island but had
spent hours with his tripod in the countryside in anticipation of

the single frame. This drive to capture the moment in its complete perfection was what distinguished his photographs.

Fuerteventura - a witch who had seduced him and made him worship her and show the world her most fascinating faces. The only woman he had not been able to resist, despite his love for Eva.

"For five years I have not looked at, nor reached out for another one on this island, with all these women around, attractive and open to adventures, " he told me. "This is what it means to commit to a woman. Love is a decision, discipline and respect for the sacredness of the intimacy between the two. How easy it is to try to reach for someone else, she would never find out. But I'll know. And this special thing between us will be poisoned. Forever."

I listened to him and thought about Marina and Gerd... Why didn't they know this? I would recall his words on that fateful night when Carla found Enrique and me in Kiwi and the pain pouring out from her weeping eyes hit me like a wave.

Miguel

First I feel it. Then I experience it. Finally, I start writing it. And in writing it, I discover it. And in discovering it, I create it.

You created an oasis within me a blessed island;
civilisation is a desert
were faith is annoyed by the truth;
when I arrived at your rock in Puerto
as I was waiting for the last meeting
over your sea I saw the sky, all open.[26]

---

[26] Miguel de Unamuno, De Fuerteventura a Paris, Editorial Excelsor, 1925

The Writer

Emiliyan's connection to the island was a lot stronger than that of a photographer with his model. It was a connection to every part of her nature, body, spirit and soul.

After my surf lesson, he came with Darina to El Cotillo to collect me. El Cotillo was a fishing village, the seat of the tribal chieftains in prehistoric Maxorata. After the conquest of the island by the French, its former glory began to fade, and only the periodic pirate attacks marked its residual significance. Nowadays, the village has become a focal point for surfers - thanks to the powerful waves, as well as for photographers and romantic souls - thanks to its fame of being the stage of the most beautiful sunsets on the island. But it was too early for the sunset. I sat in a seaside restaurant, ordered a late lunch and started writing. Darina and Emiliyan found me there.

We descended to the square where Darina and I sat on the bench in front of yet another statue of a waiting woman staring at the ocean, while Emiliyan went to look for the perfect stone on the small beach. Nearby another man was walking, peering into the sand, and occasionally crouching.

"What are they looking for?" asked an English woman standing next to us.

"This one is looking for a gem."

"And the other one?"

"I don't know about him."

We looked around and cracked up.

Emiliyan returned with a handful of pebbles.

"Here, a perfect trio," he said, showing three stones on which the ocean had created its art, "And a shell."

"It's a tiny shell."

"Oh, are you estimating its value by its size?"

"No, just mentioning it."

"An amazingly smooth pebble. All these treasures are for you, selected with the consideration of not adding to the weight of your luggage. And these two very special stones I keep for myself. One black and smooth and the other one slightly pink."

I grabbed the black one.

"I want it."

"Oh no, forget about it!"

"Wait, wait! It is talking to me - it says it wants to be mine."

"You are mixing it up with the shell."

"I will lose the shell in my ear!"

"Oh, again, you are downplaying it!"

"No no. But I also want the black one."

"Forget it!"

I insisted, insisted and finally gave up.

We went to Fortaleza del Toston tower, where Emiliyan had had an exhibition recently. We climbed up to the rooftop and I sat down on the flat stone, facing the sun, peeking behind the clouds. The ocean was a living creature. Huge. Boundless. Dangerous. Dozens of beginner and accomplished surfers were swaying in its wavy body. I remembered my flight on the board again. I would not repeat it. It was too intense and intoxicating to be safe. One more time and I could become a captive of the feeling. I could leave Brussels, move to Fuerte, live with the call of the ocean, forget that I have had another life, forget even myself, chasing the perfect wave.

Emiliyan and Darina stood forward, facing the horizon. Words lay between the three of us, unwanted and unnecessary.

As we walked to the car, Emiliyan pulled out the two stones.

"I will always regret this moment of weakness!"

He gave me the black one, and then the pink one to Darina.

Later he showed me his personal stone. Black, round, as big as a palm. He had taken it out of a leather case, round like the stone, and had handed it to me. It was warm. I held it tight, its heat penetrated my skin. His mother had found the stone, and he always carried it with him for luck, even to El Campanario to have good sales. He had cleaned it with a toothbrush to remove the dirt and the dust. Once the stone had disappeared. They had searched for it everywhere, including the taxi they had taken back from the market, but no joy. Emiliyan had been distraught. Finally, they had found it in the bag with photographs. For the first time, Darina had seen tears in his eyes. Tears of joy. He had gone to a leatherworker to make him a special case so he would not lose it again. I gave it back to him. He carefully placed it in the case and put it away.

Miguel

"...the landscape of Fuerteventura is biblical! Evangelical, more precisely. The climate is evangelical. Here evangelical parables, metaphors and paradoxes mingle and melt in the bed of the soul."[27]

The Writer

"We came because of a dog". That's what Georgi and Katya told me when we met at El Campanario thanks to Emiliyan and Darina. "Podenco canario is a predator dog that senses the victim from a great distance. But people are more cruel and insensitive than the dog. Because the dog is driven by its instinct, it has no moral categories and no choice. But people can choose." People, however, made a strange choice - if the dog was ill, they would say it did not deserve an injection, nor a bullet, nor poison, but let it die, tied up. The homeless dogs had seven days. If in that time no one took them from the kennel, someone who would appear

---

[27] Unamuno: Articulos y discursos sobre Canarias, Este nuestro clima, Francisco Navarro Artiles, Excmo. Cabildo Insular de Fuerteventura, 1980

just like that, as if sent by the God of the dogs, they would burn them alive. Georgi and Katya had lived in Italy for twenty-five years. Their veterinarian friends had heard of one of these dogs whose time was running out. They had come to the island to save it, had fallen in love with the landscape and had moved. Because they had discovered "a reality that is not real, very calm, a lot of sand, ocean, many animals, chicks, squirrels..." They had decided to take this step to purify themselves. Fuerteventura had an effect on them like an antidote to the negativity they had faced in their life.

Miguel

On one of my rides on a camel, passing through La Oliva, I see a little girl walking alone. A heavy plait hangs on her back under a white headscarf. She looks up to me and greets me.

"What is your name?" I ask her.

"Carmen."

"Where are you going in this heat, Carmen?"

"To the field."

"How old are you?"

"Twelve."

"Shouldn't you be at school at your age?"

"I don't go to school. I have many brothers and sisters. I have to work to help my parents."

"Can you read?"

"A little."

"The richest world is that of books."

"I like the world of Via Verde."

"What do you want to do when you grow up?"

"Be a mother. I want to have a lot of children. To love and take care of them."

I am about to continue when she looks up to me again:

"What do you do, sir?"

"I write books. I taught at the university. And now I'm busy exploring your beautiful island."

"What's your name?"

"Miguel. Miguel de Unamuno. Take care, Carmen."

"Sir…"

"Yes."

"Someday I'll learn to read and I'll read a book from you."

"If you do that, you will become my dearest reader."

This meeting remained in me with the image of a child, deprived of a childhood, wise like an old woman in her innocence. Ignorance is also knowledge sometimes.

The Writer

I arrived in Fuerteventura on a January Saturday with a small suitcase, which contained my laptop, some clothes, a crumpled map of the island, two of Unamuno's books, and a notebook with journal entries. The map and the notebook were from my first visit here, five years earlier.

I opened the notebook for the first time after the early morning return of Juan and Lola when I heard them kissing. I read the small pages covered with my distorted handwriting.

10.07.2010

The sense of time is different on the island. Days flow into each other. The sea is turquoise. Like on a postcard. But real. After the darkness of the past year, it is an embrace. It heals. I can not escape my thoughts, even here. But I can hide them for a while. Despite the uncertainty of the future. I let the sea wash them away. Its colour absorbs all the black in my soul, through my eyes. This sea can not be described. It can not be photographed or painted. It must be experienced.

12.07.2010

Aloe Vera grows everywhere. Today the landlord showed me how its leaves can be used. The spines on both sides are removed. A piece of the leaf must be cut and left for the yellow, stinking mixture to leak. Then it is split down the middle. The green mucous surface is scraped into a bowl. It is mixed with the same amount of water and applied to the face and the body. It must be left to dry, no rinsing. The skin becomes silky. The hair as well.

15.07.2010 г.

Half light-blue, half purple sky. And small white clouds. Sunset. I experience it while I swim in the hacienda pool. In the distance, the sea sinks in the white fog of the twilight. The first stars appear. The landlord is watering his beautiful cactus garden. The smell of earth. In front of me is the garden, in it – the pool I swim in. Behind me is the mountain. But only the sea gives peace and joy to my soul. I am reborn every time I swim in its translucent turquoise waters.

My soul has no answers. But it takes the surrounding beauty and cherishes it. I am filled with gratitude. And with pain. Will I ever get rid of it? I do not know.

17.07.2010

The most amazing sight is the tide on the huge beach of Costa Calma. All of it has become a sea. The water reaches our knees, then our waists. Small sandy islands, remains of the beach. I swim in a natural pool next to the sea. Surfers glide across the surface of the incoming tide. Around us are shoals of fish and surfers. And people celebrating the sea. A young woman in a swimsuit with a white shirt is sitting on a strip of sand surrounded by water, bathed in light. Like in a Sorolla canvas. Another landscape I will keep forever in my memory is the dune reserve near Corralejo. Kilometres of white sand. The rounded femininity of the island. Within the sand - the road. On the side - the sea.

19.07.2010 г.

Is it possible? It seems to me that my soul has been left behind, on the island, and one day I will have to return to get it back.

I closed the notebook. Yes, the old pain can come back. But I had returned too. I only had to put my soul back in place.

That same night I pulled out the map. On it, the places we had travelled to were marked with a pen - Pahara, Antigua, Betancuria, Cofete...

Miguel

The simplicity, bareness, unpretentiousness, undisguised nature, the intransigence make my relationship with her mystical, profound, inexplicable, undesignated... No matter how many words I use to convey the feeling I experienced while I was with her, as well as the feeling of being away from her, they will always be in vain. Fuerteventura can not be told. And I can not stop trying to capture it in my words, because this is the only means I have to be able to take her away with me, to distinguish her from the geography of Spain, not as one of the Canary Islands, but as the only island, the Island. To write her down in another geography, the geography of the spirit, of the mystical spirituality, so that those who have the senses to get to know her in my words, to get to know her herself, to breathe her and live her when I will no longer be here, and so we can connect forever. This land, the sea, the desert, the moon, the sunsets, the collective soul of the Mahos, they will be here after me and after you, and I believe, I want to believe, that whatever happens to this poor but blessed island, whichever way Time shapes her destiny, her original essence will prevail over all the transient things of being, and the prehistoric mother will watch with a gentle smile the spectacle of the human passage.

The Writer

After that morning, the kitchen became an empty space. Juan came home late, prepared something for dinner and went to his room. I could hear his movements from behind my closed door. Lola, when she was not at work, also stayed in her small room with her cat Nana. We ran into each other in the shady corridor, exchanged a couple of words and quickly went out or returned to our boxes, safely detached from the world of the apartment. The ocean seemed to have blown away all my redundant sentiments, and now I was finally devoted to what I had come for - the writing of the novel. During the day I worked on the roof or in the dunes, and in the evenings I went to Mojito, where, undisturbed, I gave myself to reading and more writing. I focused on two files - the novel and a diary. I had returned to Unamuno and came upon the following thought in his "Aesthetics", written about Victor Hugo: "*He felt a great attraction to everything Spanish, but he could not say a word about Spain without blurting out something stupid. His Spanish geography, history and toponymy are terribly entertaining because of their extreme inaccuracy. He throws around names of people, stories, and village names without any understanding.*"[28] This made me think and realise that on Furteventura I had met everyone but her. How could I write about the island if I don't know her? I found the contact details of the Association Raíz del Pueblo - the roots of the village - on Google. "Roots are very important," the centenarian woman, who ate only roots had said to a writer, who had replaced writing with the image of a party animal in the film

---

[28] Unamuno, Essays, Science and Art publishing house, 1983

"The Great Beauty". Inspired by her words, the writer returned to his roots on another island to realise that his only love had happened there, in the innocence of his youth. Islands, it seems, are also very important. I called Concha and we agreed to meet the next day.

Miguel

This sky a palm of your hand,
Lord, that protects me from death,
of the soul, and the other east palm of Fuerte-
calm wind and faithful ocean.[29]

The Writer

"Corralejo is not Fuerteventura, you understand? It is a tourist place, everyone is a tourist there, aliens... there is almost no local population. What do you know about the island?"

Concha was a small, agile woman with an open, sullen face and brown eyes, which were now studying me. We sat in her office in the building of the cultural centre.

"Not much... That's why I called you. I know about the exile of Unamuno, this is the starting point of my novel. I heard of what happened during the Second World War, about the crew of the German submarines who stopped in Handia..."

"That's a legend, about the German submarine crews. Nobody knows if it happened."

"How can I learn more?"

---

[29] Miguel de Unamuno, De Fuerteventura a Paris, Editorial Excelsor, 1925

"I'll take you to the Archive. If there is any information, they will know. But this is not exactly the history of the island."

"And what is the history of the island then?"

"The past. La Oliva, Betancuria, Antigua... The history of Fuerteventura is a silent history. That's what they call it. There is some information about different periods, but not a complete narrative. Just fragments. The memory of the island is mostly the people who are still alive. There's a woman centenarian here in La Oliva..."

"But how can I understand it then? Fuerteventura?"

Concha thought for a moment. Her eyes stayed on mine.

"By building your own narrative," she said simply.

* * *

"This may be just a legend. There is no evidence that it happened. Franco might have allowed the Germans to rest on the island, but he might, equally, not have... But what is sure is that a German moved to Handia. Gustav Winter. People usually link the story of the submarines with him. Here, look at this article... it came out recently. Give me your email, I'll send it to you. But unfortunately, we have no other information. It would be best if you could go to the library in Puerto del Rosario. I'll call to arrange a meeting for you."

The man with silver curly hair, big nose and slightly narrowed eyes, looking at me behind glasses, dialled a number. He explained briefly my interest and asked when they could meet me.

"Can you make tomorrow morning?"

"Of course."

The man confirmed and hung up. He gave me his business card with the words: "Write to me if you need more information."

We stopped in front of a white building with a peaked roof. Underneath the white plaster, here and there brown bricks showed through. There was a label by the door, La Cilla - The Granary; two rectangular horizontal windows with front-facing lids were situated symmetrically under it. The granary definitely had a face, and its eyes were watching us from under its eyelids' shutters. The door opened. A swarthy girl with chestnut-coloured hair tied in a ponytail met us with a smile. Concha introduced me and left. I was the only visitor. I stopped in front of each picture and tried to get a sense of the people in it, to imagine their way of living. Women, probably younger than they looked, in dark clothes and headscarves. They were no different from the women in Bulgarian villages. A donkey looking from behind them. In front of them - a little boy. Serious and tense, as if going for an exam. An older man wearing a black hat with a brim, a big nose, and a toothless half-smile sitting on a stone. Two men with bright clothes and straw hats in front of a haystack with pitchforks in their hands. Their faces hidden under the brims of their hats. Young men in beige clothes with hats. Two of them holding the leads of two camels. Among them a woman with a shirt, belt, skirt to the knees and a brimmed hat. Under the hat - short dark hair and a smile. In her hands – a digging fork. The rocky desert landscape of the island in all the pictures as a backdrop. *The past is a buried present*, it occurred to me. These women, men and children had lived on the island day to day, had loved, made love, suffered, experienced joy day by day until the end of their days. They had fed this land with their remains, and the only thing left of them were the pictures, ordinary pictures of ordinary people, who had gained importance precisely because of the ordinariness of the being that they were illustrating. Their role in this museum was to give validity to the past as it was. They had posed for the picture on a day that, within their lives, was one and only, unique, unrepeatable. And while posing, they did not suspect that this moment would turn into eternity and that in the future it would have the status of a status quo. That was your life, day after day. You are the people of Fuerteventura of those times. That captured moment of yours has turned into fossilised time. A time that will never end. The time of your eternalised transience.

Later, Concha took me to the Colonels' House. A crème-orange-coloured two-storey building in the colonial style with wooden carved shutters on the windows, balconies in front of each of them on the second floor, and a patio. The owners of this monumental house were watching us from their huge portraits with stately expressions. The windows looked at a building with wide-open doors and windows, around which rose nine palm trees. Behind them was the reddish slope of the mountain. After Concha and I had split up, I headed to Casa Mané. The gallery was housed in two small buildings at the bottom of a cactus garden. The surrealist works by Alberto Manrique de Lara kept me for the most time with their dynamic worlds, marked with the lack of gravity, light and chessboard motif. The objects in them looked like living creatures - vibrant and animated. Even the destruction was beautiful. "*Un autor no es original por su extravagancia, sino por su autencidad,*" the painter had said. And what if extravagance is authentic? Or the authenticity extravagant?

The garden consisted of large cacti, palm trees, a pavement of pebbles, and many tin goats looking ahead, grazing, standing, gathered around the goatherd, who seemed to be heading for somewhere with a stick in his hand and a rucksack on his back. In front of them a bronze statue, a long-haired woman, naked, lying down, with bent knees and an arm, folded at the elbow, supporting her head.. Slender body, heavy breasts. Fuerteventura. An imperturbable woman who is not embarrassed by her nakedness. Calmly lying down, having turned her back on all the goats and people, leaving them to the mercy of their faith.

In the evening I went to see Emiliyan and Darina. Emiliyan was unusually silent, thoughtful, worried.

"Eva has been offered work in Sweden," Darina told me.

The question froze on my lips. Emiliyan went to the window, lit a cigarette and stared at the piece of ocean-sky. His first cigarette for the past two years.

Miguel

"Plato created, I believe, and did not discover Atlantis, and Don Quixote created, I believe, and did not discover, for Sancho, the island Barataria. And I too hope, with the intercession of Plato and Don Quixote or with the help of both, to invent, to create, and not to discover the island of Fuerteventura.

(...)

This is my Atlantis! This is my island Barataria!"[30]

I create it and share it with the world like a long kept-secret.

The Writer

I found the correspondence between Esperanza Godé and her student, Chanita Suarez[31], in the Digital Archive of the Canaries after visiting the library in Puerto del Rosario. The letters intrigued me for three reasons. The personality of Esperanza Godé, the thirty-year-old teacher, unmarried, who had come to Fuerteventura, unclear from where and had suddenly left for equally unclear reasons. The tone of her letters to Chanita Suarez, portraying her as an intelligent, hearty and playful woman. And

---

[30] Unamuno: Articulos y Discursos sobre Canarias, Cabillo Insular de Fuerteventura, Puerto del Rosario, 1980, La Atlantida (p. 66)

[31] Juan Luis Calbarro, Las cartas de donña Esperanza. Una correspondencia privada en la Fuerteventura de los años treinta como vehículo educativo y de expresión de la intimidad femenina, Cabildo Insular de Fuerteventura, 2005

the strong emotional connection between a teacher and a student. Google confirmed that Chanita Suarez, born in 1922, was still alive. I called Concha and asked whether I could meet her. She promised to ask. The article said that the educational opportunities on Fuerteventura during Chanita's childhood were very limited. There were only five schools for boys, three for girls and thirteen mixed. A single teacher, and more precisely a female teacher, ran each of them. Chanita and four of her five brothers went to study in Antigua where they lived in the house of their grandfather Juan, and his third wife "Aunt Juana". Their parents came on Sundays and left on Mondays. Doña Esperanza Godé was Chanita's first teacher. One day she left without saying goodbye to anyone. "Mostly I do not want to leave Chanita," she had said. The girl cried bitterly over her sudden departure. Not long after the first letter came from Doña Esperanza, who was by then living in the province of Ueska, Coluno. Their correspondence lasted four years: from November 1933 to October 1937. The first letter was to all students. Doña Esperanza called the girls "my dear and unforgettable little friends", asked them to allow her to embrace them and wished them "a good start to the school year." She instructed them to listen to and to love their new teacher, to follow her advice, to enjoy each moment, and to evoke in her the affection they had once elicited in Doña Esperanza. "I wish she has the luck of being near you almost always; luck that I, because of *special circumstances*[32] could not have," wrote the teacher.

The next three letters were only to Chanita. Short, affectionate, skittish. She called her "my dearest Chanita" and "my very dear Chanita," and expressed her joy that she was not forgotten. She encouraged her to continue studying. "Just one thing bothers me - that you will love your new teacher more than me. Of course, I know that you have a big heart, that you have

---

[32] Highlighted by the author

enough warmth in yourself for both of us, but if you do not ..."
"What do I say to you to repay you for all the love? What would you say about that: no matter how much you love me, I love you more. Don't you believe me? No, I do not lie to you, dear, a girl who is so rebellious and bold and who more than once got out of her seat to kiss me, has gained the affection of her teacher and before she knew it, she became a dear friend." "Congratulations on passing into another group; this news shows me that at the school in Antigua, in my dear school, there are some diligent girls. Go on like this, Chanita, and you will see how much everyone will love you." The last two letters from Esperanza Godé were from Zaragoza, where she was allocated because of the war. The first was the longest of all the letters sent by the teacher to her student. She shared her thoughts and feelings about the political situation in Spain as if with a friend, as with a person who is close to her and can understand her. "Your letter, full of love, took my thoughts to my school in Antigua, and I saw you with that red flower suit, decorated with red, with your black eyes like blackberries, pushing the whole class to foolery and ending it with the desire to kiss me, repeated so many times. And at the same time, in my joy there is a little sadness, thinking that I would still like to kiss you again today, after these four years of not seeing each other."

In the other one, she thanked Chanita for her photo, and continued: "I was looking at it for a long time, and finally concluded that you were completely transformed; you are no longer that wild (but very nice) girl, and that you have become... again a girl but wise, who has developed her good qualities and applies them to life. So far I can not send you my picture because I do not have one, as I move around... But I certainly promise you one soon." That is how their epistolary communication ended - with the promise of a photo. Nobody knew what happened to Doña Esperanza. Nor did anyone have a picture of her. Her image would have gone from the island with the memory of her students. The unsent photograph, the lack of any document describing her appearance, was a gift to those who would discover her personality through the preserved correspondence - an opportunity for all of us to invent her, to dress her in the features best suited to our perceptions of her. Here is my Doña Esperanza: medium height, upright, with a proud posture, dark, long auburn hair, tangled in heavy plaits, strong body, tight breasts, open face, dense joined brows, under which fiery eyes, an aquiline nose, thick lips, cheekbones, a warm smile... I see her laughing with her schoolgirls, hugging Chanita, packing and leaving with dead eyes, clenched lips and yet still an erect figure, the only shipwreck survivor on the island of her life.

Doña Esperanza

On Fuerteventura, I found a rocky wilderness, the whiteness of Antigua, my students and a man. Is this too little? It was enough. Enough for me to stay. Enough for me to leave. I was thirty, unmarried - to the horror of all my relatives, educated and working. In short - independent. The island sucked me in and enchanted me with its unforged and unchanging nature. The white Antigua and the totality of the bareness surrounding it left me no choice but to be myself. In those first days, weeks and months, everything was real to me. The naked body of the island. The naked hearts of the people. My own gradual undressing. And - finally - my nakedness. The one of the soul. The other one happened later. Long after the Man had appeared. But before I met him, I had got to know my students. Some of them became very dear to me. I will remember two of them forever - Destina and Chanita. Destina was a timid child, diligent and devoted. Her eyes followed me everywhere. I noticed how dark they became when I talked to another girl. Then she hid inside herself like a snail. Only her not very attractive shell remained. But for me, it was just the opposite. The hunchback, uncomely and uncertain Destina, was the dearest one to me. Like a grumpy kitten who is waiting to be caressed. I knew her mother was sick. I used every opportunity to smile at her, to encourage her, to befriend her. Then her face became brighter, if perhaps only fleetingly. And it was beautiful.

He entered my life gradually. He was the father of another student. Angela. A girl with long plaits and ringing laughter. The same fires I saw in her father's eyes at our first meeting. The sparks penetrated me and discovered the cold hearth somewhere there, under my womb. A hearth that blazed up, burned, and illuminated all the rooms of my inner home. What rooms... every corner. And on the walls of my soul, the feeling started dancing. The feeling I experienced every time at our brief meetings. Which were getting longer. He was asking me how Angela did at school, finding reasons to come and burn me with his sparks. I once saw his wife, Angela's mother, in front of the school. She had come to fetch her. The child was with her, but her eyes continued to search. They came to me. And stopped. I felt them running over me, weighing me up.

I smiled and waved. I thought she wanted to talk about Angela. Her eyes moved away. She grabbed the girl's hand, turned, and walked away, rigid. She did not appear again. One day the father found me after the classes in the classroom correcting essays. For the first time, we were alone. "I can not do this anymore," he said, grabbed my hand, the pen dropped to the floor, our two fires met... That night he came to my house and left before dawn. Fire is an element. Once it catches you, it can not be stopped just like that.

Chanita joined later. She was inquisitive, smart, and naughty. It reminded me of the child I used to be and still carried under all my layers of experience and womanhood. She was always inventing a piece of mischief that involved the other girls. She missed her mother very much. The girls tittle-tattled that she was crying for her at night. She came to me during the breaks and flooded me with questions. But the closer we became, the more Destina's gaze avoided me. She turned her head when I was talking to her, her lips trembling.

It was only later, much later, that I realised she was jealous. But then I was too busy with my happiness to see what was going on with her - I had him, I had my spiritual daughter too. I had created a family on the island – patched up by pieces that were not only mine and were not even connected, yet they made a whole thing inside me. When the director summoned me to his office, I had no idea. A few days later, a ship took me forever from the place where I had come closest to the feeling of home... I did not say goodbye to anyone.

The ship was taking me away from the island, from the naked body of Fuerteventura, from the naked body of my love and my throat would burst with tears. Water splashes streamed down my face. But... it was not for nothing that they had called me Esperanza.

The Writer

On the day I had to see Chanita, Concha called me to cancel the meeting as Chanita was not well. I got on the bus to Puerto del Rosario with the thought of going to the dunes. The sky was light blue, with a few sporadic clouds. Like in Magritte's painting. I thought about how I would spend the day on the beach, reading and writing. But a voice inside me continued to insist: "Gran Tarajal, Gran Tarajal...". We reached the dunes stop and instead of getting off, I bought a ticket to Puerto, from where I continued on another bus. Antigua was on the way to Gran Tarajal. Twenty minutes later I went down the road to its suburbs. I did not know what I needed this for, but an impulse pushed me to trace the story, to enter its setting. As if the places could tell me what Chanita had not succeeded in doing.

Antigua was like a white oasis in the desert. The locals directed me to the school. Not long after, I saw its two buildings. There was a huge yard between them where children were playing. I headed for the smaller building. In the office was a sullen woman.

"I'm looking for information about a teacher who worked here in the thirties - Esperanza Godé. I'm writing a book about the island."

"Oh, but that's a long time ago! Only someone very old can say... If there is anyone still alive... This school here is new. The old one is in the centre."

"Is there such someone?"

"One moment."

The woman dialled a number and said:

"Some very, very, very old man... A woman is asking here. She is writing a book."

At that moment, another woman and a child entered. She listened.

"Come with me, I'll take you."

We went in. A large space with chairs arranged in front of a stage at the bottom. The first three lines were occupied by young people. A girl played Sinatra's 'My Way' at the piano. A man, standing on the stage, was reading names. The young people were getting out of their seats one by one and went to him.

"Tonight is their prom night. They are rehearsing for receiving the diplomas," the woman explained.

We went out into the yard. A grey-haired man walked towards us. The woman stopped in front of him.

"This woman is writing a book about Fuerteventura. She's looking for a female teacher..."

The man looked at me thoughtfully.

"Hmm, we need to find someone old... But who could that be? Maybe the pharmacist's father-in-law. The pharmacy is... come on, I'll come with you."

I thanked the woman with the child and went with him. His name was Alfonso.

"Where are you from?"

"Bulgaria. And are you from here?"

"Yes, I'm local. From Puerto del Rosario. But I have lived in Antigua for many years. I'm fine here."

The pharmacist smiled at Alfonso.

"Rosa, where's your father?"

"My father died..."

"He died? Oh, sorry! But when did Mauro die? Oh, excuse me, Mauro is not your father, but father-in-law... I'm looking for him."

"He lives across the street. Over there."

The gate led to a house with a garden.

Alfonso knocked. After a while, the door opened and a small, wrinkled man walked briskly toward us.

"How are you, Mauro?"

"Well, thank you. And you?"

His voice sounded cheerful.

"The lady is writing a book about Fuerteventura. She's looking for information about a teacher, Esperanza Godé. She taught Chanita Suarez."

"I don't know this teacher, I haven't heard of her... But Chanita's cousin lives over there, around the corner. Number seven. She must know."

Alfonso had to go back to school. She pointed the house out to me and we parted. A white-haired woman opened the door and looked at me with interest. Her face had preserved the imprint of noble beauty, despite her age.

"I'm looking for Margosa."

"That's me."

I said that Mauro had sent me and that I was looking for information about Esperanza Godé. We walked into a dark room from where a corridor began. The windows looked out to a small, interior garden with lush vegetation. She invited me to sit down.

"I've heard of this teacher," she said slowly, quietly, "but I don't know her personally. Chanita loved her very much. Unfortunately, she isn't good at the moment."

"We were supposed to meet. But because of her condition, our meeting did not happen. How has her life gone?"

"She studied to be a pharmacist. Everyone went to her if they needed a cure. Then she graduated in psychology... She wrote her memoirs years ago. They contain also information about the teacher. There is a classmate of Chanita, still alive, Destina. She can tell you more. She lives a couple of streets away from here. Tell her that I have sent you."

I reached the church. I remembered it from before. A construction worker pointed to the building on the side, saying that it was the old school, being restored now. So that was where the friendship between the little Chanita and Esperanza had begun. Two or three streets away was Destina's home. I knocked on the door. The house was silent. I repeated. No movement. I knocked on the window covered with a white curtain. The door opened and an old woman with a scarf on her head stared at me.

"Hello. Are you Destina?"

"Yes."

"Margosa sent me. I'm writing a book about Fuerteventura. I am interested in Esperanza Godé - Doña Esperanza..."

"Yes, she was our teacher."

"Can you tell me anything about her?"

The woman hesitated.

"Doña Esperanza was wonderful, very good, very kind."

"Do you remember a story to share?"

"She invited us to visit her in Zaragoza, all of us. But I didn't go. Since the war, I have not heard anything about her."

"What memories do you have?"

"She was very nice. She invited us... But I couldn't go."

The woman looked at me suspiciously. She stepped back, indicating that the conversation was over. I thanked her, and the door slammed in my face. I had nothing more to do in Antigua. The meeting with Esperanza Godé's student had not completed the story but made her image closer and more real. I went back to the square and entered a shop named "Workshop for memories". A blonde woman stood behind the counter. She greeted me in Spanish with a German accent.

My eyes ran over the souvenirs, pictures and handmade jewels. Workshop for memories... There was something in the short meeting with Destina which disturbed me. The vulnerability in her eyes, her impatience to end the meeting, her desire to send me away. Lonely older ladies are usually happy to share their memories, to leave them to somebody, while this one... I turned around and walked back. When Destina opened again, I did not need to say anything. She stepped back and let me in.

Destina

I have not told this to anyone... But you are not from here and you will understand. It was said that we would have a new teacher. A newcomer, old and unmarried. One day they introduced her to us. In her thirties, but she looked like a girl. With a wide smile, for which I immediately loved her. She was different from our previous teacher. In the way that she dressed, in the way she treated us. Her clothes - youthful, her behaviour - like an older sister. Playful, warm and affectionate, even in her strictness. We all liked her and competed for her attention. My mother was quite different from the young teacher. A rough woman. From too much work and caring for eight children, she did not have time left for caressing. A smile rarely appeared on

163

her face, and when it did, it quickly disappeared. Always pre-occupied, knitting her brows, as if having children was the greatest punishment God had sent her on this earth, and she, as a real martyr, had to endure it. In Doña Esperanza I saw the mother I dreamt of having. Kind, careful, caring, laughing. And I decided that I definitely had to become her favourite. I started studying a lot. I had not studied so much in my life either before or after. I was ready to do anything to be liked by her. When she praised me, my heart fluttered. Just a little more and it would fly away. Sometimes I even secretly imagined that my mother dies and my father marries Doña Esperanza. And she becomes my mother. They had given her a house in our street, everything could come together quite nicely. When we did not have classes I was looking for pretexts to pass by several times a day in the hope of meeting her. It was rare, but once in a while I saw her. Her warm smile brightened her face, she waved and shouted, "How are you, sweety? Where are you going?" The whole day that smile was with me. When my mother yelled at me, I imagined that smile and it was easier to bear. But there is no cloudless happiness. At the beginning of the next school year, a new girl came to our class. It was immediately obvious that she was different from us. Serious, with a look in her eyes of an adult, she spoke in a mature way, and she was always reading something. At the same time, she was rebellious and willful, she was constantly up to some prank. Half of the girls in the class immediately liked her and wanted to become her friends. The other half also rallied around her, but they spoke behind her back that she was not so brave at all, that she was crying secretly for her mother, that she would become ugly from all this reading and would not be able to find a man. I didn't know which of the groups to join. I found Chanita, that was the name of the newcomer, pleasant. I admired her and even envied her a little. I told myself, that she could not be so perfect, that she must have some weakness that would sooner or later emerge. But I enjoyed being around her, listening to her talking, participating in her escapades. Then, however, something happened that took me forever out of the circle of her friends. It did not happen suddenly, but gradually. Every passing day confirmed my impression that Doña Esperanza Godé found her new favourite in Chanita. Now I don't know if I ever had been her favourite, but I had wished it that way. Until Chanita appeared with her direct look, books, and repulsive sincerity. In the break, she went to Doña Esperanza and showered her with clever questions. Doña Esperanza was looking at her with such tenderness that my heart was breaking. She always responded attentively to her, and she often ran her hand through her hair. Those caresses brought tears to my eyes.

Something else was also happening. Each time Chanita incited us to make pranks and Doña Esperanza would scold the perpetrator, Chanita would stand up: "They are not to blame. It's my fault!" "Well, how, Chanita? You haven't done anything!" "I encouraged them". And Doña Esperanza instead of punishing her was becoming even more fond of her. Such was Chanita. Disgustingly brave and subversively honest.

I no longer wanted to study. I lost my appetite and often got sick. One day Doña Esperanza came home to talk to my mother. They shut themselves in the living room. I did not hear anything from their conversation, but I knew it was about me. And as in those happy times before the appearance of Chanita, I lay down in my bed with a shining face. If Doña Esperanza had come, she still loved me, she cared for me and had not forgotten me completely. The next day I jumped to my feet, dressed and went to school. Chanita ran toward me, embraced me and said she missed me. Her heartiness hurt me more than if she acted arrogantly. And I hated her even more because she made me dislike myself. Everything remained the same. Doña Esperanza and Chanita always together, enthralled in their conversations. Other classmates were standing around and also participated but it was obvious how special the relationship between the two of them was. Life became painful. At home, I could see my sullen mother, and at school, my dream mother had chosen another child. Banished from everywhere, I wondered why I had to be born when I was so ordinary, unattractive and incapable of evoking love. One day Angela's father came during the break. Her mother was sick, so he came to the school when he needed to. He had helped to refresh one of the rooms under the guidance of Doña Esperanza. They went to the teacher's room where they shut themselves in. Fifteen-twenty minutes passed, the lesson had to begin, but Doña Esperanza was not coming. I was eaten by curiosity, why was she taking her time. The other girls sat down and waited. I went out, as if I was going to the toilet, passed by it, and stood in front of the teacher's room. I squatted and looked through the keyhole. And I saw something that was worse than anything I could imagine. Angela's father held Doña Esperanza in his arms and they were kissing. They were kissing like a man and a woman. It was the end of all my hopes of being close to Doña Esperanza. Even if my mother died, she would not become my father's wife because she had kissed Angela's father. And the chance that Angela's mother would die with her constant illnesses was much greater. And Doña Esperanza would become her mother. I can not describe the pain I experienced when all this became clear to me. I ran to the toilet, shut myself in and cried for a long time. I missed the lesson and when I came back for the next one Doña Esperanza hugged me and asked me if everything was fine. But her embrace made me feel even worse.

She caressed my hair and held me in her arms until I stopped crying. The other girls looked at me like a leper. Only Chanita came to me: "Please stop crying, otherwise I will cry too." The memory of the love scene continued to bore into me. And then I saw an opportunity: God had allowed me to witness this sin to give me a sign of how to end my anguish and help to restore the old order. I wrote a letter to the school board, in which I told everything I had seen and signed it: Chanita Suarez. So Doña

Esperanza would not kiss Angela's father anymore, and would never become her mother. And she would turn her back on Chanita for the letter. Then she would see me again with all my devotion and affection, and I would console her in this difficult moment. I would become like a daughter to her, the daughter she did not have. A week later Doña Esperanza came to school with dark circles under her eyes. In a trembling voice, she told us that she had to leave Fuerteventura, that she would miss us very much and that we would have another teacher soon. Our faces darkened. Chanita jumped from her desk and ran out of the room. A few days later we heard Doña Esperanza had gone without saying goodbye. Chanita's crying filled the whole schoolyard. And in my throat, a ball stuck that I never managed to swallow. Doña Esperanza wrote to everyone. Several girls sent letters in reply. I could not, no matter how much I wanted to. The shame burned inside me. Then I found out that the correspondence between her and Chanita had lasted for years. I caused evil by my action, but mostly I punished myself. It's the first time I am talking about this... Please change my name, the town is small, we all know each other... May God forgive me, seeing my suffering and remorse.

Miguel

"I have to say that one of the saddest things we have, our worm, our national parasite, is envy. Spain is one of the lands of the envious."[33]

---

[33] Unamuno: Articulos y discursos sobre Canarias, Discurso sobre la patria, Francisco Navarro Artiles, Excmo. Cabildo Insular de Fuerteventura, 1980

The Writer

A lush park of palm trees and flowering shrubs ran from Grant Tarahal's station. I walked down alongside it, took a small street and reached the promenade. In the cultural centre, I found Juan Luis Calbaro's book "The Memoires of Chanita Suarez". The beach was spacious and empty, framed by rocks. A wooden path stretched over the sand toward the sea. Two girls, fourteen or fifteen years old, walked along. They had ponytails, one blonde, the other black-haired, both in shorts. How many stories start like this - two girls, a beach and a path, stretching out.

I, too, walked down the path, relaxed on the sand and started reading.

Chanita Suarez was the fifth of six children and an only girl. She spent the first few years of her life in the large stone house in La Gira, built by her grandfather, Juan. From that time, she has kept the memory of the old tango records that her father Vicente Suarez played on the gramophone. He took her mother Zoe Lopez Rodriguez in his arms, and they danced as if they were alone in the world. She also remembered the women arriving in La Gira to sell bed sheets and tablecloths and the taste of the dates at the family grocery store. But most clearly, she remembered the beach where she ran, swam and played with her brothers. Her best friend was Tildia, a charming and wild troublemaker. That's why their friendship ended - Chanita did not tolerate shouting and quarrels. Tildia became a tightrope walker in the circus.

The brightest recollection of her childhood was the shipwreck of Wad Ras in December 1930. Years later, she would recall the three chimneys of the guard ship and hear its siren. A sailor gave her a porcelain doll, which has been accompanying her throughout her life. There was no other doll like this on the island. Short-cut blonde hair, large dark eyes, red defined lips and a tip-tilted nose. White dress with waffle sleeves. The doll was like a real girl arriving from a distant and unknown world.

Later on, her family moved to Gran Tarajal. Here she continued her studies before the years of war interrupted it.

"... I can not live far away from this beach, without seeing it every day," Chanita says of the beach I was lying on at the moment.

Now she was lying in her house, not far from *this beach*, and the street named "Nurse Chanita Suarez," was staring at the ocean from its height. And I could not stop thinking about the story told by Destina. Would her soul find peace? Would she forgive herself?

I thanked her when I was leaving, kissed the wrinkled hand and told her I was sure that one day in the future Doña Esperanza and she would meet and embrace. Her old face was wet with tears when she was closing the door behind me.

* * *

One day I hired a car and hit the road from one city to another. Pahara, Betancouria, Ajuy, La Pared...

In my trips, I found a resemblance between the naked body of the island and the landscape around the Rila lakes when I first saw them in October. Sandy golden colours, no vegetation. For weeks I brought up this image in myself. The yellow of the mountain and the azure of the lakes - mirrors facing the sky. When I went back a while later, driven by longing, it was different. Another season, other colours. This was my reference point on Fuerteventura, where familiar and foreign merged and trembled with the common vibration of the feeling of home.

I was driving along a spiral road. A breast-shaped hill always stayed in my sight, its tip like a nipple. The spiral is the official symbol of Fuerteventura. Like the snails, like its roads, like the sun that gently warms it.

Ajuy welcomed me with a triangle of palm trees and white houses in the Arabic style, with blue around the windows. Its beach was different from the other ones on the island. It was dotted with large, colourful stones on one side, and with many small pebbles on the other. It looked like a huge stone artwork. *A real gold mine for Emiliyan*, passed through my mind and I smiled inwardly.

The ocean here was wild, rebellious and dangerous. The waves reached the beach in full height. On both sides, the bay was surrounded by rocks on which they crashed angrily. They called it the Beach of the Dead because of the drowned bodies that the currents throw up on it. It was here that the Norman Jean de Betancourt arrived in 1402 to conquer the island for the Spaniards.

At that time, Fuerteventura was divided by a wall into two territorial parts or "kingdoms" - Handia and Maxorata, headed by King Guise and King Ayose. Perhaps the division was the result of strong competition for cattle and pasture. According to some historical sources, the former wall is today's La Pared in Handia. Despite the enmity between the two kingdoms, when the Normans arrived their inhabitants fought side by side to save their island.

"The conquest of this island required more time than the previous one because there were many people fighting boldly, preferring death to surrender," says the Ovenes Chronicle.

The names of two women appeared in the sources - Tibiabín and Tamonante, mother and daughter. Tibiabín was a "fortune-teller and a very wise woman, who, through communication with the demons... foretold a few things that happened... she led the ceremonies and rituals as a priestess," and Tamonante "solved the disputes arising between kings and captains, and they treated her with great respect... "[34]

Guise and Ajose valued them a lot and turned to them for advice. Tibiabín foretold the invasion of the outlanders.

"Ah, if only we could call up the roaming spirits of the prophetess Tibiabín or the fortune-teller Tamonante, wandering through the tragic peaks of this island, thirsty for fresh water, they would tell us what this division was with the wall of Handia ..."[35], had written Unamuno.

Ah, if only we could, indeed...

I sat at a respectful distance from the shore but the waves threw themselves ever closer to me. I shuddered. Their strength scared me. But it also soothed me. My excitement of the recent days seemed like the foam being absorbed in the sand. Sinking deep inside me, dissolved in the sands of my inner life. It was as if I were carrying inside me models of the desert, the ocean, the island. The more I sank into its fragmented history and the sense of integrity carried by the landscape, the more I took them into myself. I was yet to find out what external manifestation this interpenetration would become. But for now, I refused to analyse it, it was unnecessary. Needless. All my other life realities were pushed far, far away from Fuerteventura.

Miguel

"This miserable island of Fuerteventura, where between the peace of the sky and the sea we write this comment about the life that passes, and about the life that remains, is one hundred kilometres long from its most northern to its most southern point and at its widest is twenty-five kilometres. At the southwestern point it is an almost unpopulated peninsula, through which, among the naked loneliness and the loneliness of the earthly poverty, a few

---

[34] Museo Arqueológico de Betancuria

[35] Unamuno: Articulos y discursos sobre Canarias, Discurso sobre la patria, Francisco Navarro Artiles, Excmo. Cabildo Insular de Fuerteventura, 1980

shepherds pass. On this peninsula which is known as Handia or La Pared, the wall, perhaps the wall that gave the name to the Handia Peninsula and from which there are preserved parts, was built by the locals to separate the two kingdoms into which the island of Maxorata, that of the mahoreros, or Fuerteventura, was divided, to stop the raids from one to the other kingdom. And here, in this piece of the Sahara desert in Africa thrown into the Atlantic, it was allowed to have a peninsula and a wall, like in China, in the historical sense.

(...)

It is assumed that the two kingdoms into which the island was divided were two hereditary monarchies. And this division was the reason for the primitive Fuerteventura to become historical: it was the root of its incipient illiterate civilisation."[36]

The Writer

La Pared. I parked next to a restaurant overlooking the ocean. Here again, the bay is framed by rocks. One of them looked like a wall erected in the ocean. The waiter, a young boy, brought me honey rum with cream, popular on the island.

"Where is the wall?" I asked.

"That's the wall," he pointed to the sheer cliff.

"No, no, that wall from ancient times."

"There is no such wall."

"Its remains..."

"There is no such wall. The place is named after this rock. Because it looks like a wall."

"And the wall that the chronicles talk about?"

"There is no such wall."

When I got home, Juan was having dinner in the kitchen.

---

[36] Unamuno: Articulos y Discursos sobre Canarias, Cabillo Insular de Fuerteventura, Puerto del Rosario, 1980, Los Reinos de Fuerteventura

"Where have you been, Writer?"

"I was travelling. La Oliva, Ajuy, Pahara, Betancuria... I passed by the Grain Museum again, I was in the Archaeological one in Betancuria and in Dr Mena's House..."

"I had no idea that there were such museums at all..."

I asked him about his work.

"It's okay. But life is not very interesting."

"Why?"

"There is nothing to do. I like the tranquillity, the nature, the water sports... but, apart from that, there is not much variety and entertainment. That's why I travel once a month. I need this escape. Otherwise, I wouldn't survive it."

"How much time do you have left here?"

"Three years. A long time."

"Do you like what you do?"

"I like it. But I don't feel the passion. I began to study medicine by chance. Then I started to like it. I found myself here too by chance. I wanted to get away from a woman. So I chose Fuerteventura. My life is a string of happenstances that I follow. And my role in it is passive."

"And fleeing from a woman, you found yourself trapped with another one."

"Pardon?"

"Nothing. You can always make another choice."

"How about the lost years?"

"How about those that you are still going to lose?"

"The risk of losing everything is great."

"There is always a risk when one follows one's self and what one wants."

"But I'm unclear exactly what I want..."

"Perhaps you will find out with time. Then you will know what to do. Good night, Juan."

Miguel

One morning as I was writing, the receptionist knocked on my door.

"You have a visitor."

"A visitor?"

"A woman."

She stands by the reception and looks out. She radiates the stillness of a Greek statue. On the floor beside her is her travel bag. The young writer K. R. She is no more than thirty. We had seen each other a few times. We had had discussions in which her sharp mind, calmness and clear thought became apparent. She once asked me to read her short novel. It was about a relationship between a student and her teacher. Written with talent. I closed my eyes for some obvious similarities, praised her for the style and advised her to seek inspiration in more social themes, of which in our present there is an abundance.

"Social is transient, while love in its essence, being a universal human experience, is eternal," she answered, looking boldly in my eyes.

"The transient can become a constant in a human life. I did not mean giving up love as a topic but contextualising it. Relationships do not grow on their own. They have soil, environment, humus. Love between a teacher and a student is a banal plot. What is unique in your story? What makes it different from all the other similar stories?"

She blushed, took the manuscript, and thanked me dryly. We had not seen each other since. And now she was here. All the questions were unnecessary and therefore unavoidable.

"K., what are you doing here?"

"Can I get a cup of coffee, please?"

She left her bag in the reception and we went to the nearby café. She had a sip of the coffee and rubbed her eyes.

"I came because of you."

"Because of me?"

"I heard that they sent you into exile."

"How did you get here?"

"On a boat."

"How did you get access?"

"I have some useful acquaintances. As soon as I heard about it, I organised my trip."

"Why are you here?"

"To share your exile. So that you are not alone. I do not expect anything from you. Whenever you want me to leave, I will."

She looked down at the table and, when she uttered the last sentence, her lower lip quivered.

"K., I am not alone in this. You shouldn't have come. I want you to leave immediately."

Silence. Her gaze had turned heavy when it met mine.

"Are you sure?"

"I'm sure."

"Can I stay with you until I find a boat for the continent?"

"No. I do not want to give grounds for speculation. You know I'm married. But I will ask some of my new friends here to put you up."

She took a deep breath but did not cry. She looked me proudly in the eyes and stood up. At the hotel, I asked the receptionist whether she could accept the young lady at her home. She nodded, without asking questions, explained to her how to get there and gave her the key. Five days later she told me that the lady had left. Love is indeed the most tragic in this world. I wrote in an essay - "love is a child of deception and generates disappointment." But what blindness had brought that young woman to this God-forsaken place? How could she imagine that I would accept her? That I would betray Concha? A pretty and educated lady indeed, and talented, but how her beauty, youthfulness, education, and talent could replace everything that Concha, who is not only my wife and mother of my children but also my sister, companion and mother, has given me?

This episode, which I was not going to share with anyone, briefly broke the peace of my solitude and my deep conversation with the island. But then time took it away, disappearing like the circles formed on the surface of a smooth lake from a stone thrown into it.

The Writer

The employee in Unamuno House Museum had told me of a woman who followed him to the island. I remembered this in the evening when Juan said he had come here to move away from a woman. Unamuno had not chosen to come to the island. Nevertheless, by arriving he had moved away from the young lady. His retreat, however, was not accepted as an obstacle, but as an opportunity. The lady, crossing the ocean, had done the impossible. But sometimes the impossible is not enough. Only the possible is.

I saw her on the deck of the ship, which had to get her closer to the answer to her sleepless nights. With hair flying in the strong wind, dashing towards the island of strong winds. Full of determination, hope, and a difficult to express feeling. The feeling.

K.

The feeling that does not leave me while I pack my luggage, while I travel by train to Madrid and then by bus to Cádiz... The feeling that keeps me going, while I board the ship to Tenerife and then to Las Palmas and finally to Fuerteventura... The feeling of destiny. Once I knew of his deportation, I called my father and asked him to use his contacts with the government so that I could follow him. How he tried to dissuade me from doing it. Finally, I said, "If you do not help me, I will find a way myself." He knew I was not kidding. I am his daughter, after all. My mother died when I was five. He only has me. For me, he would do the impossible, even if it means sending me to a God-forsaken island in pursuit of love. Love. I devoted my first short novel to it. To him. To this fate I have been sensing since the moment I met him, after I had read through all his philosophical works, heavily underlining, memorising whole passages. I believed that in this way I would possess something of him, of his extraordinary intellect, mind and spirit; that in this way I would draw him closer to myself, for our souls to bind together. I introduced myself to him after a literary discussion at the university. Now he knew of my existence. The first step towards the target had been passed. The first step is the most important one. Every succeeding step is easier if the first one is overcome. Our acquaintance has opened the way for communication. We met a couple of more times, again at such events.

We had long conversations about contemporary Spanish literature and philosophy before I asked him to read my novel. He accepted in his generous, sophisticated way, and I almost lost my mind with excitement. Now he was to have something of me. Something of my innermost self. It was to penetrate his thoughts, and perhaps his emotions and soul. I gave him my book as if I were giving myself to him. Its fluttering pages which he would unfold with his noble hands were my trembling body. Two weeks later I waited for him after a lecture and asked if he had read it. His dry reply was a desecration of the body of my book, of my naked body from which he had diverted his eyes because it was not perfect enough. His advice that I write on social topics was offensively ridiculous. Hasn't he himself written that "Love is the most tragic thing that exists in this world and in life." It is, therefore, most worthy of being shared, told, expressed... In all possible forms. Write on social topics! How can you force yourself to write about something? Does he write by his will and not by the vocation of his mind and soul? I said nothing. He did not like my book. All right. This would only stimulate me to write the book that he will like, and which will compel him to look at me with other eyes. I would write a novel that will touch his soul, and make him feel the fate that pushes me to him.

But while I think about the plot, the message of his deportation comes. It means years without seeing him, without access to him, without the possibility of slowly but surely building the invisible thread that will connect our destinies forever. Years that will erase the memory of me, will bury under the sand those steps I had made to get me closer to him.

Then the solution just comes to me. It's simple, I clearly have to follow him. This deportation is my chance. There, banished from anything familiar, close and dear, he will need a soulmate. He will need to share the pain, to pour it, to transform it. And what is more transformative than a new love, a forbidden, hidden, comforting, of exile. A love of a young woman, of a woman-artist who understands him, admires him, honours him, is ready to fall at his feet, to give herself to him right away without any preconditions and demands. No one would know. Even if this love lasts only days, it is worth it. Because love never ends - once it has emerged, it lives in one form or another until the end of days and even after their end.

The wind blows in my face, the ship cuts the waters, and I am overwhelmed with determination and hope. He cannot send me back. He can not help being touched by the power of my gesture, by the courage, by the days and nights on a gruelling journey, the gift I want to offer him, to give all that I have, without wanting anything in return. I will be in his destined exile time, which is beyond ordinary time, as if it doesn't exist, and therefore everything that happens during that time would be as if it has never happened. His compassion would not let him reject me. He would be shaken by my strength and vulnerability. It can not be any other way. But if... If he turns me away, at least I would know that I have tried, I have crossed the ocean of this love.

I arrive at a rocky land and find his hotel. Everything is a dream. A rock in the ocean, a town, the prison-hotel. Surreal. Have I really done this? Yes, I have. Here he comes. He is surprised, but not as much as I expected. He seems calm and peaceful. Not tormented as I imagined him. In a restrained manner, he asks me what I am doing here. I don't answer but ask for a coffee. I do have the right to a coffee. He takes me to a café and I tell him there. I say I came here because of him, that I do not want anything but to accompany him in his exile. And I will leave when he wants. But he wants that right now. Right now! He refuses to accept me at the hotel-prison so that people do not gossip. I did not expect such provincial thinking of such a great mind. Who cares what people say? The volcanic rocks of this desolate island would crackle with tenderness or pity in front of the vulnerability of a woman who forsakes her pride, her honour, everything she has, but not him. He is kind, but insistent and indifferent. Like a wave that washes the shores of the island out of habit.

I am ready to fall to my knees and beg him. I do not, I suspect it would be in vain. Yes, it is in vain – he tells me nothing would help. Better to save what remains of my dignity. One thing is sure: he will remember me. Not weeping and begging, but with admiration and amazement. Proud, not, though it is what I am, insane.

Marina, the receptionist, is an angel, sent to me by the merciful God. She offers me shelter at her home, gives me the keys. I find it without too much wandering in a neighbourhood on the outskirts. A room with a large bed and a few pieces of old furniture. I sit on the bed and let everything pour out. When I have cried myself out I wash my face, go to bed and fall asleep. Marina's arrival wakes me up. She changes her clothes and starts cooking.

She does not ask questions. She was born on the island and has never been away. I learn that while we are having dinner. I ask her whether she is not interested in seeing other places. Maybe, but not necessarily. She feels good here. You have to see the island, she tells me, before you leave. She would ask her uncle to give me his car. The next morning she goes to work, and I get in the car and drive through the rocky, then sandy, desert surrounded by volcanic mountains. Yellow-beige landscape. Biblical. And as I am driving, something extraordinary happens. The pain which possessed me even in my sleep, diminishes. And with every kilometre, I feel more and more myself, more and more mine. I pass through La Oliva, Betancuria, Pahara to Ajuy, where I park and walk down to the pebble beach. Waves like walls fiercely overwhelm the shore. The wind pushes me, but its roughness is a caress compared to the philosopher's quiet and courteous dismissal. I sit on a stone and look at the ocean for a long time. At once frightening and alluring. Tranquillity goes deeper inside me. I drive back at sunset. A sunset that blossoms in shades of yellow-gold-orange-pink. The orange light penetrates me to the bottom of my tormented being. After that, there is only bliss left. I now understand the philosopher's radiance. How silly I have been! How vain! To invent his martyrdom so that I would be the one saving his soul! But his soul had found its home! Now mine follows it. That's how we would meet, he and I. Not with bodies, but with our souls, on the island, recognised by them as their true homeland. This thought gives me consolation. I have not made this journey in vain. By not reaching him, I have captured him. He would have liked this contradiction with his taste for duality and counterpoint. My face is wet again with tears, but tears of happiness and gratitude. This is the philosopher's gift to me. Without knowing it, he has repaid me for all my aspirations, anguish and efforts.

The next day I drive to the other end of the island - Handia. I stop briefly in Antigua and light a candle in its white church. A thanksgiving candle for my transformation brought by the island. I walk on the vast beaches, letting the mystique of the landscape fertilise all my senses. This is the novel I will write. A novel about a woman who arrives on the island in love with a man, and leaves the man in love with the island.

On the fifth day, the ship comes. I hug Marina firmly and get on it, windblown and renewed. I look back at the island. I am not going back. It is already in me.

The Writer

Unamuno was brought to the island by force, but what should have been exile had turned into love, into a sacred experience of connecting with himself through his union with her. He experienced her and created her from a distance with his powerful writing quill, seeing himself as Don Quixote on Fuerteventura, sowing the idea of a future book and writing several more; he had discovered his Atlantis and had clearly and boldly declared it to the world. He had warned his wife not to follow him and sent away the woman who dared.

Juan had arrived to escape from a woman. And he never stayed with one single woman.

Emiliyan had to leave because of a woman. And to, probably, never stay in any one place.

As if Fuerteventura did not endure rivalry. As if all the other loves here became unnecessary or impossible. She, the island, ruled over all the intimate space, was the intimate space herself, and where there is intimacy there is no room for a third. Warm, soft, embracing with her nakedness, sweeping away with her winds, intoxicating with her sunsets, Fuerte is a sorceress who wipes out the memory of everything before her, to stay alone, the only and omnipresent one, like a book you never cease to read, like the Bible.

Emiliyan was preparing to leave. To do the unthinkable. To separate from his tripod-bearer Darina, to leave his camera on a bench, and to throw the stone-talisman in the ocean along with its leather case.

He had not told me anything. But our brief encounters during the days following the news of Eva's new direction showed what was happening even though he was trying to sound as before. To joke and be cheerful. But deep in his eyes, the absence was spreading like mould. The void that would remain after the flight, which would deprive him permanently of the orange light. His dark eyes were taking in the island. They lingered on each of her features to savour them for as long as possible, to take away a mental image of her... but was that possible? How could her image and likeness replace her, the island, the most inimitable?

"Sweden is very beautiful. You'll have a lot to photograph..."

"It's done, the photographing. Here it began and here it will stay. I can not photograph another one... other places. Do you understand that, Writer? I-can-not. Here is my inspiration. Here is... all that I have. I will go back to physiotherapy. I will offer Bulgarian massages to the Swedes. To move the blood in their cool northern bodies," he said sardonically.

His smile was different now. It could easily turn into thunderous, universal weeping. No, not weeping. Roar. Like the loud suicide of the waves in which it would sink and find consolation. I fantasised. I did not know yet that consolation was doomed with the appearance of the idea of it. Fuerteventura has marked the souls of all of us, its pilgrims-residents-writers-poets, forever. It was not us who lived her. She lived us. And she called us out from her depths like a siren, so that she could last forever through us - her imperfect, yet passionate and yearning projections.

Miguel

A telegramme from Puerto Cabras, July 8, 19.40, handed over to Fernando.

"I'm leaving tonight on a brig wait for me there hugs Miguel."[37]

The Writer

Gustav Winter had also chosen her, Fuerteventura. Among all the islands - her. Here he built the house that would give birth to legends, circling the island like bees but returning to the hive for decades.

There is a whole chapter devoted to him in the Memoirs of Chanita Suarez. The article, which the man from the archive sent me, used it as a starting point, completing the information with even more detail. The main spices in Winter's story were mystery and guesswork. Charismatic, self-confident, opportunist. These were the most often used adjectives to describe him.

Born in Zastler Loch near Freiburg on 10 May 1893, he died in Las Palmas de Gran Canaria in 1971. He graduated with honours in electrical engineering at the University of Freiburg.

When he was nineteen he went to Argentina where he installed electric fences on large ranches. There he met his first wife with whom he had six children.

On returning from Argentina in 1914, when the First World War had already begun, the British Army stopped his ship,

---

[37] Cartas del destierro, Entre el odio y el amor (1924-1930), Collete y Jean-Claudde Rabate, Ediciones Universidad de Salamanca, 2012

detained him, and transferred him to a prison ship in the port of Portsmouth. According to some sources, the reason for this was the suspicion he was a spy. In February 1915 he managed to escape. He embarked on the Dutch transatlantic ship SS Hollandia, travelling to New York from Amsterdam. He went ashore at Vigo and sought asylum in neutral Spain. He had no money at all and requested support from the German Consulate. After the refusal, he used his surname, which could also be interpreted as British, along with his impeccable English, and received a small financial subsidy from the British Consulate. With this money, he reached Madrid, where he immediately found a job thanks to the Spanish engineers he met during his studies in Germany. By 1917 he was already the director of an electro-chemical factory in Tarragona. After the end of the war, he decided to stay in Spain.

In Madrid, he completed his engineering studies. He undertook various projects for thermoelectric power plants for the Spanish government in Tomeioso, Valencia and Zaragoza. The electric factories were the first of this kind in the country. This success, however, was not enough for the ambitious German and in 1925 he moved to Las Palmas de Gran Canaria to electrify the entire archipelago. One of the most influential people in the country at the time, Antonio Goykoehea-y-Konskujuella, a famous politician, helped him to get the enormous project. He managed it and Miguel Primo de Rivera himself arrived for the official opening of the factory on October 12, 1928. Winter worked as general manager of the factory for eight years and during his free time he travelled over the Canaries with his boat "Argo". That is how he came to Fuerteventura in the thirties. The decision to buy Handia turned his life around. The law prohibited the sale of land to foreigners, but Winter was able to conclude a lease contract with Alfonso de Keralt-i-Gil-Delgado, the last descendant of the Counts of Santa Coloma, the lords of Handia. He took possession of it on October 1, 1937.

They signed the contract in Burgos, the Fascist capital. His decision was risky because if the military were to lose the war, the agreement would not apply. Hence the legend that Franco allowed Winter to purchase Handia so that the Germans could organise a secret military base. However, it is unlikely that Berlin had already been planning WWII and, hence, building strategic bases in the Atlantic Ocean.

Even those who do not believe in the conspiracy theories about Winter agree that the structure of the house in the Cofete is weird, with its cellars, a long corridor with eight small rooms on both sides, claustrophobic, without windows except for the door crystals, with a maximum capacity of twenty-five people.

The house was built under strictly secret conditions. The workers were taken there in the morning and back in the evening. Winter built a road between Horos and Cofete and a runway not far from the house even though he did not have his own plane or pilot skills. According to his family, he built the runway to react quickly in case of urgent medical aid being needed. Others say that the aim was to provide a landing space for German planes during WWII.

Winter met his second wife, Elizabeth Althouse, in June 1945 at the German consulate in Madrid. She worked there as a secretary while studying medicine at the university. Elizabeth was twenty-eight years younger than him. The two left their respective work and studies and settled in Handia. They had five children. There was fifty years difference between Winter's oldest and youngest children of his two marriages.

Both Elizabeth and he acquired Spanish citizenship and changed their names to Gustavo Winter Kinhele and Isabelle Althaus Schreiber.

At the end of his life, Winter donated solar batteries to recently married couples and 73,000 square metres to the Francisco Franco patronage for homes for the most deprived. He also donated 85,000 square metres to the Pajara municipality for social, sports, institutional, sanitary, religious and school equipment.

The name Winter appeared along with a hundred and three other names, in the blacklist of German spies in 1945, in the main archive of the Ministry of Foreign Affairs. However, in 2002 the office of Simon Wiesenthal, the famous pursuer of Nazi war criminals, reported that there was no evidence of a connection between Winter and the Nazis, and even less so of his participation in war crimes.

Chanita Suarez has a positive recollection of Winter: "I can testify for Don Gustavo Winter's humanitarian activity in the sphere of health, so scarce in those times." In his house in Moro Jable there was a complete set of medical equipment, used to alleviate the suffering of the inhabitants of the whole area. Chanita went there periodically to give vaccinations to the children. This took place at Winter's home. The aerodrome in Handia was used in cases of emergency when an aeroplane had to land to evacuate a sick or seriously injured person to Las Palmas.

About Isabelle Althaus, Chanita says she was a good and very beautiful woman.

* * *

Unamuno, his anonymous follower, Esperanza, Winter, Juan, Emiliyan, the whole guard of nameless surfers, tourists, artists... and now me.

I was sitting on the roof of the building with a laptop on my knees. Where had I come from? I did not remember. Where was I going to? It did not matter.

I was. Here. Her. The island. Our Atlantis.

THE CYCLICAL NATURE OF TIME
OR
THE TRUE STORY

Miguel

"The legend is the true story, and a legend is what people believe has happened. And what one believes has happened affects their actions more than what has really happened."[38]

Gerd

She did not say a word. That disturbed him most. Her silence, as if nothing has happened. And her disappearance which preceded it. He woke up and did not find her beside him. Maybe she was in the bathroom. But when he realised she was not and an anonymous voice kindly informed him that there was no connection with this number, his anxiety increased. She had not been to Indy. He had a coffee and left. He could not stay still. He went around all the places in Corralejo where they had the habit of hanging around. Carla was gone.

In the afternoon, exhausted of these efforts, he lay in the room when he heard a key turning, and Carla appeared at the door. She looked calm, although her eyes were moist.

He stared at her with a drawn face and waited. She, without saying a word, undressed, lay down beside him and kissed him. They made love with gentle fierceness, then fell asleep in each other's arms.

Only later the thought of Marina came back. Their evening was suddenly over and the anxiety, overwhelming both of them, replaced the self-oblivious love of the previous hours. But Carla's silence was paralysing him more than if she had made a scene or if they had talked about what had happened. It entangled him with invisible ropes and made him incapable of acting. As if, should he not initiate anything, he would erase, like with a

---

[38] Miguel de Unamuno, De Fuerteventura a Paris, Editorial Excelsor, 1925

rubber, that he had cheated on her in front of her eyes, not only with his body but also with his heart; that he had even considered leaving her.

The next morning they surfed with Enrique. This more or less brought him balance. The board gave him more sense of a firm surface than the land. The concentration needed to keep himself on the surfboard freed him from other thoughts. It was only him and the ocean, with just the board between them. If he could conquer this element, he would manage everything else. As he rode yet another wave, the joyful ease returned. Nothing had happened. Life would continue without disturbance and traumas with its integrity intact, just like before. Between the tranquillity of Freiburg and surfing on Fuerte. Wonderful in its simplicity. He sat on the shore for a short break, ate the sandwich made by Carla, and observed her in her stubbornness to keep herself standing longer, not to submit herself, to try with the next wave. He felt tenderness toward this steadfast young woman who had devoted her life to loving him as he was, swallowing the pain that this feeling caused her. No, he did not want to hurt her anymore. He will not call Marina.

Marina

Two days of obsessive expectation have passed with no news. *"Imagine that I was your daughter, that it was happening to your daughter..."* Carla's words echoed in her head. That was right. It would be best if he never contacted her again. But with the possibility of not seeing him again her throat dried up and she could hardly breathe. She lay awake in the darkness, trying to calm herself, to silence the thoughts, and with them her feelings, not to fall back into the abyss from which she had just begun to escape. Meeting Gerd was like a thin rope coming from above, from a bright place she had not inhabited for years. With his silence, the rope was becoming ever thinner, and there was just a little left before it broke. And then... She fell asleep, but dreams did not give her peace - in them the past, the present and fantasies mingled in a dark vaudeville. The awakening from which was the beginning of its next act. On the second day, Gerard suggested a trip and she agreed. They went to Pahara and Betancuria. They found them pretty and deserted. In Pahara, Gerard told her about the arrival of general Betancourt on the nearby Ajuy beach, in Betancuria - how the city had been founded by him. Marina was trying to listen to him and even felt grateful. His stories disconnected her from her painful thoughts. She imagined Betancourt on his ship after weeks of sailing on the ocean, the battle with the local population, his feelings after the victory. Gerard described the events with the pride of a descendant of discoverers and conquerors. "*But the island would have existed without being conquered,*" Marina thought. "*The beginning created by the French was an end for the locals.*" It passed through her mind that it was the same in love, when two couples overlap – for the existing couple this is the end of a life, a collapse of a whole world, while for one of the partners and for their discoverer it is a new life, a novelty, a future. She felt even more compassion for Carla. She was entitled to her island with Gerd. Marina was the one who had set foot on it, experiencing the excitement of the access to new territories. "*It's better this way,*" she told herself, "*It is better for him not to call. It is better for me to forget*". From this moment on she stopped waiting for his call. And she started to wait for oblivion.

The Writer

Her phone rang. It was Concha.

"Can you come tomorrow afternoon to meet Carmen?"

"Yes, of course."

"I'll wait for you at two-thirty."

Her Spanish was good enough to manage a simple conversation, but would it do the job with this old woman, who might even speak a dialect? She had missed calls from Marina in the past days; perhaps she could help.

"Hello, Writer," she heard her soft voice.

"Hi, Marina. Where do I find you?"

"In Betancuria."

"I have a request. Tomorrow I have to meet an elderly woman about my book. I don't know if I can handle it with my Spanish... Could you come? "

A brief silence.

"Yes. When is the meeting?"

"At two-thirty in La Oliva."

"I'll fetch you at two from Corralejo."

"Thank you very much. See you tomorrow!"

"See you tomorrow."

Carmen

The white car stopped, and the Writer got in. She noticed that Marina's dreamlike expression from their last meeting had disappeared. Her face was tired and had sunk back into its previous inaccessible distance. She stared at the road, but she drove the car mechanically, absentmindedly.

She put the address in the GPS with one hand while holding the wheel with the other. "Her hands are like broken wings," thought the Writer.

Concha was waiting for them. They followed her car. They passed the La Oliva sign and entered Via Verde. They turned left towards the valley beneath a hill on which two windmills rose up.

To a white house, in front of which a small old woman with a black headscarf sat on a bench. "White, tidy cottage ..." But there was no linden tree here either. A man and a woman in their sixties were sitting beside her. Concha introduced the Writer and Marina to Carmen. The others were her children. Two of eleven. Nice people, with open, good faces and a dignified warmth. The Writer sat next to Carmen, Marina in a chair opposite. The "children" sat on a nearby wall. A car arrived and two more women got out. Two more children who sat down next to the others. A woman came out and brought doughnuts and water. The doughnuts she had made especially for the guests, were still warm. The Writer and Marina took one each, then one more. Carmen smiled gently and looked at them with her veiled eyes. Concha said goodbye and left.

The Writer leaned towards Carmen.

"I am writing a book about Fuerteventura. Can I ask you a few questions?"

"What?"

"She does not hear well," her son explained and turned to the old woman. "SHE IS WRITING A BOOK ABOUT FUERTEVENTURAAAA. SHE WANTS TO ASK YOU A FEW QUESTIONS."

"Go ahead," Carmen smiled.

The Writer switched on the recorder in her mobile.

"What do you like most about the island?"

"Pardon?"

"WHAT. DO YOU. LIKE. MOST. ON THE ISLAND." The son stepped in again.

"I like most my house. I like it best to sit outside the house. There is shade, the sun passes on the other side, it is calm... I love La Oliva, the sea, the beach, the mountains here. One time I left it to go to Moro Jable with my son. We were looking for one of my daughters. Once, I saw Fuerteventura from a plane and I didn't like it. I don't like travelling, I'm not used to travelling. My husband drove the car around and I wouldn't stop him; I took care of the children; I did my work. I've been to La Lajita, to Posso Negro... but I haven't seen anything else on the island... Then immediately home."

"What has changed over the years?" The Writer shouted.

"Today there is a lot of traffic. People don't stop, they go wherever they want. In the morning I'm there, at noon I may be elsewhere."

"How did you have entertain yourselves before and how now?"

"We fed the donkeys, we rested, we fed them, we got hungry, and we stopped to eat too. And it happened again and again, and we did it with great joy."

"What gives you joy now?"

"There were no roads before so we didn't go much for a walk. We toiled the mountain... And now there are roads, people and buses. Now only the memories give me joy".

"We were her only entertainment because she only had us," added one of the daughters.

"I have eleven children. Only the last one was born with a disability. I came here on October 4, 1940. And, as they say, here I saw green and ripeness. Always working, just working. I worked in a bakery selling bread to my neighbours. When the soldiers came to La Oliva, they came from the sea... they came to me for bread, no one else sold it."

"How was it during the war?"

"Life during the war... On July 18 it began, and it lasted a long time. It began in 1936 and ended in 1939. We all had someone in the war. All our men were taken from us, and for some, when their men were sent to war, peace came to them. Everything was calculated. For a month we had half a kilo of sugar, and they gave us gofio – no matter how many children you have, it was the same ration. But we managed. We only ate the gofio. They gave us a small piece of ham each month. It was a bad time."

"And did good things happen? Or only suffering?"

"We had no water. It was a joy when it was raining. We put out large containers to fill up."

"And during Franco?"

"There are many people who complain, and many who are supporters. We did not experience anything bad. There was no hunger. The younger children have never starved. Only this daughter," she pointed out the one who had made the doughnuts, "and one other child experienced the hunger. There was work, there was money."

Marina listened intently. Her face had changed. The distance was replaced by interest.

"How old are you?" The Writer asked.

"101 years, two months and - today's day is not counted because I am still living it – twenty-two days. Here I win the Via Verde award. 101 years with a fresh head. I was born on March 30, 1913. If I reached 102, I'd be happy," Carmen said, laughing.

"Like Van Gogh," the Writer uttered, "March 30th."

"Pardon?"

"Nothing..."

"She had never seen a doctor. But when she was 92 she got sick and a doctor came to see her," the daughter with the doughnuts stepped in again.

"I ate what was there, broth, fish, I lived as the Lord wanted. Within seven months two of my children died – at 67 and 66 years old. Huge pain. One child died at 37. And two more in between. I'm still managing. I manage to go to bed myself, get up, go to the bathroom, go to the kitchen, but the children come to support me because they are afraid that I might fall."

"I did not hear that," the Writer said to Marina.

"She said ... she said that five of her children had died, two of them... in recent months. She does everything ... " Marina's voice trembled.

"Marina, are you okay?"

"Yes, yes, it's nothing, sorry, I'm sorry... for the lost children," she said.

The children looked at their feet or at the horizon. Carmen stared at her face. Marina wiped the corners of her eyes.

"How do you live, how do you pass your days?" The Writer asked.

"Before breakfast, I sit in bed, I say my prayer. At seven. This is my oldest habit. I never wake up after the sun."

"What do you remember from your youth?"

"On Fuerteventura we danced isas. I can start right now. And the folias. It was great. All the old people were watching us. The married men were on the side with the elderly, and we just sat and looked at each other. We were courting only with a look. Lelito. A special look. Somebody liked to dance, somebody else - no. Who did not like it, just watched. My husband...," Carmen laughed. Her laughter was fragile.

"How did you meet your husband?"

"At the dance. Every eight days there was a dancing party, and every eight days my father did not let me go. This one time was an exception."

"They did not allow going out, even for a walk, alone. Her mother always went with her," says one of the daughters who did not starve. "She did not let her exchange a word with her boyfriend."

"Suddenly there were roads, buses, and young people were everywhere," Carmen started speaking again. She thought, and added, "I live as the Lord wants and it will always be this way. It seems to me that young people do not know the simplest prayer."

"Do you have many visitors? Do people disturb you?"

"How could they disturb me? They disturb me when they don't come. Who likes to stay with their mouth shut, and with a closed door with no-one going through it?"

"What is your best memory except for having the children?"

"Youth is the best. At 21, my youth was over. You live in some moments better than in others, and so life is flowing."

"Have you ever left the island?"

Carmen stared at her incomprehensibly.

"HAVE YOU. LEFT. THE ISLAND." repeated the son.

"Yes. I was in Canada. But I stayed only for fifteen days. I had a son there whom I had not seen for four years, and finally, I went. He died seven months ago. I had a visa for one month. We went with my other son, he took leave for a month. But on the fifteenth day, I told myself, "Let's go home". I missed what I had left behind. There were such high buildings in Canada. They reached the sky. With the car back and forth I liked it, now I realise that I liked it. There were some large puddles of water that was supposed to be sweet. Lakes. I'm saying: it cannot be sweet! They took my boots and trousers off and I stepped into the water because I wanted to check if it was sweet. I drank. It was really sweet. There were also people who were surfing. Yet I remembered what I missed at home. I was returning by plane and the sun was ahead of us, ahead of us, in front of us, but it ran faster than we did. Apart from Canada, I was in Tenerife. For a year, when I was twelve years old, with my brothers who worked there. Then we went to pay some bills by ship, and when the captain saw us coming back on the same day, he asked, 'Why are you coming back so quickly? Didn't you like it?' We wanted to go home."

"What do you dream of?"

"No matter how much you dream, these things are not true. I have dreamed, but who trusted me? I dreamed when I was young and I saw myself dead, dressed in white, and they were putting me in a coffin, it stayed in my mind... but nothing happened."

"What is the most important thing in your life?"

"Religion, don't you hear," her daughters said in one voice.

"Your greatest desire?"

"To keep my big family. The worst is that five of my children died."

"What else do you still want to do in your life?"

"I want to go to school and complete my studies, learn to write and read better. There was not much time. They were showing us letters on a wall and didn't bother to explain... Once a man passed on a camel. He looked smart, educated... He said he was a writer. I promised him some day to read something he wrote. But whether I will manage... And I've forgotten his name."

"Unamuno, Miguel de Unamuno," the son said.

"It was something like that, yes."

At that moment a man of indefinite age arrived. His face had the innocent expression of joyous wonder that is special to some people with Down Syndrome. He approached the guests and shook hands with them vigorously. Then he sat down on the wall next to his siblings.

"Has she met Unamuno?" The Writer asked.

"That's what she says... We have been hearing this story ever since we were children. About the writer to whom she promised to learn to read. It coincides with the time of his exile here. But whether it was him... only God knows."

"Can I ask her something?" Marina turned to the Writer.

"Of course."

"How long... how long does love last?"

"It depends. At fifteen, I began to feel it, and it evolved and stayed, so that people were wondering what those old people still have to say to each other. I bore with him, he bore with me. At fifteen I felt that feeling... love lasts a lifetime. It doesn't last only until someone does not want it to."

"I've been with my man for sixty years, happily. There's no way that time doesn't have an impact, but it's up to the people to keep that feeling between them," said the daughter who had brought the doughnuts.

"Twenty-four years ago her husband died. Our father. She always mentions him, and whenever she prays she rises from her chair and goes to kiss his photo. They were together for fifty-nine years. Twenty-four years without him – that's the life of a young man," the son said.

Six elderly children sitting next to each other on the wall. Behind them the mountain. Above them - the spirits of their deceased siblings. And the two mills on the hill.

The Writer and Marina got up to say goodbye. They invited them to see the house. It was spacious, with an interior courtyard with lush greenery. On the wall above Carmen's bed hung an icon of the Madonna and Child and photographs of all her children. The Writer and Marina looked at them, then at each other, and their eyes said more than words could express.

When leaving, the Writer thanked Carmen and her children. Carmen smiled:

"A fiancée can not offer more than what she has."

The Writer and Marina embraced each of the children. When they reached Carmen, Marina knelt and kissed the back of her hand.

Marina

She was driving back and her face was wet with tears.

"Marina, what is it?"

"I am thinking about this woman and about... all the children she's lost."

The tears overcame her. She stopped the car and covered her face with hands.

In a moment she lifted her head, wiped her tears and said:

"I have not talked about it for three years."

It was a day like any other day. No intuition nor premonition for misfortune. Angel and Neda were about to go out. They were going to a children's party in Borisova Gradina, Boris's Garden. They were at the door, I washed the dishes. Neda turned around, ran, hugged me, and kissed me. My angel... They were out for a long time. I thought Neda must have been absorbed in playing with the other children. Hours later the key turned. Angel. Alone. His face... I can still see his face. Terrified like in Munch's painting.

"Where is Neda?"

"She's gone."

"What do you mean – she's gone?"

"I don't know where she is. She disappeared in a moment."

"What do you mean - disappeared? She's not a needle, is she? WHERE IS MY CHILD?"

I screamed and struck him. He squeezed my wrists, hugged me strongly, and cried aloud. I broke away, I was mad. I put on my shoes.

"Where are you going, Marina?"

"What do you mean - where? I'm going to search for my child!"

200

"Marina, I walked through the whole park. I've been looking for her for three hours. It's pointless. I called the police."

"What's pointless? How is it pointless? What's pointless is to stay here when my child is somewhere out there alone."

I ran away, he followed me. We scoured the park. We called her name. We stopped people and showed them pictures on our mobile phones. No one had seen her.

We went back home around midnight when we couldn't do anything more. We didn't close our eyes until dawn. Only then did he tell me what had happened. He was with her. She was playing with some children, there were a lot of people. He was around her, watching over her. He met a former classmate that he had not seen since their school graduation. They spoke. For a little while, he claimed. A few minutes. No more than five. Then he realised, she wasn't there.

He left his classmate and ran to look for her.

At dawn Angel's mobile rang. It was the police.

He said almost nothing. Only "where" and "yes".

He hung up and looked at me, but I already knew it, knew it, knew it...

They found her, he said. They found the body. And he cried again.

My Neda had become a body.

We had to identify her. Angel did not want me to go to the morgue. But there was no way he could stop me. You can not stop a mother from seeing her child, whatever the condition. Even when it's already only a body.

Marina paused, breathing heavily, large tears slid down her neck and soaked in her dress. The Writer was silent, her eyes were fogged. She made a gesture towards embracing Marina. This time she allowed herself into it. She wept long in the Writer's arms. She pulled away, wiped her eyes, and watching the yellow wilderness of Fuerteventura continued:

Her blonde hair on the white sheets. Bruises on her hands. And around her neck. Her face, however, was calm. She had not become a body in death, my Neda, no. She had become an angel.

Raped and strangled, the pathology report said. Death occurred at 3 pm. They found her in the bushes in the upper part of the park.

My child, my only child, lived through this. She didn't live through it.

And I still can not live through it. Day after day I feel the horror she experienced, and I imagine the scene..., that monster! And that moment, that very moment when my life ended, when Angel came home. Alone.

And this woman has buried five children. Two in recent months. And she laughs. How? How?

"Faith," the Writer whispered, "you heard it. Faith helps."

"I called Gerard right away," Marina continued as if she had not heard her, "and he arrived that night. After the cremation, I left with him."

"Angel?"

"I have not spoken with him, nor seen him since. We divorced from a distance. I have not returned to Bulgaria either. They never caught the monster, even though the case is not yet closed. I don't want to have anything to do with a country where little angels are being raped and killed," her voice subsided.

"This happens not only in Bulgaria. Also in Belgium. And elsewhere. As for Angel, he went through this horror as well. The guilt. And the pain from you leaving him."

"Yes, exactly. He did go through them. Someone told my mother that he had married the same classmate who played a decisive role in my child's death. They had a son."

"Life goes on, Marina. And for you, it must go on too. Do you know that Unamuno also lost a son and was depressed? In a forum, I read that Winter lost a son as well, so he bought the isolated Handia in search of peace... And your parents?"

"They spend a few months a year with me. They were devastated. But they understood that I could not stay in Bulgaria, that if I stayed, they would have lost me as well. And Neda I took with me. In a small box, in the bedroom."

"Have you thought about having another child?"

"My periods stopped then."

"I understand. And with your lost child by the bed..."

"What are you hinting at?"

"Nothing. We can not have a present until we release the past, can we? Angel has managed to move on. But the guilt will always pursue him. Unless..."

"What?"

"He receives forgiveness."

Marina looked at the Writer, made an attempt to say something, but only dropped a sigh.

"I will send you a link to a film. Watch it," the Writer said when she was leaving.

Marina pressed the throttle towards her hotel.

The Writer went home and took the key to the roof terrace. Just in time for the sunset. Saturated, radiantly cutting through the clouds, dramatic and short... Like life.

The Writer

"Where have you been hiding?" Juan watched her impishly from behind the kitchen counter.

"In the lives of different people."

"And your life?"

"Good question."

"How's the novel going?"

"It's writing itself."

"Am I in it?"

"You have not given me enough material."

"Oh, how's that possible?"

"Like that. Okay, have a nice evening. I'm tired."

"Have a nice evening..."

Miguel

"Because living is one thing, and knowing - quite different and, as we shall see, there may be such a contradiction between the two, so we can say that everything vital is anti-rational, not only irrational, and everything rational is anti-vital. And this is the basis of the tragic sense of life."[39]

Marina

In the evening, Marina found an email from the Writer. She had sent her the film. She went to bed with her laptop and played it with earphones. The film was called "Nostalgia For The Light". It was shot in Chile's desert Atacama, where the world's largest telescopes are located. A young astronomer talked about the speed of light. "The moonlight takes a little more than a second to reach us," he said, "the sunlight - eight minutes. We do not see things in the present moment. This is the trap: the present does not exist. "

The man explained that the only present that may exist is the one of our consciousness, it is closest to the absolute present. And

---

[39] Miguel de Unamuno, Essays, 'Science and Art' publishing house, 1983, „The starting point'

still not completely, because it takes time for the signal to move between the senses.

"The past is the main tool of astronomers, we work with the past. We are accustomed to living in past times. Just like archaeologists and geologists. And historians."

"The past is a straight line. A blow would destroy it," the man continued.

There was footage of mummified Indians, since before Columbus, in the desert, and women who for twenty-eight years have searched for the remains of their loved ones killed by the Pinochet regime and buried God knows where. Day after day, they went out into the wilderness with small blades and searched for parts of the bodies of their husbands, brothers and sons to connect to them again, if not through life, then at least through death.

The women, with weather-beaten faces and swallowed tears, shared the experience of discovering or continuing to search without result, but with hope. One of them had found her brother's leg. She was saying how she recognised the sock, the shoe.... "This foot was last in my house," she said. How she had got up during the night and caressed it - that leg, and she had had the feeling that she was back with her brother, and she had felt both a great relief, and a great deal of pain, for she knew then that he was dead for sure.

"If these huge telescopes could be pointed towards the ground instead of the stars and look there, to find the remains of our loved ones. I am only fantasising," another one said.

Finally, they invited two of them to an astronomical station. The small women climbed into the big telescope and stared at the stars. Marina was suddenly convulsed by waves of tears. Gerard looked at her out of the corner of his eyes but continued to read his book.

The last shots showed a young woman, mother of two children, and an astronomer at one of the stations. Her parents had been killed when she was one year old. Her grandparents had raised her.

"It's all part of a cycle that will not end with me, nor with my parents or my children," she said. "We are all part of a cycle of one energy that is recycled. Like the stars that must die so that new stars, planets, life can emerge. In this context, what happened to my parents has another dimension. It acquires another meaning and releases me a little bit from this enormous suffering, because I feel that nothing really ends."

The author ended with the words: "I am convinced that memory has a gravitational force. It constantly attracts us. Those who have memory can live in the present fragile moment. Those who do not have it, don't live anywhere."

Marina watched the closing titles through tears running down her face. A new wave of sobs shook her. Gerard left his book and pulled her into his arms. When her crying faded, Marina took her mobile and sent a message to the Writer: "Thank you."

The Writer

Intrigued by what she had read about Winter, she looked at pictures of his house with an increasing eagerness to penetrate it, to feel it, to enter into its secrets. The house invited her, it called her silently, enticed her... One night she dreamed about it. Its gate was half-closed. She pushed it slightly and walked in. The courtyard was full of elegantly dressed people with glasses in their hands. Like a Brussels after-work gathering. Gerd and Carla, Enrique, Marina and Gerard, Juan and Lola, Emiliyan, Eva and Darina, Alma and Kumar, all were there. Dressed up, smiling widely, carefully holding the fragile stems of their glasses. She stood at the door, indecisively, when a man with gleaming white hair, black glasses, and dandy clothes approached her. Gustav Winter. An enormous black dog stood beside him and stared at her suspiciously. Winter smiled, offered his elbow gallantly, and said, "How long have I been waiting for you, Writer!"

Her stomach knotted, and the only thing she felt like doing was escaping. She woke up with a dry mouth.

A little later she entered Indy. Enrique raised his head and his face lit up.

"We thought you'd left without saying goodbye."

"How about a trip? With a mission."

"Based on experience, I know our missions don't succeed."

"This one is going to be different."

"Where to?"

"Cofete."

Gerd

It was just after their best surfing for that stay when Gerd and Carla decided to stop. They had been in full possession of the feeling. And they wanted to keep it. To close it in the memory box and inhale it from time to time like an opiate, to satisfy their hunger for surfing until their next return.

There was one more day before their departure. They decided to go to Cofete with Enrique and the Writer. Even though Winter was from the same neck of the woods like them, they wouldn't have crossed the island just because of him and the surrounding him mystery, had they not seen the long, deserted beach.

At first, they spoke energetically. The Writer was afraid she might feel awkward, but Carla acted as if nothing had happened. Gerd also seemed natural, only occasionally his gaze was becoming pensive as if he did not follow the conversation. Enrique was excited, witty, and ostentatiously gallant.

The silence of the landscape gradually settled inside them. Its roundness reminded Gerd of Marina's body. A shiver of memory passed through his body. He realised he could not leave without seeing her. Just once. Just one last time. Even those sentenced to death have the right to one last wish, don't they?

To see her. Just this. Just one last time.

Carla

In the days after her disappearance, Gerd was gentle and loving, but nonetheless detached and distant even in his tenderness. It seemed to her that he had decided despite himself to be like this. Perhaps he was still infatuated with the Bulgarian. It needed time to pass, so he could return to his usual self in relation to her without making an effort. She understood that. She could not wait to return to Freiburg and leave Fuerteventura behind, at least for a while. Freiburg, the anchorage of their lives, their family, their friends - they would become the bond between them again, the same bond that had been the island till recently. She felt his pulling away again, as they travelled. It did not worry her, it was natural. But his sudden cheerfulness disturbed her. Was it related to her? So soon? Hardly. She believed he was not in contact with Marina. Then what?

The turns curled like a snake, occupying the border between the sacred mountain and the abyss. As they drove down, the rough ocean and Cofete with its majestic desolation unfolded before them.

Carla stretched her hand towards Gerd and gripped his. They looked at each other. This is the place.

The Writer

They stopped by the monument of Gustav Winter and his faithful dog, accompanying him even in his bronze eternity. After the brief visit to the mysterious man, who had chosen the most impossible place for his castle-like house, they returned to the car and drove to it. In reality, it was even more impressive than in the pictures. Built on several platforms with stone struts to align with the mountain slope, stretching towards the ocean. Its sand-coloured stones looked like a huge web.

The only witness to everything that had happened here was this building, whose interior probably contained its own story, full of oblique signs and conjectures, more authentic than any legend. The Writer slid her hand along the wall and stopped in front of the door.

"You want to go in, don't you?" Enrique was behind her.

"Yes."

"Then what is stopping you?"

The house was located between the mountain and the ocean like a border post. Its threshold was a boundary between reality and legend.

The Writer grabbed the handle and pushed it down. The door quietly opened. And like in her dream, she crossed the doorstep and entered.

Gerd

After deciding to see Marina again, his sensations became more intense. It was as if he was on drugs. An exhilaration, almost an exaltation, seized him. The dramatic landscape and the mysterious house made him feel like a hero in a film. That's what was happening: a film. The meeting with Marina will be its end. Then life will continue as before. Perhaps they would never return to Fuerte again. They could find another place to surf. Or make a journey with Enrique in pursuit of the perfect wave. Everything was possible. After. Now... Now just one last meeting.

He saw the Writer and Enrique entering the house. The violation of the rules, norms, and law were alien to him prior to this holiday. In his orderly life, he would not cheat nor invade someone else's property. But the island brought out something in him, whose existence he had not suspected. Something shady, flighty and free. He waved to Carla and followed them.

Carla

The view of the Writer and Enrique entering the house took her out of her inner languor. She wanted to shout, to stop them, but her throat was dry. She looked at Gerd in the hope that he would do something. But he just waved to her and followed them.

The lightness of this gesture hurt her more than his crush on the Bulgarian. The ease. How instantly the responsible, caring, and discriminating man, with whom she shared her life, had made the decision to cross the boundaries, to enter into a foreign possession, to break the law. Just like that. Without much thinking. Without *any* thinking. Spontaneously.

But aren't we our truest selves exactly in spontaneity? With whom then had she spent all these years?

She had wanted to believe that his infidelity had come after a tough and painful struggle with himself in which he had been defeated. That it was impossible for him to resist. An exception. It can happen to anyone once in a lifetime to succumb, to be weak, to make a mistake. But when they realise their mistake, to overcome their weakness, to return to the person whom they have always been. The instant when Gerd entered the house, Carla had an insight that she did not know who this person was, that she did not know him at all. The way he had entered the house, he had also embarked on the affair with Marina. Without thinking, *spontaneously*. As spontaneously he could leave her tomorrow. With a wave and a few steps leading him to another, forbidden and enticing world.

And she? She had remained alone in this bare, harsh landscape of Fuerteventura, of her life, of the world... It was as if Gerd, the Writer and Enrique had never existed. As if she had invented them. That's how she felt as a little girl when she heard that her parents had departed forever for a lovely country where they would meet her on a day, far ahead. Abandoned. Alone. Later it seemed to her that she had invented them and that she had to give life to this fantasy every day until the end of her days. She could not bear to experience this again. She came out of her numbness and walked to the house. The door was invitingly half-open. She walked in.

The Writer

A small courtyard with a garden revealed itself. A piece of land surrounded by a short fence. In the middle, an installation of the rusty chassis of a truck mounted on two rails, and on the top of that, placed across it, a wooden green plane with a missing cockpit. Three or four small banana palms grew on the bare land. In front, the word "COFETE" written in stone. On the left side, a fig tree complimented the setting. The rectangle of the garden was surrounded by the white wall of the house, with arches. A narrow, green path circled the wall. The rooms of the house were only behind it, in the shade. A stone kerb, about fifty centimetres high, curved around the wall like a snake. Young aloe vera plants grew behind it. The house seemed decayed, shabby and... inhabited.

Enrique stood behind her, Gerd also came in. They glanced at one another. The Writer walked down the green path, followed by them.

Gerd

Outside the house seemed more impressive than inside. The yard was empty, except for the ridiculous construction linking the structure of a truck and a small plane. In a museum, this could pass for modern art. Here it looked nonsensical. But, despite the disappointing first impression (what would have been more exciting? a courtyard overgrown with plants and a snake skimming down the fig tree? dense cobwebs connecting the sides of the arches like curtains?), his excitement did not diminish. The Writer had told them about Winter and the mystery of the house. And now they were in it. At the very place. In the domain of the legend.

Carla had stayed outside. The Writer and Enrique walked along the path leading to the interior of the house. Gerd pulled out his mobile and quickly wrote: "I'm leaving tomorrow. I have to see you. Tonight? Please!" He entered Marina's number and pressed "send".

The Writer

She saw stairs and climbed up. They led to a spacious room, whose walls were covered with household tools, fishing rods, bells, goatskin... A strange museum. Next to one wall was an ancient bookcase with luxury volumes behind its glass. A heavy table with four chairs in front of it. A fireplace with a grid on the opposite side, and two old armchairs with black damasks of roses. A plaster head of a man with a straight, imposing nose,

212

tight lips and deep wrinkles was resting on a stand next to one of the chairs. A pipe hung from his mouth, his eyes were hidden behind dark glasses, a white coarse wig half-covering his forehead. On it - a straw bowler hat. A golden rectangle of cloth with a print of colourful, spiralled twigs was his garment. Gustav Winter. A lady's straw hat with a ribbon was attached to the armchair beside him, a sign of Elizabeth Althouse's former presence.

The Writer approached Winter, squatting, staring at his dark glasses.

Enrique and Gerd looked at the tools on the walls behind her.

"I don't remember inviting guests today."

The Writer jumped in surprise and turned. In the door frame stood a large, dark man.

Carla

The yard was empty. Her eyes ran over it and she walked towards the house. She climbed the stairs and found herself a few steps away from the back of a big man with a white shirt and beige trousers. The Writer, Gerd and Enrique, were facing her. They seemed startled.

Carla stepped back slightly and pressed herself close to the outer wall of the room.

The Writer

The man's face was thunderous. Thick knitted brows with a deep wrinkle between them, a fleshy nose, thick lips, dark dense hair to the ears, deep blue eyes.

The Writer stepped towards him.

"Do you live here?"

"What do you think?" His voice was coarse.

"We're sorry... My curiosity is to blame."

"Haven't you heard that curiosity killed the cat?"

"I've heard that cats have nine lives."

"How smart you are."

"What do you want from us? We should have not entered a private property, but we were tempted because of the legends. We do apologise!" Enrique stepped forward and stood in front of the Writer.

"We do apologise," the man imitated him in an ugly manner. "So what?"

"What do you want?"

"What if you find some strangers in your house, what will you do? Will you let them go just like that just because they apologise?"

"Enough! This is not fun," Gerd said. "We aren't criminals, you can see this yourself. Nor are we children, for you to scare."

"If you were children, I'd have spanked you by now. Still, you did not answer my question. What if you had come across some strangers in your house?"

"Look, I'm writing a book about the island. It was inevitable I would come to Winter and his house. And yes, we entered... Now, as we're here, could you tell us something about it?"

As she was saying this, the Writer was walking towards the man. At the word "it" she stopped in front of him and stared at his blue eyes. His hard look didn't scare away hers. For the first time, he smiled faintly.

"I like you. You're not a coward. You're a journalist?"

"I'm writing a book. A novel."

"I'm fed up with journalists. They come, pretend to be tourists, gather information and then distort my words as they wish. Everyone is looking for a cheap sensation."

The Writer did not answer. She just kept looking at him. Eventually, he grinned broadly, revealing even teeth, with one gold upper and lower.

"All right. I was joking. I wanted to scare you. But, obviously, you are not easy to scare. I'm almost a guest in this house too, even though it belongs to me by right. Come on, I'll show you around."

Carla appeared at the door.

"It's been a while..."

Carla

She listened to everything with bated breath, ready to escape and call the police, if necessary. But after the last words of the man, she decided to come in.

Despite the change in his behaviour, she still felt restless. He did not evoke trust in her with his roughness, the primal power he radiated, and the way he acted when they met. Practical jokes, at which no one else but their author laughs, were not her cup of tea.

She wandered around the house absent-mindedly, listened for a while to Winter's possible Nazi ties, but this did not interest her. At school since an early age, they had been encouraged to be humble, modest and measured in their behaviour. They owed it to the world. They were born indebted. The German guilt was wrapped around their necks like an umbilical cord from their first scream. The original sin for them had another time dimension. Pre-born was their sin, passed down from generation to generation as an unwanted inheritance, genetic disease or omen. She did not need to be reminded of it on her last day on the island.

They went out onto a natural terrace on the other side of the house, from where a view to Cofete opened. Gerd pulled out his camera and took a few shots.

Carla approached him:

"Let's go to the beach."

The Writer

After the initial thrill of being caught at the scene of the crime had passed, the Writer marvelled at the opportunity given to her by Destiny. To meet a descendant of the first inhabitants of the house! The lineage of the people hired by Winter to live in and manage it, witnesses to its life, to the pompous feasts organised by the German and his young wife during their sporadic visits, and to all that fed the legends, the gossip and the fantasies of people... Eighty-five years had passed since the house construction and the right to inhabit it has been passed on from generation to generation with an unwritten decree, long after the death of the elegant German. However, the moral right and the right of the law were not the same. The heirs of the first inhabitants of the house were declared by law to be squatters. Pepito had turned out to be the most business-oriented of all his predecessors, turning the house into a private museum without official status. The tourists, hungry for the sensation, had the feeling of ending up in a real adventure. And they generously gave him cash when leaving.

Now he was walking with the Writer and showing her various sights: "Over there," he pointed at the distance, "was the runway for his private plane, here the tunnel that goes down to the beach begins, here are those circles of grass, burned grass, that have never grown again, here are the signs in the corners of the roof, all different and sending encrypted messages that this was a Nazi base, that's the kitchen, it's huge, isn't it, here they did plastic surgery on Nazi leaders right after the end of the war..."

Enrique moved next to the Writer like a shadow. Gerd and Carla would be waiting for them on the beach.

Winter and his young wife came to the house once every few months. They arrived in a car with an open roof, both of them wearing dark glasses, he with his silver hair but still masculine, she - the same age as one of his sons, beautiful, refined, a real frau. The black dog always sat proudly in the back seat.

Winter and the dog had become part of the island with their statues. But not the stunning frau. The most outstanding thing about her was her status as the wife of a mysterious man. And this is not enough for eternity.

They arrived together with other cars, full of people, elegant in their look and colourful by presumption. With them, came servants with bags full of fresh products, from the Majos who were expelled from the peninsula when Winter became its tenant. Again and again... until the night when the girl died.

"What girl?" The Writer asked.

She had read the articles about Winter, she had followed long discussions on internet forums, but there was no mention of a dead girl.

"I've never told anyone that story...," Pepito looked at her hesitantly.

"Of course. Because you waited for me."

The man grinned and showed his two gold teeth.

"You do not lack self-confidence."

"That's why I'm here. For this story."

Pepito grinned even more. Then he became serious.

"I'm writing a survey on the traces of Winter's Nazi activity in the house. It is taking a lot of time. In fact, I have no time for anything else."

The Writer reached into her purse and took out a ten-euro note. The man cleared his throat.

"I'm afraid for my life. No one has any interest in the results of this study coming to light... No one has any interest in me proving that Winter had a relationship with the Nazis."

The Writer put back the ten-euro note and pulled out a twenty euro.

"That's it. You won't get more. Now the story."

The man reached for the banknote, but she quickly closed her palm.

"First the story."

"What a woman you are, que ba!"

The Writer smiled and looked at him with narrowed eyes.

"Sitting would be better."

Pepito smiled faintly and signalled Enrique to follow him.

They came back a moment later with one of the armchairs and two plastic chairs.

"Please, Your Majesty," Pepito offered her the armchair with a theatrical gesture.

The three of them made themselves comfortable, facing Cofete and the ocean. They saw Gerd and Carla moving along the beach - small figures in the setting of a universe so perfect in its nakedness, severity and unity of water, earth and sky that it was impossible to be true - not in Europe, not here, not now. But Fuerteventura was not quite Europe, was it? The energies of the two continents had met for an eternal tango. Europe and Africa. And from them, Fuerteventura. Daughter with two mothers.

"... any other."

"Pardon?"

"Writer, where have your thoughts taken you, again?" Enrique smiled slightly.

"Here. Would you start all over again?"

"It was a January night like any other. Again the masters arrived with their important guests, again there was plenty of food and drinks. The fiesta swirled as usual. The only difference was a presence..."

"A presence?"

"Yes. The presence of a Majorera who did not belong to these circles. A local peasant girl. Very beautiful."

Carmen

Don Gustavo the German, as everyone called him, came to Fuerteventura in the early thirties, looked around and decided to stay. His intention to buy Handia came to him sometime around my birth and is a silent harbinger of my death twenty years later. The arrival of this mysterious man in the prime of his life, who always wore black glasses and was accompanied by his black dog, became a subject of long and exciting conversations in the otherwise uneventful life of Majos. Everything showed that the self-confident German maintained close ties with the powerful of the day, and even with God. All obstacles to his taking over the peninsula vanished as if with a wave of a magic wand. Until his arrival, Handia had been a place forgotten by God, and although the wall separating it from Maxorata was long gone, its ghost continued to distinguish this part of the island from the other, and from the world at large. Having overcome the barriers to taking what rightfully belonged to him (because his wishes and the law usually coincided), he placed Handia on the map of Europe. Winter signed the lease for the peninsula on October 1, 1937, just when I turned three years old.

The following summer he arrived with a group of compatriots on a German fishing boat and spent days circling the area, took pictures, smoked cigars, while music floated from their boat until late. It was said that, in order to acquire Handia, in addition to what he paid, he had to deprive himself of his favourite car, which ten years later he found in Argentina and bought again after it had passed through two owners. Winter was a sentimental man and did not give up on what belonged to him.

Or at least not forever. After becoming the only master of Handia, he began to build a road, and a little later, his own runway. At that time, I was about six, and I heard my father saying to his friends, Pedro and Sancho, that this Winter was a Nazi spy. They discussed this with hushed voices. And then I saw him for the first time. He passed our house in La Pared in his cabriolet, with wind-blown hair, dark glasses, and the black dog sitting beside him. A boy sat in the back. His blue eyes stared at me and did not move until the car disappeared into the dust.

An air of animation filled Handia. More and more cars passed, light-haired Germans walked around, and I could hear their incomprehensible speech reaching me through the windows of my room. Sometimes women came with them. Gorgeously dressed, with high heels that clacked on the cobbles, holding the arms of their handsome husbands. They were photographed against the background of La Pared and the cliff that spread out in the ocean like an outstretched hand. They dropped by our small farm to buy goat's milk and cheese. We had two goats - Sandra and Susana, mother and daughter. Thanks to them and the vegetable garden we had enough food, and with the arrival of the Germans, we even started to earn some pesos. They praised our cheese by nodding contentedly, with their faces turned red from the sun, repeating: "Schon, schon," and "Bueno."

One day, Don Gustavo's car stopped in front of our house. He, himself, was behind the wheel. A beautiful young woman sat next to him. The black dog behind them. He got out and introduced himself to my father as if we might not know who he was. The two of them went to one side and spoke briefly. The woman was waiting for him in the car. Her dark glasses turned towards me, and she smiled broadly, revealing her even, white teeth. I also smiled at her a little. I felt embarrassed around strangers. My mother had died at my birth, and the person with whom I had communicated most was my father. I was accustomed to the few neighbours who came for a chitchat, but apart from them, I had no other contact with the world beyond La Pared.

Don Gustavo got back in his car and they headed to Moro Jable. We again saw his car approaching about two weeks later. The German was with a young man. He also got out of the car and Don Gustavo introduced him as his son Mateo. His blue eyes stared at me, and only then did I recognise the boy I had seen years ago when his car had passed our house like a mirage. Both men wore shirts and trousers. They were different from the local men not only physically, but also by the sophistication and wealth they radiated. Mateo asked me my name. I answered and sat to one side in the shade. As our fathers talked, Mateo did not take his eyes off me, and when they were leaving, he waved to me. I was approaching seventeen, he was some ten years older.

My father seemed hopeful after their visit. Don Gustavo was introducing some new rules according to which we would work more, produce more cheese and earn a little more money.

More or less a month later Don Gustavo came again with Mateo and another German, whom they called Joseph. Joseph was older, perhaps Don Gustavo's age. The black dog always there. Mateo greeted me, asked me how I was, and all the time looked at me, while I wondered where to turn my eyes. His gaze made me sweat, it was more scorching than the midday sun.

From that day on Joseph came by car every three days and loaded the boxes of cheese, giving my father pesos. Dad was keeping the money in a box and said that someday we could buy a car and make a tour of the island. I dreamed of going to Puerto de Cabras, to the far end, to wander around and buy a dress like the ones of the Germans.

I grew up without a mother or other female presence. There was no one to teach me how to be a woman, I had to find out all that alone. Nature was my mother and teacher. From the low and high tides, I had learned that where there is a swell, then there invariably follows a withdrawal, again and again... When the

German women appeared in their dresses, heels, scarves and coloured lips, I wanted to be like them. And to walk around arm in arm with a smart man in a shirt and trousers, with dark glasses and hair combed back. Perhaps Mateo would be my husband. I blushed from this thought, and I immediately ran to splash my face with water. Mateo and his father, however, disappeared and did not show up for a long time. Only Joseph continued to come for the cheese, but he was old and I did not imagine walking around with him.

I was superficial, naive and silly. Young.

Don Gustavo began to build a huge palace in Cofete. The people who lived there were displaced to other parts of Handia, the construction was guarded by Germans with rifles. It was said that the prisoners at the concentration camp in Tefia, convicted of criminal physical closeness to other men, were building the castle. From a God-forgotten place, Handia was turning into a place full of half-spoken things, untold stories, and unshared secrets. I felt unknown excitement, a presentiment that something great and exhilarating would happen.

A year later another car stopped in front of our door. Mateo was driving. A young man sat next to him. I stopped milking Sandra and went out. Mateo got out of the car and gave me his hand, gallantly. My fingers were dirty with milk. I wiped them in my skirt, embarrassed, before I caught his hand. He gently squeezed it as he stared into my eyes like before. The other man came down and approached us. He was tall, blonde-haired, bright-eyed. Broad forehead, fine nose, the upper lip slightly thinner, a mole over its left corner. He gave me a hand, his eyes laughing, and then the mole rose in a smile. I felt a pulsation low in my stomach, as if the smile had penetrated my womb and shifted something in it. Gary. I heard his name coming from somewhere far. I had entered a trance. For a moment everything was gone, and the only thing I could see was his grey-blue-green eyes.

The next moment I heard Mateo speaking and concentrated. He was inviting me to a fiesta in his father's house, the Cofete castle. The feast would be three days later.

I had heard from my father and Pedro about those parties, with sophisticated guests who drank champagne from crystal glasses and used silver cutlery... I did not know what to answer. Gary was smiling at me invitingly:

" Your presence would give us great pleasure."

Nobody had addressed me with such gallant words. And his voice... I could close my eyes and listen, and just that made my body alive in a new way.

I said, "I have to ask my father."

"I'll talk to him," Mateo reassured me.

Father had gone to get something from Pedro. The Germans sat on the bench in front of the house to wait for him. I offered them fresh milk. Two pairs of eyes ran over my face and body. Mateo's intense, Gary's laughing. And it seemed as if they were not looking at me, but caressing me, and something deep inside me would explode with elation.

My father came back and his face subtly tightened as he saw them. He rubbed his hands on his trousers and shook theirs. Mateo asked him how he was and then moved on to the matter. My father listened to him with an earnest expression, looked at me, read the request in my eyes, and said:

"All right. But you will bring her back before midnight."

Matheo promised, we agreed that he would pick me up at eight pm on Saturday, they kissed my hand as if I was a real lady, got into the car and set off.

I was overwhelmed with happiness. I felt the beat of my heart in my whole body. My father stared at me. Finally, he said:

"Carmen, these gentlemen are older than you, they have more experience, they are from another society and class. I allowed you to go to the fiesta because you have no entertainment in your life... But please, do not lose your mind. Do not believe everything you hear from them. Their goals and your wishes are probably not the same. Be smart and do not let them fool you... You know what I mean..."

"No," I said. I really could not understand why my father wanted to poison that single moment of complete happiness in my life with his lecturing.

My father sighed and looked sideways. I felt sorry for him. He appeared to me old with his white hair and a wrinkled, sun-burnt face. A strong flow of love overwhelmed me.

"Don't worry. I will be fine."

My main concern over the following days was what to wear. There would be all those beautiful, dressed up German women, and I did not have a proper dress. I was embarrassed to appear in my old-fashioned clothes. I went through them one by one as if I were seeing them for the first time, but none appeared to be right. I shared these concerns with my father. He called me into the bedroom and opened a chest. My mother's clothes, carefully folded, were in it. Excited, I began to take them out - dresses, skirts and blouses, and embraced them. I noticed my father's eyes moistening; he left the room. My mother used to be a city woman. She lived in Moro Jable, was able to read and knew how to dress. My grandfather worked in the city hall and my grandmother was a nurse. My father went to Moro Jable for a document from the city hall, and she had popped in to visit grandpa. They saw each other in the corridor, he asked her something, they spoke... My father said it was love at first sight. Her parents were against it, but mother married him nevertheless and moved to La Pared. She did not make contact with her parents again. A year later, at my birth, she died.

I did not know my father still had her clothes. I began trying them on until I reached a yellow dress, clinging to my body just so, as if it were designed for me. I was like a German lady. Only my hair was dark and curly, not like theirs, golden and straight like silk threads. The shoes also fitted. And I found a small bag. My father had waited for the right moment to give them to me.

I only had one picture of my mother. From her wedding with my father. A very beautiful, smiling woman. Medium height, with a strong body and full breasts. My father said I was like her. She looked happy in the picture. My father too. I had never seen him so radiant.

At a quarter to eight on Saturday evening, Mateo parked in front of our home. I was ready and waiting for him, sitting on the couch, nervously cracking my fingers. My father was pretending not to see my anxiety. I almost did not go. I did not know what I was going to do there, what I would say, how I would behave. It seemed to me that I was going to a terrible test which, if I failed, would ruin my whole life. I was given one chance only. There would be no other.

I sat next to Mateo in the jeep and we headed for Cofete. The road was steep and rocky, the ocean far below us. The jeep kept jolting. I gripped the door handle and prayed to get there safely while trying to talk to Mateo. He was amused by my fear.

"Everything will be fine. We'll be there soon."

And as he said this, he stroked my face lightly. I did not dare move. First the abyss, and now this caress, which opened another abyss in me.

Ten minutes later, the car descended along the slop at the inner side of the mountain and a huge house, Winter's castle, appeared before us. The house was lit up and there were cars in front of it. We parked and walked in. In the large, tiled living room about forty people, all dressed-up, spoke in groups. Some of the men were smoking cigars, women - cigarettes. They held fine glasses with drinks of different colours. The main language, floating in space, was German. Don Gustavo and his wife, the same young woman I had seen in the car, turned to us with a smile.

"Welcome, Doña Carmen. Make yourself at home!"

I thanked them awkwardly and followed Mateo to the drinks table. He poured some red liquid into a round glass and handed it to me. I sipped and wrinkled my nose - it was bitter.

"What is this?"

"Campari. Do you like it?"

"Not particularly."

"You're not used to it. You will see that you will grow to like it."

I did not like it, but I continued to drink it and did not protest when he poured a second glass. For the first time, I drank alcohol and I immediately felt its beneficial effect by the calmness that had replaced my nervousness.

As soon as I entered, I started looking around for Gary, and it was not long before I noticed him. He was talking to an attractive lady who was tilting her head toward him conspiratorially. After a while, he left her and came to us.

Our eyes met, and I felt once again that warmth that had come over me when I first saw him. I could not compare it with anything I had ever experienced before. He told me I looked stunning. Someone called Mateo and I stayed alone with Gary. He spoke Castilian well enough for us to understand each other. He told me he was from Freiburg. A son of an old friend of Winter. He met Mateo when Don Gustavo, his first wife, and his children took a trip to Freiburg to visit his birthplace. Mateo and he had stayed in touch, and he had now taken the opportunity to visit him on the island. He was twenty-nine, working as an engineer. Don Gustavo had told him he could include him in one of his projects. He was very impressed with Fuerteventura; he said it was a very special and unusual place, a place that could be the backdrop of a romantic novel or film. When he said that, he was staring at me. He raised his hand and touched my face slightly, as Mateo had done earlier. But my body's response to his touch was different. I felt my feet softening; I could easily fall into his arms.. Apparently, I swayed lightly because he asked me in a concerned manner if I was well. I told him it was very hot. I was dizzy from the alcohol. He suggested we go outside.

We walked down to the beach. Gary held my hand, I squeezed his. Like the German ladies, I too was wobbling on my heels walking on the stones. The wind jostled us forward, my hair covered my face, I could not see anything, I felt Gary's hand in mine, and followed him, trusting him completely. The energy of his hand passed through my body, filling me with ease, exaltation, and a stunning happiness. It was like a dream. An amazing dream I did not want to wake up from.

Gary, in his grey suit, with a white shirt, beautiful like a prince, me in the yellow dress of my mother whom I had not seen but who, thanks to this dress, was with me and gave me her blessing, our bound hands, the clasp of the wind...

We reached the sand. Huge waves collapsed on the shore. I shivered. Only now did I feel cold. The chill of the wind, the ocean, the night. Gary pulled me into his arms. My body clung to his as if we were long lost parts of each other. I do not know how long we stayed like this. He caressed my hair and gently kissed my cheeks. "You are wonderful, wonderful...," I heard him whisper: "My Majorera." There was no greater happiness on this earth than being his Majorera. Forever his Majorera.

He took his face from mine, held my chin and kissed my lips. I no longer felt the wind, the ocean, the chill... Heat swept over me. I answered his kiss uncertainly. The feeling was of a wave that passes through my body and crashes somewhere deep inside, sweeping away everything that was; that I had been. There was no uncertainty anymore. My lips knew. My body knew. My dress fell to the sand. For a moment my father's warning passed through my mind. But my father did not know.

Then everything became searching lips, hungry hands, a single body, a single moan...

It was craziness. It was uncontrollable, like a natural force. It was love.

"I love you, I love you, I love you," Gary whispered, and nothing was left of my body. Just an intense sensation.

I was lying in his arms, our breathing was calming down, he stroked my hair. The wind whirled over us, the monstrous waves crashed closer and closer, but nothing could penetrate the shield created by this fateful feeling.

I had drifted away. Footsteps took me out of my trance. I turned around and saw Mateo's anguished face. He held a glass of champagne in his hand. Next to him was his father's black dog.

I looked around for my dress. It was thrown to one side. His blue eyes slid across my body, cold and slimy. I tried to cover myself with my hands.

Gary pressed me close to himself and said: "Mateo, go back to the house. We're coming in a moment."

Mateo did not move. His face was a distorted mixture of pain, anger, malice.

"Why her exactly? Of all the girls around, why her exactly? Couldn't it have been somebody else? Anybody... else..."

His voice was hoarse and strong, stronger than the wind.

"Mateo, you're drunk..."

"Don't tell me, you son of a bitch, what I am and what I am not!"

He hurled his glass to a large stone. It crashed into a thousand pieces, splashing us with champagne. The dog snarled.

I clung to Gary, trembling.

"Mateo, calm down...," Gary's voice was pleading. "Let's talk tomorrow."

"Oh, no, why wait until tomorrow? Why not talk now? For example, what are the plans for the young couple? Or will you first notify your wife in Freiburg about your island beloved?"

"Mateo!" Gary's voice became angry.

The dog started barking and jumped towards us.

Suddenly it became very quiet. Only the words "the wife in Freiburg, the wife in Freiburg, the wife in Freiburg" echoed in my ears. Slowly I pulled back from Gary, turned my face to him and looked in his eyes. A terrified child in me was desperately praying that he would deny it, would attack Mateo for the lies, for this disgusting slander. Gary looked down.

"Wow! It seems you'd missed mentioning this tiny detail... Oh, you son of a bitch! And you, little fool, why did you open your legs so fast? Even a prostitute would first negotiate the price, and you threw your one-and-only honour to the wind. What for? For a married coward! What does he offer you? Twenty minutes of pleasure in the sand. I have been in love with you for years, from the first moment I saw you back then by the road. What for? For nothing! For a wretch! I'm the fool!"

I sat on the sand, naked, no longer touching Gary, with a downward glance. I was crying. I was crying bitterly for my ruined life. For a moment, everything became clear to me. Mateo was right. I was a fool, a wretched nothing, dishonoured forever. What had I imagined? How would I get home? Look in my father's eyes? Hide what happened?

Gary jumped up and threw himself on Mateo.

"Don't you dare insult her, loser!"

The dog started barking, showed his teeth and attacked Gary. Then I saw another huge dog, one of those who strayed across the island, podenco canario, moving fast from the other end of the beach. His long thin legs moved quickly, as if it was flying. A moment later it reached us and threw itself on Don Gustavo's dog. It left Gary and turned to him. The dogs snarled and stared at each other with bloodshot eyes. The next moment they threw themselves into a fierce battle. Mateo shouted in a desperate attempt to separate them. Gary began to dress hurriedly.

My head was whirling. Any moment Don Gustavo and his beautiful wife, and other guests, could come from the house and they would all witness my shame and my nothingness. My poor father would not survive this.

I stood up and headed to the ocean. No one noticed. Only the waves, enormous, strong and mighty, ran towards me, inviting me. As if they were my sisters who wanted to comfort me, to wash away my shame, to give me shelter in their embrace. The cold water lapped around my feet. The first wave knocked me down and dragged me with it. Somewhere behind me, I heard a shot, followed by Gary's and Mateo's voices. They were calling me. For a moment, my head came to the surface, I took air before the next wave hit me and dashed me into the deep. "I'll become a wave...," was my last thought before I flew into the starry sky where my lost mother was surely waiting for me.

The Writer

She was staring at the ocean. The small figures of Carla and Gerd were reduced to dots, blending with the landscape.

"How do you know this happened?" she asked after a while.

"I know. Because my father, then a curious child, followed them. And he saw everything. But he didn't tell anyone. He was afraid that the gentlemen would kill him... The whole situation was very delicate. The master's son was involved. Everything was covered up. In the morning Mateo went to Carmen's father and told him that she had disappeared during the fiesta. That they had been looking for her all night. The poor man never received the body. My grandfather claimed she was buried somewhere on the beach. No cross, no service, no gravestone nor any other sign... So her spirit remained restless. And every year, in January, she takes victims at Cofete. She is waiting for her German couple, my grandfather said. Her revenge. For all the lies, for her lost youth, and for her father, who, my grandfather told me, went mad from grief."

The Writer shot a glance at Enrique and shifted restlessly.

"Enrique, shall we go? Carla and Gerd must be waiting for us."

"Have you become scared, sugar? Don't be afraid, it is just a story, you can hear all sorts of things... People drown all over the island, and not just in January. Your friends are not so crazy to get into this raging sea..."

Pepito's wide smile gave her shivers.

Marina

Marina reached the high dune where she had met Gerd a couple of weeks ago. She stared into the ocean and took in all its moods. The joyful, the serene, the dark, the frightening, the tranquil, the deep - all were hers.

She pulled out her mobile, turned it in her hands for a long while as she stared at the colours of the infinite water.

There was no answer. She was about to hang up when she heard a man's voice. So close. So remote. Coming from another life or from beyond.

"Hello."

"Angel..."

"Marina?"

"I'm sitting on a dune and watching the ocean. Thinking about it being bigger than us. Greater than life. Its waters are able to wash away everything – any sadness, insult, loss..."

"Is that what you're calling me for? To tell me this?"

"No. Not only..."

"What then? After you left, just like that, as if it were only your loss, as if I were that monster... It's not just your loss, you know! My life was over too. The guilt will eat at me for the rest of my days..."

"I'm sorry. I am really sorry. But I could not do otherwise. I had no other move. Only this way could I survive, physically survive. My life was over, yes. And my survival began, which is continuing today. You at least managed to move on, to build something..."

"I loved you insanely. You and Neda. For one day, I lost both of you in the most brutal unimaginable way. If it was not that woman who shares my days..."

"*And because of whom our angel was brought to heaven,*" passed through her mind, but she gritted her teeth and did not say it.

"I know. I'm sorry. I could not keep seeing you every day. I could not stay in this city, in this country... I could not. But today, today, I want to tell you that... I forgive you. I've forgiven you. And I ask you to forgive me too."

Silence.

"Why now? Why today?"

"I don't know. Perhaps because of this island that brought me back to life, to the desire to live. I met a woman, a centenarian, who had buried five children, two of whom in recent months. If you could see the grief in her eyes when she talked about that. If you could hear her laughter, despite all this. For three years, Angel, I lived our life before that terrible day. To leave was the only way to continue living with you. I have not separated from you, from her. Now I understand that. That's why I'm calling you. To part. And to forgive each other."

Silence. Swollen tears of a man who loses everything.

"Angel..., let the guilt go, please. Because of her. She would not want that. And I do not want it. This happened. If I was with her, it would probably have happened too. It was meant to be that way. Now it seems to me that if we don't give each other forgiveness - true, deep, heartfelt - her spirit will also never rest."

Silence.

On both ends of the line, two people share everything without words. Their common past. And a tragedy that separates them. But also brings them together. They know this conversation is the last one. That's why they are silent.

Finally, Angel speaks.

"I have nothing to forgive. I did not blame you. Take care of yourself. And stop surviving. Life is... to be lived."

"It was hard to start this conversation... And now it's even harder for me to finish. I will count up to three. We hang up at three. One..., two..., three."

Marina pressed the key. End. Something that seemed to have ended had now ended. With the pressing of a key. Just like that. That is how simple it can be.

A message appeared on the screen. Gerd.

"I'm leaving tomorrow. I have to see you. Tonight? Please!"

This time her hesitation was shorter.

"It's better not to see each other again. Thank you for bringing me back to life."

Pressing the key. Just like that. That is how simple it can be.

She got up and walked back.

Carla

They descended on the winding road that led them to the huge, almost empty beach. Only here and there one could see a couple. Four or five youngsters were taking photos of themselves with a tripod. A dark-haired young woman fell into the sand. A young man outlined the contours of her body with his foot, the way they do it with crime scenes, and began to take photos of her.

They went to the right towards a cliff that stretched out into the ocean like a hand. The wind was lashing them, suicidal waves were throwing themselves to the shore. There were no more people around. They walked, walked, and still did not reach it. It was as if the rock was a mirage. They walked silently, did not touch each other, there was no connection between them. Carla's feeling from the morning solidified. Gerd was far from her. But she could not and did not want to do anything more. For the first time since the beginning of their relationship, she felt powerless. She wished that he could sense the distance between them and cross it. At least for once. But Gerd was too engrossed in his own thoughts. They walked parallel to one another. The ocean, the beach, the mountain, and two lost souls. The rock continued to stand in front of them, and still they did not near it.

Gerd broke the silence. "Do you want to go back?"

"No."

As if by reaching the rock, they would achieve something. A turning point. A point of return. Carla had no idea what this would mean, but it was important for her, that the two of them cross that distance, overcome it, find themselves alone on a rock at the end of Fuerteventura, Europe and the world. Were they to discover there whether the end of their world had come? Were they capable of a new beginning? She did not know, she had no premonition, only a desperate hope, and compulsion to keep walking. She felt the place, its biblical beauty gave her a sense of calm acceptance and eternity.

Nothing mattered anymore. Just to reach the rock.

She let all her thoughts go with the wind. She was empty, windblown, ready. Ready for an end. Or for a start. At least that was what she thought. The turning point. The turning rock.

At last, they arrived. The rock gleamed wet under the January sun. The waves crashed at its end. Now what? What after they have arrived? There was the return in front of them. Everything was in front of them. Everything that remained.

But now that they were here, at the end of Fuerteventura, Europe and the world, perhaps at the end of their world, Carla wanted Gerd to remember. Her. Them.

To notice her. To see her. To recall.

He pulled the camera out of his rucksack and started taking pictures. The ocean, the beach, the rock.

The rock.

Carla jumped on it and walked towards its edge. The wind blasted her, splashes of the waves' broken bodies reached her and soaked into her jeans.

"Carla, come back!" Gerd called after her.

She did not react. She kept going until she reached its end. From there on was the ocean. The waves threw themselves just centimetres from her feet.

"Carla!"

Gerd had also got up on the rock and was walking toward her with the camera in his hand.

"Take a picture of me!"

He hesitated. He picked up the camera and froze with it, staring at its screen. At that moment, a wave rose above all the others and covered the rock. Carla swayed, struggled, but kept her balance.

"Carla, enough! Have you gone mad? Let's go back!"

Now her legs soaked with water to her knees. The wind threw a lock of hair over her face. She put it up. Her gaze contained everything unspoken over the past days.

"Take it!"

Gerd

The ocean had gone mad. The wind had gone mad. Carla had gone mad.

She stood in front of him, soaked, with her hair over her face, and frenzied eyes.

The only way to end this performance was to take the damn picture.

He picked up the camera and stared at the screen. His finger moved to push the trigger, and then he saw it - a huge, powerful, preying wave moving ahead with a whid rush. He tried to shout, but his voice stuck in his throat. An instant, and Carla and the wave disappeared. As if they had never been.

His body responded faster than his mind. He dropped the camera, ran and jumped into the water, foaming like champagne. The last thing he sensed before leaping from the edge of the rock was the vibration of his mobile in his small leather bag. The vibration from a new message coming. *What has...*

The Writer

She held the glass of water and stared at the still surface. She shook it gently, the water rippled to its edge. Does the storm in a glass of water produce waves, killer waves that take victims?... But if this storm is so small as to fit into a glass of water, surely the victims are just as small, insignificant, miniature compared to the vast body of life... But wasn't the entire vast life contained in this glass?...What is left out then?

"Please come with me to the room."

"Pardon?" The Writer said.

"Into their room. I don't want to go alone. Or else I may never come out. I will always expect the door opening, their voices in the kitchen..."

"Come on. Let's go in." The Writer walked along the corridor.

Another corridor. To life preceding death? To the explanation of why them, why today, why here?...

She put her hand on the door handle and pressed. The light suffused them. The windows gaped – toothless laughing mouth. The sheets were smoothly straightened. "Carla," thought the Writer. She sat on the bed. Enrique slumped down at her feet and started wailing. She took his head on her knees, stroking his hair, until his weeping obeyed her caress, calmed, got lost in the shady thicket of the space beyond time. The time that stopped...

Enrique

He lifted his head and saw the white face of a woman, a bright spot in the dusk. A woman who might have been his mother or Madonna, or maybe the Writer... The Writer?

"How long have I been sleeping?"

"An instant."

Enrique lifted himself, climbed up her body, grasping her knees, arms, breasts, her trunk, her branches, the tree she was, his fingers reached her face, touched her lips, felt her damp tongue... She stood motionlessly - this woman, open and accessible, his lips replaced his fingers, and his tongue penetrated her mouth, met her tongue, his fingers undressed her, leafed through her like a tree, turned over the pages like a book, the book she was and in which he wanted to get lost, among the shady leaves, over the perfectly straightened sheets, the smooth surface of a sea in a glass in which the two of them were causing waves, at that moment when the waves were born, in which they had become a wave, in which a powerful wave swept both of them...

"Enrique?"

"Yes."

"Please don't call Marina... They left today."

The Writer

She took a farewell walk in Corralejo. She reached the junction to Buena Onda. She passed it but then stopped and returned. The table was free. She sipped the sangria and narrowed her eyes. Gerd, Enrique, Carla and Gerard talk about surfing, she chats with Marina. The air is full of excitement, light tension, a promise. The moment has frozen. There is no need to hurry. It enjoys its own perfection, without realising it completely. As if it anticipates this other moment in which the togetherness of these people would be unattainable, that next moment that would make it impossible in the face of an obscure and immense eternity.

Let's not hurry. Let's stay here. Let us have our drinks and talk about surfing, writing, Unamuno, whatever, just to delay the impending... The sounds of cheerful music. Laughter burst out behind her. She wiped her tears, paid, and left. She saw Emiliyan and Darina sitting in the "office". Emiliyan waved.

That night, the three of them parked by the dunes and went down to the ocean. The Writer and Darina sat under the lee of a rock, while Emiliyan walked further and stopped over the darkened waters. A moment later the cord flew, made a thin curve in the air and sank in the ocean. The Writer held her face between her palms, her eyes tired from crying, and stared at the blurred border between the ocean and the sky.

"An instant," she dropped. "And they're gone. I do not understand it."

"There's no way for it to be comprehended."

"I travelled all over the island, geographically and historically, I went back in time, read, searched... what? I tried to meet her, to get to know, to grasp her... And what came out of it? That, meanwhile, her nature was revealing itself in front of my eyes."

"Or maybe Fuerteventura is a huge mirror of our souls. She's what we make of her."

"And only I have seen all those love triangles and unfulfilled loves?"

"Yes... But there are also other stories, right? Those that are fulfilled." Darina nodded toward Emiliyan's straight figure.

"Why don't you turn your back to all the pain and write such a story?"

The Writer sighed and said nothing. The two listened to the ocean, which was reading aloud the consecutive night of Fuerteventura.

At dawn, she heard movement in the flat. Juan was leaving. They would not see each other again. She went to him in the dark corridor just as he was about to go out.

"When will you come back?" he asked her.

"I don't know."

"I'll wait for your book... and you."

"See you soon, Juan."

"See you soon."

The Writer reached out and kissed him on the lips. It was a light, butterfly kiss. She returned to her room, into the embrace of the warm bed.

She sat on the top of the high dune and, looked at the ocean. The camel she had seen a few days ago emerged before her eyes like a mirage. She recognised her by her wise look and knowing smile.

Its rider was a man with glasses with fine frames, through which piercing eyes looked at her. He had an intelligent face, silver hair, thinning on the top of his head, well-formed chin and moustache. He was dressed in a dark suit with a white shirt and black shoes with laces.

The man pulled the lead and the camel stopped.

"A perfect day for contemplation," he spoke in Spanish, and his eyes smiled.

"It seems they are all like this here."

"Exactly. That's why I came back. And because of the book. 'Don Quixote on Fuerteventura.' We should not leave our books unwritten, right?"

"We should not."

"How far did you get with yours?"

"To the dunes..."

"Very good. The best stories are born among the dunes. The sorceress sea whispers them."

"You think so?"

"I know."

The man leaned forward and stretched out his hand gallantly.

"May I invite you for a short ride, señorita? I would like to introduce you to a couple of friends. Tibiabín and Tamonante."

"With pleasure."

She took his hand and climbed behind him on the back of the camel - a high, uncertain, wonderful place. The man pulled the reins and they slowly set out through the deserted beach. The wind splashed around them like an invisible cloak.

"You know, Iris, what is the best thing about this island?"

"What?"

"That whenever and wherever we are we can be back to it. Whenever and wherever..."

* * *

"To Juan Cassow
in Paris

Fuerteventura accompanied me to Paris; right here in Paris, Fuerteventura has dissolved in me and, with it, the most intimate, the most important aspect of Spain, which the blessed island of strong winds symbolises and concentrates in itself. Here in Paris, where there is no mountain, no bare spaces, nor sea, here the religious and patriotic experience of Fuerteventura has matured in me."[40]

---

[40] Miguel de Unamuno, De Fuerteventura a Paris, Editorial Excelsor, 1925

A year later...

Marina was changing Mina's nappy when her mobile rang. An unknown German number. Gerd? She hesitated.

"Hello?"

"Hello, Gerd's mother calling."

"Gerd's mother?"

"The last message in his phone was from this number."

"The last message? What do you mean?"

"Don't you know?"

"What should I know?"

* * *

The cold wind-driven rain blew into the Writer's face like tears that she did not want to wipe off. She walked quickly. She passed another canal and found herself at the Museum of Photography. She closed the umbrella, walked in, left her belongings in a locker, and continued into the museum. In one of the halls, there was an exhibition under the title "Brilliant in their absence", in memory of Frido Troost. An exhibition of photo corners and frames of missing pictures. The photo corners resembled small wandering birds. The Writer remembered her childhood albums, in which she put black and white pictures in such corners. There was an inscription underneath the outline of a missing picture. Written on a piece of wrapping paper "I wish you many happy returns of the day, July 18, 1951". How many returns had past before the space became empty? And how many after? *It is ridiculous, this expression. The day will always return, but we will not always be there to wait for it. Many happy 'live to see the day' makes more sense, doesn't it?* But that was not important in this case. What was important were the portraits of absences and their possible dimensions. Shining in their absence. Were not all experiences in life marked by someone's absence? Absence also had shape, boundaries, density, emotional value, backed by memories from another time when there was a presence instead. A presence, almost inevitably connected with someone else's absence.

Presences, absences... coupled vessels in the emotional system of the world. *In our absence sometimes we are even more present.* Below the last cardboard pad was a crumpled white paper with a few orange spots, and under the brown outline of the frame - a handwritten inscription: *the last picture. There is always one last picture.* Frido Troost, who had died at the age of fifty-three, was still shining in his absence. His departure must have opened a huge emptiness for those who knew him that the glow, no matter how strong it was, could never fill. That was what the Writer thought as she was leaving the museum. Later, ironically, she found out that she had lost her camera full of pictures of the North Sea; pictures of dunes, birds, dead starfish, and a blue sky, crisscrossed with white vapour trails.

She remembered the exhibition a week later at an art fair in a luxury hotel at Stephanie Square in Brussels, when she reached large canvasses with many small human figures seen from above, roaming in the course of their day like ants. There were empty spaces around them, bathed in sunlight. Pedestrians and cyclists. *Ants with small lives, to which we attach such great importance. Whose was the perspective? Of a merciful and compassionate God, or of Providence, being entertained by our useless efforts?* She lifted her head and saw a square canvas in yellow-orange tones. A couple was painted in its left upper corner, also seen from above, taking a selfie. The boy wore a backpack and had embraced the girl. In his other hand, he held a camera. Behind them, their shadow looked like an elephant. The Writer froze.

There is always one last picture.

"What does this yellow space mean?" she turned to the artist.

242

"Happiness. Yellow means happiness."

Fifteen minutes later, the Writer went out with the wrapped painting and headed for Marolles. A fine drizzle wet her face, hair and clothes, but she did not feel it. She carefully carried the painting, which had captured countless loves, reflections, deaths, immortalities, presences, absences, last pictures, lack of pictures, the end of a book, her and she, the island, all within the yellow, which means happiness.

Acknowledgements

Actual historical figures who have lived on Fuerteventura in different periods appear in 'She, the island'. But in the book they should be seen as part of its fiction. There, their stories, apart from quoted sources, come from my imagination alone.

The novel wouldn't have been the same without my encounter, turning into friendship, with the photographer Emiliyan Draganov, Daniela Valcheva and Evelyna Todorova. I am also grateful for the expertise and responsiveness of Concha Maria Fleitas Perdomo from the cultural association Raíz del Pueblo. And then there was the centenaire Carmen, who sadly had died before the book was published, the writer Juan Luis Calbarro, three surf teachers in Corralejo and the local people who were always ready to answer my questions and to guide me in this exciting journey. I also gleaned invaluable information from the staff at the Municipal Archive in La Oliva, the Municipal Library in Puerto del Rosario, Miguel de Unamuno House Museum in Puerto del Rosario, and the Archeological Museum in Betancuria. Heartfelt thanks to all of them as well as to my Bulgarian editor Mitko Novkov for the merciless and stimulating feedback, to my English editor Ric Giner for his patience and efforts to find those words which both made sense and preserved the heart and music of my novel in English and to the Welsh poet Phil Madden for further polishing the style - making it shine – as well as to the illustrator Nevena Angelova for the beautiful cover and book design.

By the same author

'Pelican Feather'
A novel

The novel tells the story of Martin, a ten year old boy who spends a summer with his mother and grandmother in the seaside city of Burgas after his father has left the mother for her best friend. Martin is the main narrator. His narrative is interwoven with monologues of the seven adult characters showing their deepest feelings and life experiences which have influenced them and their views. The novel also gives a fascinating glimpse of the world around Burgas's salt and mud pools and the lake with its rich birdlife. The city itself becomes a main character.

I want to write a tale about the pelicans. A tale so enchanting that it would replace all the tales about swans. I want to write it with the pelican feather. I want it to tell it to me.

"'Pelican Feather' is a panorama of contemporary Bulgarian society. It covers political protests, ecology, confusion in moral values, poverty, but also goodness, friendship, and the reaching out of hands. Life in the book is colourful, authentic, true, full of sounds, and above all alive. The story is so real that at times you have the feeling it is happening in front of your eyes. You are a witness but not from a distance. An involved witness; a witness who somehow actively feels for the characters as they are close to you, as you are close to them… Proximity of feeling – perhaps this would be the best short definition of the novel 'Pelican Feather'."

Mitko Novkov, literary critic and editor

"'Pelican Feather' is a story of romantic love told by the ten-year old Martin after the separation of his parents, It depicts the experiences of his mother at the end of her marriage, her wry and brave path to recovery, contrasted with Martin's first experience of romantic love-gauche, idealistic but still very real and intense.

Set during a summer by the sea, the novel is spiced with vivid accounts of contemporary Bulgaria and just the right sprinkling of magic realism."

Phil Madden, poet and editor of the English translation

About the author

Irina Papancheva was born in the Bulgarian city of Burgas. She holds an MA in Czech language and literature from Sofia University "St. Kliment Ohridski" and in European Politics and Social Integration from Vrije Universitet Brussel (VUB). She is the author of the illustrated children's book 'I Stutter' (Ciela, 2005), the short novel 'Almost Intimately' (Kronos, 2007), the novels 'Annabel' (Janet 45, 2010), 'Pelican Feather' (Janet 45, 2013) and 'She, the island' (Trud, 2017) and the novella 'Welcome Nathan!' (Fast Print Books, 2019) as well as of short stories and the play 'About a hippo' (2016).

Her work has been published in English, French, Arabic and Persian.

Website: ipapancheva.com

Printed in Great Britain
by Amazon

64124885R00142